ACCOLADES

I thoroughly enjoyed DECO DAMES. A lovely trip down memory lane to the Jazz Age. I chuckled at Jazz and Nathan in a high-speed chase in a rusty Model T, racing at 25 mph through the streets of Galveston. Ms. Collier did an excellent job of painting a picture of the 1920s, when Prohibition was in full swing. I could imagine the clothes, the hats, the manual typewriters, the elegance and the rough neighborhoods. An excellent book!
  —*Teresa Watson, Amazon*

DECO DAMES has a ghost bride, a gypsy fortune teller and plenty of adventures that kept me riveted. A page-turner, for sure.
  —*Noreen Marcus, Amazon*

VAMPS was superb. A fantastic and delightful read from page one until the very last page. I couldn't put VAMPS down. I love the characters and the trouble that they get themselves into....this (series) is rich in historical detail and humor. I always find myself laughing at Jazz's antics and admire her gumption and determination to put wrongdoers to task.
…I love this Jazz Age series because it is unique and different from other historical mysteries. This series is fun and sassy and always has me on my toes. If you haven't discovered this brilliant series, then you are missing out on a fun read. I simply cannot get enough. If you want a heroine who is smart, funny, and sassy, Jazz Cross is the one for you.
  —*Kimberlee, "Girl Lost in a Book" Blog*

I loved this. Quite simply, it's a lady's version of the show *Boardwalk Empire*. GOLD DIGGERS is full of mobsters, shady deals and dirty policemen, and you never fully know who's trustworthy. Jazz is feisty, fearless and doesn't give a jot what the chauvinistic men around her think. She's great! The author really seems to know her stuff, gently weaving in details without overwhelming or confusing an uninformed reader. The characters all have plenty of 'moxie' and are well thought-out and likeable. There's a constant sense of mystery keeping you turning the pages, with a pace that's spot-on.
  —*Charlotte Foreman, BestChickLit.com Blog (U.K.)*

Ellen Collier's novel FLAPPERS is set in one of my favorite locations, during an era when Galveston was one of the wildest on the Texas Gulf Coast. Spunky society reporter Jasmine (Jazz) Cross gets involved with murder right off the bat, and her breezy voice carries the narrative along at a bright clip. Great Galveston period setting and atmosphere.
  —*Bill Crider, Author of the Sheriff Rhodes mystery series, etc.*

Ellen Collier's novels would make exciting movies or a cable TV series.
—*Haskell Morris, Goodreads*

Jasmine Cross is back in all her feisty independence. Once again, Ellen Mansoor Collier does a great job of putting us in the Roaring 20's where we experience vaudeville, Prohibition, fashion, and Galveston. If you're ever accused of murder, you want Jazz on your side! You'll find mystery, intrigue, and a lot of fun in VAMPS.
—*Amy Metz, "A Blue Million Books" Blog, Goose Pimple Junction mystery series*

I was totally taken with BATHING BEAUTIES, the second in the Jazz Age series following the spunky, intrepid flapper-reporter, Jazz Cross. Collier combines historical trivia with a cozy mystery beautifully, and I'm falling in love with her 1920s Galveston. Jazz is wonderfully empathetic in a way that felt authentic, not modern. (She passes my I-want-her-to-be-my-friend test!) The perfect mix of historical detail and zippy plot to keep me happy...it captures the dangerous allure of glamour, fame and easy fortune.
—*Audra Friend, "Unabridged Chick" Blog*

BATHING BEAUTIES' exciting and glamorous setting is hugely beneficial for this colourful and enjoyable novel.... With all its fun, chemistry, authenticity, plotting and ease in style and slang, this is very recommendable. An elegant and hugely entertaining mystery set during Prohibition times in Galveston. Great style and a fantastic sense of authenticity....Well-written, cleverly-plotted and very enjoyable.
—*Christoph Fischer, Top 500 Amazon Reviewer (U.K.)*

GOLD DIGGERS is so much fun it should be illegal.
—*Noreen Marcus, Amazon, freelance reporter and editor*

What a great read! Collier's smart and classy writing style keeps the familiar cadence of a "whodunit" novel or film noir. With all the moxie of Lois Lane, Jazz Cross is the kind of strong female character you find yourself rooting for. Full of rich historical detail and colorful 1920s slang true to the era, Galveston—the "Ellis Island of the West"—jumps off the pages.

A fun and entertaining mystery drives the plot along, but it was the story world that really won me over. Every aspect—from the cultural climate to the perfume and cosmetic cases—is fully realized and I couldn't have asked for better world-building. It was a special treat to learn so much about Prohibition-era Galveston while having the pleasure of enjoying the story. Hardcore history and mystery lovers alike will fall head over heels for this series, and general readers will be enlightened and entertained.
—*Regina Vitola Mader, "ME ReadALOT" Blog*

DECO DAMES, DEMON RUM AND DEATH

A JAZZ AGE MYSTERY (#5)

ELLEN MANSOOR COLLIER

Text Copyright © 2018 by Ellen Mansoor Collier

Cover Art Work: Vintage Photos and illustrations (1920s)

Cover Design Copyright © 2018 Ellen Mansoor Collier

Interior Page Design: Ellen Mansoor Collier and Gary E. Collier

DECO DAME PRESS

All rights reserved. Published in the United States by Deco Dame Press

ISBN: 978-0-9894170-4-4

First Edition

The text of this book is Garamond 12-point

CONTENTS

Read the Complete "Jazz Age Mystery" Series

By Ellen Mansoor Collier:

FLAPPERS, FLASKS And FOUL PLAY
A Jazz Age Mystery #1 (2012)

BATHING BEAUTIES, BOOZE And BULLETS
A Jazz Age Mystery #2 (2013)

GOLD DIGGERS, GAMBLERS And GUNS
A Jazz Age Mystery #3 (2014)

VAMPS, VILLAINS And VAUDEVILLE

A Jazz Age Mystery #4 (2015)

DECO DAMES, DEMON RUM And DEATH

A Jazz Age Mystery #5 (2019)

PREFACE

By: Ellen Mansoor Collier

Before Las Vegas, Galveston, Texas reigned as the "Sin City of the Southwest"—a magnet for gold-diggers, gamblers and gangsters. Inspired by real people and places, **DECO DAMES, DEMON RUM AND DEATH** is set in December, 1927 Galveston, where businessmen rubbed elbows with bootleggers and real-life rival gangs ruled the Island with greed and graft.

During Prohibition, the Beach Gang and Downtown Gang fought constant turf wars for control over booze, gambling, slot machines, clubs and prostitution. To keep the peace, the gangs tried to compromise by dividing the Island into two halves: Bootleggers Ollie Quinn and Dutch Voight headed the Beach Gang, south of Broadway and on the Seawall. The infamous but long-gone swanky Hollywood Dinner Club on 61st Street and the Turf Club on 23rd Street (which became the gang's headquarters, renamed the Surf Club in the novel) were located in the Beach Gang's territory.

Colorful crime boss Johnny Jack Nounes and hard-boiled thug George Musey ran the Downtown Gang, the area north of Broadway. Nounes once partnered with Frank Nitti, Al Capone's legendary enforcer, who tried but failed to muscle in on the local turf.

Like many port cities, Galveston greatly profited from Prohibition—bar owners, businessmen and bootleggers alike—until it was nationally repealed in 1933. Enacted in January, 1920, the Volstead Act prohibited "the manufacture, sale, transport and possession of intoxicating liquor or distilled spirits containing more than 0.5% alcohol for beverage purposes." The Treasury Department employed hundreds of Prohibition agents to enforce the new law, but that proved futile as most local police and the public refused to follow the not-so "Noble Experiment."

PREFACE

The Maceo brothers, Rosario and Sam (Papa Rose and Big Sam), were Sicilian immigrants who eventually took control of the Island, known as the "Free State of Galveston" for its vice and laissez-faire attitude, for roughly 25 years, from 1926 on, until the Maceos' deaths. Sam Maceo died in 1951 of cancer, and Rose Maceo passed on in 1954 due to heart failure. **DECO DAMES, DEMON RUM AND DEATH** is loosely based on actual events, fabricated to protect the innocent as well as the guilty, leading to the Maceos' gradual take-over in the late 1920s and early 1930s.

The *Galveston Gazette* is a fictitious newspaper, but is based on *The Galveston Daily News*—the first and oldest newspaper in Texas, founded in 1842 and still in publication. Since many of the gangland crimes and activities went largely unreported and/or under-reported, the main characters and circumstances in the novel are fictitious and not intended to malign or distort actual persons or cases, but are purely the author's imagined version of possible events.

Author's Note:
By the way, for fact-checkers, I took a couple of liberties in this novel: According to local legend, a ghost bride does haunt the Hotel Galvez, but rumors are she died in the 1950s, not the 1920s, on the fifth floor. For my purposes, I created a 1920s ghost bride who drowned in the ocean in front of the hotel.

I imagined the Broadway Cemetery as an overgrown Gothic Dickensian graveyard and also mentioned Mickey Mouse, who was formally introduced in mid-1928 (six months later).

While most of the characters and events are fictional, I've included a few real people and places, and researched the history and settings to the best of my ability.

CHAPTER ONE

The plump gypsy woman caressed my hand, studying my palm as if it held the map to Lafitte's pirate treasure, rumored to be lost in Galveston Bay. Madame Farushka certainly looked the part in her colorful scarf, flowing hair, a fringed shawl wrapped over her peasant blouse and skirt. Was she an actress or a clairvoyant or a fake?

Flickering candles dotted the dimly-lit room, strands of sparkling beads and crystals criss-crossed the windows, the strong scent of sandalwood floated from an Egyptian brass incense burner. A crystal ball gleamed in the center of the table, beckoning like a jewel from King Tut's tomb.

The fortune-teller cleared her throat. "You face a lot of struggles as a working woman, with many challenges ahead."

I bit my tongue to keep from blurting out: So what else is new? Every dame I knew had problems.

"I see a lot of changes in your life," the seer chanted, gazing into the crystal ball. "Upheaval, uprooting." She closed her eyes, swaying from side to side. Suddenly her dark eyes flew open and she looked up in alarm. "Someone close to you is in danger. Are you married?"

Her kohl-rimmed gaze bore into my skull, as if reading my mind, daring me to reveal my secrets. Wouldn't she already know them if she truly was clairvoyant?

I shifted in her silk slipper chair, tapping my fingers. "No, why?"

"A loved one then, a sweetheart or a family member. A young man. He's in grave danger." Madame Farushka gripped my hand, her voice a hoarse gasp.

I tried not to be fazed by her theatrics, but I had to admit, I was worried. "What kind of danger?"

She peered into the crystal ball. "Terrible danger. Life or death."

"Can you be more specific?"

"I'm sorry, but that's all I foresee."

OK, so now I was curious. "What does the man look like?"

She stroked her temples, rings of gold bracelets jingling on her arms. "He's tall, handsome, young...with a dangerous occupation."

That described my two favorite fellas: my fair-haired Prohibition agent beau, James Burton and Sammy Cook, my black-sheep half-brother. Sammy served as maître d' of the Hollywood Dinner Club, the swankiest spot on the Gulf Coast.

"Is he blond or dark?"

The seer shook her head. "I'm sorry. I lost the vision."

In other words, my dollar was all used up.

What a load of hogwash. Sadly their risky jobs always put Sammy and James in danger. This phony-baloney hadn't told me anything new.

"Is that all?" I stood up, annoyed that I'd wasted a whole dollar on ten minutes of trivia.

"You'll have to come back for a second reading." She held out her palm, fishing for a tip. When I gave her a nickel, she scowled, as disappointed as I was. Now I wondered: Was she a fortune-teller or a fortune-hunter?

Why in the world had I let my boss talk me into a reading with this so-called seer? What did she actually see, besides the obvious?

"She's the newest attraction in town," Mrs. Harper had raved. "All of the society bigwigs invite her to their parties to read palms and predict the future."

"Really? Does she cast spells on them too? Create love potions?"

She frowned over her spectacles. "That's enough, young lady."

I'll bet they paid Madame Farushka a pretty penny to spout tall tales of happy marriages and prosperous futures or to trumpet tragedy. Why did I have to be the unlucky gal who'd gotten such a dire prediction?

A month ago, the editor-in-chief, Mr. Thomas, had promised to put me on the city beat, writing hard news about crime and corruption in Galveston—no shortage of stories there. Instead, here I was in a remote Victorian mansion, forced to write yet another silly society story for my social-climbing boss.

"Tit for tat," Mrs. Harper told me by way of explanation.

I wondered about her choice of words. Did that mean for every puff piece I wrote, I got a chance to write real news?

When I asked, my boss dismissed me with a wave of her hand. Clearly, she and Mr. Thomas conspired to keep me chained to my desk, toiling away like a servant.

I'd received some minor acclaim for my recent vaudeville villains article—my big break, or so I thought—and I was dying for more adventures and bylines. Despite my ambitious articles, my bosses refused to give me any more stories that required actual reporting and investigation.

I stomped outside to find Nathan waiting in his Tin Lizzie. Madame Farushka strictly forbade any observer from entering her parlor during a reading, especially a newspaper photographer.

"What a waste of time! That charlatan gave me such a canned spiel of baloney it can apply to any dame." I failed to mention the "life or death" part since it sounded so melodramatic and corny.

"What did you expect—a trail to the Holy Grail?" He cracked.

"Why not? Say, sorry you had to wait out here doing nothing."

"Nothing? While the diviner wasn't watching, I canvassed her place, shooting photos through her windows."

"Gotta admire your gumption. See anything interesting?"

"Only the usual flim-flam, Tarot cards, a crystal ball or two. And did I mention a couple of shrunken heads?"

"What? Where?" I jumped back in alarm.

"Just pulling your leg." Nathan grinned. "Let's hope the photos turn out alright. She sure has a lot of lit candles in there."

"I'll say. All part of the dramatic effect, to help convince her customers that her hocus-pocus is real." She had to be a fake, didn't she? Thank goodness I wasn't a superstitious or gullible gal. Still, what if James or Sammy were actually in danger—and they were the last to know?

CHAPTER TWO

A couple of newsies stood outside hawking papers with gusto when I returned to the *Galveston Gazette*. I settled down at my desk, grinding my teeth and figuring out what to tell Mrs. Harper about my faux fortune-telling experience. Luckily she seemed to be at one of her fancy-pants ladies' luncheons, unlike most of our good-old-boy staff who preferred liquid lunches over actual meals.

Mack, our cranky senior reporter, had taken a "leave of absence"—a nice way of saying he was on probation until he could lay off the liquor. Of course I felt relieved, since Mack seemed to be living in the Stone Age and expected women to be chained to their stoves, not to their desks.

At times I wondered that if I focused on hard news and "the seamy side of life" as Mr. Thomas, the editor-in-chief, put it, I could end up like Mack—jaded and bitter. Maybe it wasn't such a bad idea to balance frills and frivolity with a mix of murder and mayhem?

I heard a commotion and our two cub reporters bustled in, talking excitedly, making a beeline for their desks. "What's the ruckus?" I asked Pete, the least obnoxious of the young newshawks.

They eyed each other and Chuck made a zipper motion across his lips.

"We're not even supposed to know," Pete told us. "The press isn't allowed inside the courtroom, and we heard the story is hands-off to reporters."

"Courtroom? Is there a trial going on?"

"Not yet." Pete motioned me over. "Swear not to tell anyone?"

Impatient, I tapped my foot. "Well?"

"Word is, Johnny Jack was caught confiscating a load of booze from a Cuban rum-runner."

My ears pricked up. What a lucky break for Sammy!

"Nounes is always getting in trouble." I shrugged, pretending I'd heard the scuttlebutt. "What else is new?"

"The Coast Guard caught him buying ten grand worth of booze from a Cuban bootlegger in the bay, and arrested him for violating the Volstead Act," Pete said, voice low.

"You don't say." Why hadn't I heard about this from Sammy or my Fed Agent beau? Wasn't capturing bootleggers and rum-runners part of his job? "Is he in jail now?"

"He's out on bail. He has to appear before a grand jury this week and the lawyers are keeping quiet. After hearing testimony, they present the charges and the jury decides if there's enough solid evidence to go to trial."

"Why a grand jury? Why not a regular trial?"

"Law enforcement doesn't want the public to know since it may affect the outcome," Pete explained. "Johnny Jack is so slippery, they may rush the trial before he tries to skip town."

I tried not to get my hopes up. If the case went to trial and he was found guilty, then that let Sammy off the hook—at least for a while. Like Houdini, Johnny Jack had a knack for making jailhouse escapes—not by any crafty magic tricks or sleight-of-hand illusions, but by paying off the right people.

"Johnny Jack always manages to get away," I pointed out. "He bribes the judges and they dismiss the charges. Why will this time be any different?"

"Apparently there's a key witness who's going to testify and make the case against him. Must be a brave fool on the inside, who's familiar with the Downtown Gang's dirty dealings."

My throat went dry. Casually I asked, "Anyone we know?"

Pete shook his head. "To reveal his identity could mean death."

"Boy, this sap sure has balls to testify against Nounes," Chuck smirked. "Whoever he is, he must have an ax to grind—right in Johnny Jack's back."

Nathan glanced at me and I knew he read my mind.

My brother Sammy? Is that who he meant?

"How do you know so much about this grand jury hearing if it's supposed to be so hush-hush?" I asked the newsboys.

"What do you think?" Chuck said.

"Let me guess. Mack?" By their expressions, I knew I was right. "I thought he was on leave. Why is he still chasing leads?"

"Just because he's not here, right now, doesn't mean he's lost his touch, or his sources." Chuck sounded defensive. "Mack is freelancing these days, writing for the *Galveston Daily News*."

Our big rival—the first newspaper in Texas. A bit on the stodgy side, but with a stellar reputation, while the *Gazette* was the fresh upstart in town.

"Good for him." I smiled, glad he seemed to be recovering from his latest bender. "Mack may return to his old job sooner than later."

"Hope so." Pete leaned closer. "Keep this under your hat, OK? Don't breathe a word to anyone."

I tugged on my red felt cloche in reply. Despite Mack's downfall, he always proved solid with his leads and his stories. Trouble was, since Pete and Chuck were secondhand sources, how could I confirm the rumors and get more information?

Rattled, I returned to my desk, making a mental note to confront Sammy as soon as possible. Truth was, I was more worried about my brother than I cared to admit. In Galveston, small-time crooks came and went, but the Beach and Downtown gangs continued fighting their turf wars over booze, bootleggers and bars.

Sammy barely escaped the Downtown Gang and Johnny Jack's clutches, only to join the Beach Gang and work for his rivals, the Maceo brothers at the Hollywood Dinner Club. Nounes would never forgive the Maceos for stealing Sammy right out from under his turf and control. Sadly, Sammy was a wanted man with a bloody bull's-eye on his back.

Trying to eavesdrop, I twirled around in my banker's chair, but the newsboys changed the subject. How could I focus on upcoming holiday parties and Christmas galas worrying about Madame Farushka's warning? Could Sammy be the key witness in Johnny Jack's grand jury hearing?

Mrs. Harper showed up an hour later, and stopped by my desk. "How was the reading? What was Madame Farushka like?" she asked breathlessly. "Did she look...you know...like a real fortune-teller, with the long hair, colorful scarves and gold jewelry?"

"Yes, she did. Very flamboyant, almost like she was wearing a costume. Unfortunately, she didn't allow Nathan to take any photos...inside the house."

"That's not surprising," Mrs. Harper clucked, missing my dig. "She only wants believers present or it might break her spell." Believers—me?

"So what did she say about you? Did she predict your future?"

"She told me things any gal might hear. Nothing earth-shattering." At least I hoped not. "Sorry, but I'm not convinced she's the real McCoy." My boss considered this a plum assignment, but to me, it was a real lemon.

"Don't be so hasty. My friends swear by her. Now they consult her before making any major decisions—and she's always been spot-on." Under her breath she added, "Sadly, she's usually right."

Now I was interested. "Right about what, for example?"

"Mum's the word." She lowered her voice, as if this was top-secret gossip. "One wealthy debutante planned to marry a dashing bachelor from Colorado, who claimed he was a mining baron. After seeing Madame Farushka, she discovered the scoundrel was wanted for bank robbery in two counties. He simply changed his name and appearance, and proposed to the first rich Southern belle he met in Galveston. Poor Emma Lou," she sighed.

Poor Emma Lou indeed. "How'd they find out?"

"Her family hired a private detective and sure enough, he was a fraud—as fake as the handlebar moustache on his handsome face."

Lots of con artists came to Galveston, hoping to get rich quick, making their fortune off booze, bets and broads. "OK, I'll give her a second chance. I'll try to see her this week, if she's not too busy with her society clients."

I had to add that last jab. Maybe Madame Farushka did have some insights and advice that might help Sammy?

Suddenly the phone rang on Chuck's desk and Mrs. Page called out: "News desk! Police!"

Every time I heard her shrill, nasal voice and the word "police," I froze, dreading the next crisis.

When your brother works for the Beach Gang and your beau is the town's only Prohibition agent, you have to be on your toes. Pete rolled his banker's chair over to the phone and both fellas nodded, wide-eyed, as they listened. I craned my neck, trying to overhear.

"Last night? Caught red-handed?"

Bank robbers? Killers? Bootleggers? Curious, I strolled over to their desks. "What's the rumpus?"

Nathan appeared out of the darkroom and I motioned him over, knowing they'd be more willing to talk with their pal by my side.

"Here's a strange scoop," Pete whispered. "The guard at the Broadway cemetery said he caught a couple of grave robbers last night, in the act."

"Grave robbers—in the act? Are you kidding? I thought they went out with Dickens and the Victorian era," I gasped.

"Obviously not," Chuck added. "The groundskeeper caught 'em waist-deep, holding a fistful of gems."

"In a grave?" Shocked, I made a face. "You mean while they were removing items—from a *corpse?*"

CHAPTER THREE

"The groundskeeper claims the grave robbers were covered in dirt, leaning over the coffin, stealing pearls and jewels from a decrepit old woman's body," Pete said.

"How'd they know the victim had anything worth stealing?"

"Does the name Bailey ring a bell? The guard believes it was a relative who resided in a modest gravesite. Those thieves sure uncovered a lot of dirt to find her," Pete said, as he and Chuck jabbed elbows and snorted.

"You're a riot," I frowned, shocked as well as disgusted.

"We're going to pitch the story to Mr. Thomas," Chuck said smugly. "The public will eat it up."

"Good luck." I raised my brows, doubtful that our down-to-earth editor would approve such a salacious story about the Bailey family. Not only could it upset the status quo, the high and mighty society set might want to dig up and move the family mausoleums out of town.

The Baileys practically owned or controlled half of Galveston and the rest was for their taking—except the gangs' turf. Though the prominent, proper family didn't approve of or condone any illegal activity, they were smart enough to do business with the likes of the Maceos, Ollie Quinn and Johnny Jack Nounes—from a safe distance, of course.

Old-money General Bailey eagerly accepted the local mobs' new money into their banks and establishments. Bailey had no problem loaning cash to the bootleggers and gangsters for their next booze supply—coupled with high interest rates—knowing the mobsters would pay them back in spades.

Trying to eavesdrop by the door, I watched the cub reporters try to sell the story to our boss, to no avail. Clearly disappointed, they slouched out of his office and returned to their desks.

"What happened?" I asked innocently, shuffling my papers. "Did Mr. Thomas buy it?"

"No dice. He told us to keep mum and not tell anyone outside of the newsroom." Pete looked perplexed. "Hell, I thought we were doing a public service, warning people their family's graves could be decimated. But he thinks a story about local grave robbers will create a huge scandal!"

Mr. Thomas was right. Not only was the topic sordid and unseemly, the old Broadway cemetery was a source of great pride and comfort to the citizens of Galveston. Generations had been laid to rest there and the families knew where their ancestors were buried. Sadly, the six-thousand-plus victims of the Great 1900 Storm didn't have that luxury. The bodies were either washed out to sea and never recovered or crudely burned in massive funeral pyres.

Still, the fellas looked so crestfallen I tried to cheer them up.

"Why don't you ask the groundskeeper if any other graves have been robbed? Maybe it's the Bailey name that worries Mr. Thomas. He doesn't want to tarnish or taint the Bailey family in any way."

Pete nodded. "He said it was the tall tale of a lone guard—that he needed proof."

Nathan showed up at my elbow. "Proof? I could bring my camera but I doubt they'd pose for pictures."

Chuck slapped Nathan on the back. "Thanks, pal. If you're serious, we could visit the cemetery tonight, watch and see if any robbers come back."

Nathan winked at me. "You mean a stake-out? To catch grave robbers? What about ghosts?"

Chuck said, "Sure, if you're not chicken."

"I ain't afraid of no ghosts!" Nathan replied.

Pete turned to me. "Say, Jazz, what about you? Are you up for a midnight rendezvous with ghosts and goblins?"

"Why not?" I pasted on a brave face. "How about tonight?"

The last thing I wanted to do was spend the night in a cemetery looking for grave robbers, but I pretended to be "one of the boys."

"OK, you're on then. We'll meet you by the Broadway entrance tonight by the angel, say around eight o'clock?" The newsboys exchanged sly looks.

Nathan and I nodded. "Sure. See you there."

I could tell he didn't exactly relish the idea either. I smiled to myself, wondering if Nathan was more afraid of ghosts, goblins or grave robbers—or all of the above.

At five on the dot, Nathan stopped by my desk and asked, his voice low, "Sure you want to meet those jokers tonight?"

"Gotta admit, I'm kinda curious. Let's see if they're pulling our legs." I paused. "First I need to call Aunt Eva to tell her I'll be late." My spinster aunt was the type who worried nonstop, especially about my "dangerous job" as a journalist, though high teas and charity balls could hardly be called living dangerously. While my mother was away in Europe, she felt responsible but still treated me like an unruly child at the ripe age of twenty-one.

As Nathan and I started for the door, Mrs. Page yelled, loud enough for everyone to hear: "Jasmine! Agent Burton is calling you!"

Swell—why didn't she put it on the front page? She didn't need a foghorn with that booming voice.

"Jasmine! Your sweetie pie is on the phone!" Chuck mimicked.

"Jazz, a knight in shining armor is calling you!" Pete chimed in.

"Maybe you want to date him too?" I shot back, then louder: "I'll pick up in the break room."

Turning to Nathan, I held up a finger for him to wait, ignoring Chuck and Pete's smug faces.

"Hello, beautiful," Burton said, smooth as ever.

"Hello to you, too." I always perked up at the sound of James' voice, though after his semi-proposal, I admit, I'd gotten cold feet.

"Want a ride home? We can grab a bite to eat on the way."

"I've got an assignment," I fibbed. "We have to go cover some society shindig. On Broadway." Partly true, but I left out the graveyard setting.

"Don't those society types ever get tired of parties?" He snorted. "Count me out. Maybe we can get together tomorrow?"

"Sure, see you then." Not wanting to explain, yet, I hung up the candlestick phone, hoping Mrs. Page hadn't been listening. She was almost as bad as my boss, Mrs. Nosy Nellie herself. Without bothering to ask for "permission," I grabbed my purse, coat and notepad and headed out.

As we left, Nathan called out, "See you tonight!" winking at Chuck and Pete, the only editorial staff still there, besides my boss.

"I dare you!" Chuck smirked.

"I double-dare you!" Nathan retorted.

Inside his Model T, Nathan asked, "Are you buying their story? Those two saps may be trying to bait us."

"I wouldn't be surprised. First, can we take a small detour?"

He brightened. "Want to hit the juice joints?"

"How about the Hollywood Dinner Club? We can see Sammy, eat a quick meal and catch up. What d'ya say?" I admit, I had an ulterior motive.

"I say we can't afford the water. Can he get us any free food?"

Leave it to Nathan to try to scrounge up a free meal at the ritziest, glitziest place in town. The Hollywood was the place to see and be seen on the Gulf Coast—acclaimed as the first air-conditioned nightclub in the country.

Frankly, I was afraid the Downtown Gang might target Sammy if he ever left the safe confines of the Hollywood. One step outside and he'd be like a tin duck in a shooting gallery. Burton's close call there reminded me of that fact.

"Do you want to get him fired so soon? Now that he's practically part of the family, maybe he can give us a discount."

"Which family do you mean? The Mafia or the Maceos?"

"Both." Tell the truth, Madame Farushka's words had gnawed at me all day: 'Someone close to you is in danger.'

I had to know: Was Sammy the key witness in Johnny Jack's grand jury hearing?

CHAPTER FOUR

At the Hollywood, I felt a bit self-conscious in my work clothes, a rumpled tweed jacket and skirt suit I'd bought at Eiband's on sale, though it was only a casual weeknight crowd.

Sammy seemed surprised when he greeted us at the door, looking natty in a tuxedo with tails, his dark hair slicked back Rudolph Valentino-style. "Evening, Jazz. Nathan. What brings you two here?"

He forced a smile, wary. No wonder. The Hollywood was the kind of glossy, glamorous place you reserved for special occasions— not for interrogating your brother about a possible mob trial.

"We were in the neighborhood and wanted to say hello," I said.

He didn't buy that for a minute since he knew the *Gazette* was across town.

"Well, hello to you too. Where's your...steady?"

"Probably out raiding some bar. You remember those days."

His handsome face broke into a genuine smile. "Hope Agent Burton has learned a thing or two since then. He wouldn't scare a poodle with that routine."

"I think he's improved with experience," I bristled. "When the gangs try to take pot-shots at you, they mean business."

Why did I feel the need to defend Burton? He and Sammy weren't exactly the best of pals, but they had an understanding. Mostly because of me.

Since it was early, the crowd seemed sparse, with only a smattering of the usual high-hat high-rollers. A jazz band played with flair, and I recognized the tune: *Melancholy Baby.*

Honestly, I wished I could ask Burton to join us instead of chasing grave robbers at the Broadway Cemetery.

Still, I was on a mission. Somehow I needed to confront Sammy without scaring him off. From experience, I knew that a rat-a-tat-tat Tommy gun approach rarely worked. "What's new with you? How's the nightclub act?"

"The show is still going on. Slow night." He shrugged. "What can I get you two to eat?"

"Is there anything we can afford?" Nathan said, then stopped when I poked his ribs.

Sammy winked at us. "Here, take a table by the kitchen. I'm good friends with the chef. Let's see what we can do for my friends."

"How about a quiet table? I don't have my glad rags on tonight."

"You look fine." He led us to a table in back, away from the jazz band and dance floor—a far cry from the royal treatment Agent Burton and I usually got. Ever since he saved the day during the "Bathing Beauties Pageant" performance there, Sam Maceo was one of his biggest fans.

Like a proper host, Sammy pulled out our chairs and retreated to the kitchen. A column semi-blocked my view of the bandstand, but I noticed a few older couples doing the tango and foxtrot to strains of *When You're Smiling*.

After Sammy left, Nathan grinned. "Nice to have a pal at the Hollywood, even if I don't rate."

"Sure you do, Nate." I nudged him. "You're like family."

"Gee, thanks." Nathan twirled a finger in his dimple like a celluloid street urchin. "That's what all the reporters say. I'm like their kid brother."

"Don't worry, it means they trust you. Take it as a compliment."

"Oh yeah? I think it's more of an insult," he said, scowling.

Sammy returned with two big plates of lasagna, then pulled up a chair. "Leftovers from last night, courtesy of the chef."

"Oh, boy! Nothing like having an in with the staff." Nathan dug in like he hadn't eaten in a week, while we watched, amused. "Thanks for the grub, pal. Best dish I've had in a while."

"My pleasure. So what are you two doing out in the boonies?" Sammy knew full well the Hollywood wasn't exactly on our way home from work.

"Just a friendly social call." I pulled my chair aside. As Nathan gulped down his food, lost in ecstasy, I tried to broach the subject.

"Say, what's new? How are the Maceos treating you?"

"Sam and Rose are swell. They've been showing me the ropes, explaining how their operation works." He lowered his voice, glancing at Nathan, too busy wolfing down his pasta to pay attention. "Unlike Johnny Jack, who threw me in a black pit and expected me to crawl out on my own."

"Figuratively speaking, I hope."

"I've heard of a few sad sacks who disappeared without a trace."

"You don't say." I winced. "Has he tried to stop by here?"

"Not over my dead body."

"Dead body?" I made a face. "Please don't say that. You're scaring me."

"Sorry, Jazz. Luckily I'm not alone at the door. Big Sam and Rose post bodyguards and bouncers all over the club. After what happened to Burton, they have guys watching the entrance, back exit and the parking lot."

"Good to know." I let out a sigh of relief.

"Give my compliments to the chef," Nathan raved. "If he has any more leftovers..." I kicked him under the table, embarrassed by his lack of finesse.

Sammy smiled, his even white teeth lighting up his dark features. "I'll be sure to tell him."

"Excuse me, I've got to powder my nose," Nathan joked. "Which way's the little boy's room?"

Finally, my chance to confront Sammy. After Nathan left, I said, "I hear Johnny Jack might face a grand jury hearing soon. Are the rumors true?"

"Who told you—your newsboys?" His olive eyes flashed and he glanced around as if the walls had ears. "Why? Is it for the paper?"

"I'm worried about you, why else? I'm sure Johnny Jack wants payback after you left the gang. In fact, reporters aren't even allowed in the courtroom."

"Safer for everyone," he said. "So what?"

"Are you involved at all?" When he didn't reply, I clutched his arm. "Tell me, Sammy. You're not going to testify, are you?"

He shook his head, meeting my gaze. "Hell, no. That's like signing a death warrant. Why risk my life when I know that bastard will bounce right back? He'll pay off the jury when no one's looking."

"Good for you. Do they already have a witness lined up?"

"I hear they found some sucker to volunteer, probably promised him a big pay-out and protection." He let out a snort. "Sure wouldn't want to trade places with that poor patsy."

"I'll say." I felt the tension in my back dissolving. "So how are Frank and Dino doing over at the Oasis?"

"Those knuckleheads are finally learning to run a bar, but I do check in weekly, make sure everything's A-OK."

"Glad they're shaping up. Any trouble with Johnny Jack? He's such a hothead, no telling what he'd do."

"Not yet. His goons show up all the time and try to shake them down, but so far no real threat. Even Buzz won't take their guff."

I knew Sammy had to keep his distance from his own bar, to make sure his staff remained safe and sound, for now. Who knew when Nounes would try to get revenge?

Nathan reappeared, and shook Sammy's hand with vigor. "Thanks again for the meal. You've got a swell set-up here."

"Dinner was delicious," I added, though I barely ate a bite. "See you soon. Take care." No need for Nathan to know Sammy was my big brother.

At the door, I gave Sammy a quick hug. "Jazz, give my best to Amanda," he said. "Stop by anytime."

Apparently, since Sammy started working for the Maceos, he and Amanda were on a "break," for her own security, he insisted.

To date, no one had escaped the Downtown Gang and joined the Beach Gang and lived to tell the tale. Now Sammy was like a wanted man—wanted by both gangs.

CHAPTER FIVE

Nathan's old jalopy stuck out like a rusty old sign surrounded by neon marquees. After I climbed in, he asked, "What were you and Sammy jabbering about? Everything copacetic?"

I stared out the window as he drove down Beach Boulevard, white foamy waves flowing to shore, debating how much to tell him. "I asked if he'd heard about Johnny Jack's grand jury hearing."

"Is Sammy involved?"

"No, thank God."

"Good to hear." He eyed me. "Sure you don't mind creeping around the cemetery tonight?"

"Beats sitting at a desk all day, surrounded by Neanderthals. Except for you, naturally." I forced a smile. "Besides, I don't want to give Chuck and Pete a reason to razz us all week."

"Between us, I don't trust those two jokers one bit."

"You said it. Say, got anything I can slip on?" Surely he didn't expect me to delve into the muck and mud in my office outfit.

"Lucky for you, I happen to have an old jersey and jeans on hand. Sometimes I like to play baseball with the guys after work."

"Swell." Yet one more reminder of why I wasn't a member of the all-male news club. "No peeking!"

Quickly I changed clothes, then tucked my bobbed hair under a cap and wiped off my face paint.

"Oh, boy. Now you look like a skinny wino," Nathan joked.

My stomach was in knots as we neared the cemetery, foreboding with its majestic mausoleums and Gothic headstones.

What was I thinking, coming out here in the dark, hunting down grave robbers? Fortunately the Victorian street lights along the boulevard beckoned us like Aladdin's lamps, illuminating the way.

After Nathan parked, he held out his flashlight like a sword.

Tree branches resembled witches claws in the dark, shrubbery looked like hunchbacked ogres. Slowly we made our way to the entrance where we'd agreed to meet Chuck and Pete. Tiptoeing through the tombstones, I wondered about the lost lives, the names engraved on the markers: A whole graveyard full of stories! Yet now wasn't the time to mull over buried bodies or buried secrets.

Our breath came out in frosty puffs as we stood shivering by the imposing monument, afraid to speak. No sign of the fellas.

"You think they stood us up?"

He shrugged. "I figured those two lollygaggers were no-shows."

A bright beam of light cut through the shadows.

"Who goes there?"

Nathan and I flattened against the statue's base, holding our breaths, like telltale clouds of smoke in the cold night air.

"What if it's the grave robbers?" I whispered.

"Relax," Nathan replied, but he didn't look relaxed at all. "It's probably just the groundskeeper."

The light flashed across the statue, illuminating us like coal-miners in a cave. A soot-streaked oaf with big dirty hands held up the lantern. "What are you kids doing out here at night? Not safe to be here after dark." The burly giant stood over us, a ragged wool cap on his head, his lantern swinging back and forth.

Nathan found his voice. "We're here to pay our respects to Aunt Matilda—it's her birthday."

"Well, you boys be careful. We've seen some shady characters out here lately. You never know who they'll come after next."

Boys? My disguise worked!

We skulked back to find a place to hide near the gate, in case we needed to make a quick exit. Hard to avoid stepping on graves in the dark. I shivered each time, hoping not to disturb any lingering ghosts. I'm not superstitious, but I wasn't so sure about the afterlife. Who knew if it existed?

Luckily a huge mausoleum provided a perfect hiding place in case the guard scoured the grounds again. As we waited for Pete and Chuck, we heard a motorcar drive up and stop on Broadway.

"Is that the fellas?" I asked, craning my neck.

Under the bright Victorian lamps, we saw a flatbed truck park by the entrance. Two hobos in overalls got out and started to fiddle with the truck's tailgate. One tall man climbed in the back of the truck and began shoving a wood box toward the burly man on the ground.

Curious, Nathan and I crept closer to the truck, ducking behind bushes. Who were these guys—and what were they doing here at this unholy hour?

"Be careful!" We heard one fella yell while he struggled with the long container. The tall fella jumped off the truck bed and helped the other man place the wood box on the ground. I blinked in surprise.

Jeepers! No doubt about it—it was a coffin.

I watched while they pulled out shovels and began digging a grave for the poor sot. Seems they'd planned this burial in advance.

"Who buries bodies at this hour?" I whispered to Nathan.

"Gangsters, that's who."

CHAPTER SIX

"Let's scram before these goons decide to dig two more graves!" I yelped. A tad melodramatic, but I was scared to death.

As I turned to leave, Nathan reached out to stop me. "Not yet."

The men resumed digging and I swear I heard one singing an Irish tune. How could they be so cheerful surrounded by death?

"If we blow, we need to be able to locate the graves later," Nathan said.

"Why? So we can be next?"

"Don't you want to know who's in that coffin—and why these wiseguys showed up here after hours?"

He was right. Despite my trepidation, I was tempted to stick around to find out. Nervously, I moved closer, trying to get a good look at the men. What was the whole story? Was the groundskeeper connected? Or were they simply digging a pauper's grave, trying to find a proper resting place for a poor pal?

Tell the truth, I didn't believe that theory at all.

With the soft gray puffy clouds and graveyard full of sweet angel statues and grand mausoleums, I felt as if we were in a Victorian novel—rather, a Bram Stoker horror story.

The cemetery felt eerily silent while the gangsters took a break, smoking cigarettes and talking in voices too low to understand.

"I'm getting my shovel." Nathan headed toward his Model T.

"Don't leave me here alone!"

A sliver of a moon cut the dark sky, barely illuminating our way. I tripped over a tree root and fell onto a grave, crying out in pain. Quickly I glanced at the headstone: "Eliza Hamilton, Beloved Wife and Mother, B. 1852 D. 1888 May She Rest in Peace."

Oh no—if I didn't get up, and fast, Eliza was sure to haunt me tonight. If not in spirit, then in my dreams. "So sorry, Eliza," I told her grave. Now I was talking to ghosts?

Nathan helped me to my feet and I limped slowly to his car, stopping to rub my ankle. The air was calm, the night silent. Only a few seagulls soared overhead, squawking to each other.

Nathan picked up his shovel from the trunk. "These guys don't seem at all worried about being caught by the guard. Say, where'd he go anyway?"

"He may be on the take, paid to look the other way." I pointed to his glove compartment. "Do you have a gun in there?"

"As a former Boy Scout, I always come prepared." He grinned, holding his flashlight by his face, giving an otherworldly man-in-the-moon effect.

"Hope those goons finish soon so we can mark the spot and go," I said.

Gingerly we crept toward the fresh gravesite and stopped in our tracks. Now the men appeared to be unloading another long wooden box from the flatbed truck.

Was I seeing things? *Two* coffins?

CHAPTER SEVEN

"Oh, my God!" I gasped. "Why are they burying two coffins in one grave? You think they're hit men?"

"Maybe a gangland slaying—or double murder. Say, two hired hits," Nathan said. "You know, a two-for-one special?"

"Fine time to joke about murder. That's two bodies, too many."

Hiding behind the mausoleum, we watched the men bury the second coffin right on top of the first one. Economical and efficient, even for killers. Finally the gangsters finished digging and leaned against their shovels, taking a cigarette break, talking and laughing. Surely they wouldn't hang around for long, waiting to get caught—unlike us fools.

"These thugs act like they're playing in a sandbox. No remorse," I whispered.

As we watched, the men patted down the graves as if making sure the bodies didn't escape their coffins. One grabbed a liquor bottle from the truck, perhaps to celebrate their handiwork or toast their fallen friends. They passed the bottle back and forth, taking swigs, slowly getting plastered.

"This could take all night," I complained. "I'm getting leg cramps from crouching for so long."

After what seemed like ages, the two gravediggers drove off in the truck. Undaunted, Nathan picked up his shovel and began to attack the fresh dirt. "Wait till I tell the guys what I dug up!"

"You wouldn't dare dig up fresh graves! Let them rest in peace."

"So what? I can take some great pictures."

"What if we get caught? They'll accuse *us* of murder!"

A fancy car—a Cadillac?—turned around on Broadway, headlights beaming into the cemetery. Did they see us? Frozen in place, Nathan dropped his shovel and we hid behind the bushes. Luckily the car kept driving.

Desperate to leave, I looked around for something, anything, to help mark the graves. Then I spied an empty bottle of rum thrown carelessly into a shrub. "Let's use this bottle as a marker, OK? We'll need permission, and a whole crew, to dig up these graves, not just one shovel." I placed the bottle on top, and tried to memorize the area, noting the monuments and shrubbery.

"Guess you're right." He looked disappointed. "Sure wouldn't help our careers to spend a stint in jail."

Nathan fancied himself a famous photojournalist and often got carried away on a story, rushing into danger without thinking. During a booze bust, he once dashed into a raging fire, risking his life to take pictures for the paper.

"Come on, let's skedaddle!" Anxious, I sprinted toward his car and slid into the Model T. "I wonder if there's a turf war going on between the Beach and Downtown gangs. When two bodies turn up dead, it's no accident."

Nathan started his car, checking his side mirror before easing onto Broadway. "I'll ask the fellas at work what they've heard."

"Sammy didn't mention a new gang war, but he rarely confides in me."

"Why would he tell *you* anything?" Nathan eyed me. He still had no idea Sammy was my brother and I planned to keep it that way.

"Maybe they're goons for hire who do the gangs' dirty work, like get rid of dead bodies," I suggested.

He nodded. "I've heard they fix problems for the mob, and clean up any incriminating evidence at crime scenes. Mack calls them fixers." Nathan honked at a sleek hayburner that moved into our lane. "I wish Mack was still working at the paper. He always knew about the gangs' latest feuds."

Mack again? "Probably because he has a criminal mind like they do. When is he coming back?"

"When Mr. Thomas gives him the A-OK. Considering his condition, that could take a while." A nice way of saying Mack had the DTs and needed to dry out. Sure, we'd had our ups and downs but despite our differences, it was sad to see his decline.

In fact, Prohibition seemed to have the opposite effect that the Women's Temperance Movement and the Drys had intended: By forbidding the sale, transportation and manufacture of alcohol—but still allowing drinking or *consumption*—the Volstead Act had turned the country into a land of lushes. People considered the lame law an excuse to imbibe at speakeasies in public or throw elaborate cocktail parties in private.

"Should I tell James...Agent Burton about these coffins?"

"Why spill the beans to the cops?"

"Burton isn't an ordinary lawman, as you know." Why did I have to keep explaining his job to Nathan? "He's as suspicious of the local cops as we are."

"Well, consult me first if you decide to blab to Burton."

"Blab to Burton?" I bristled. "Since when do I need your permission to talk to my boyfriend?"

Nathan gave me a sly smile. "I think that's the first time you've ever admitted that Burton is your fella."

He was right. Blushing, I changed the subject. "Better head back home. Aunt Eva will be worried." By now it was almost ten and I wondered if James had tried to call. Fine if he was keeping in touch, not checking up on me.

After Nathan stopped at the boarding house, I got out and leaned over the window. "Mum's the word until we can go uncover more evidence." I grinned, giving him a taste of his own cornball humor. "See you tomorrow."

"Can't wait to razz the guys at work, the big sissies."

A smile seeped across my face. "OK, but don't mention the gravediggers or the coffins yet. This might be my chance to scoop those blowhards."

CHAPTER EIGHT

After I tiptoed inside the boarding house, Amanda stopped by my room. "Where have you been? You look like Boxcar Bertha."

I hesitated while I peeled off Nathan's dirty clothes.

"What's going on?" she persisted.

"The cub reporters wanted us to help them catch some grave robbers, but they never showed up."

"Grave robbers? Are you bonkers? I can't imagine spending more than one minute in a graveyard at night. I only stay long enough to pay my respects and flee. See any spirits?"

I was tempted to tell her more, but I knew what a chatterbox she was. "Believe me, it was so spooky, I got the heebie-jeebies."

"Be careful out there, Jazz," Amanda warned. "You never can tell who, or what, might appear. Ghosts, goblins, gangsters..."

"Let's just say I know where the bodies are buried."

The next day, I was late to work since I hardly slept a wink. When I did fall asleep, I dreamt the Downtown Gang chased us across the cemetery, arms outstretched like Frankenstein's monster. I must have screamed because Amanda said, "Poor thing. No wonder you're having nightmares."

By the time Chuck and Pete strolled in, Nathan and I had our story straight, or so I thought. "Where were you last night?" Nathan asked. "Jazz and I waited an hour for you two 'fraidy cats. Guess you got the jitters."

Chuck and Pete gulped. "You were there? Sorry we missed you. We didn't see any grave robbers so we got bored and left early."

"Says you. Boy, did we get an eyeful," Nathan said, but I tugged on his jacket to shut him up.

"Oh yeah? An eyeful of what?" They leaned in to hear.

"Oh, Nathan's just joking," I broke in. "All we saw were a couple of mourners, and the groundskeeper."

"Nothing fishy?" Pete asked.

"Only a few bats and rats," Nathan said. "No fish."

Changing the subject, I asked, "Say, have you heard about a recent gang fight or slaying?"

"Nothing new. Same old turf war. I'll ask Mack what he knows." Chuck gave me the once-over. "Hey, don't you have any fancy weddings or charity balls to cover? How about recipes and household hints to write up?"

"Recipes? I can't even make coffee," I bristled, which was true. "I'd rather look for leads myself than depend on Mack, like you two lazy dewdroppers."

I glared at him before returning to my desk. What a louse. Mrs. Harper frowned at me over her Underwood typewriter and I knew I'd better get to work, fast. "Miss Cross, there's a short stack of stories that might interest our readers," she said, waving at my desk.

Half-awake, I perused through the usual tidbits of society gossip—upcoming Christmas parties, church potlucks, charity fundraisers, engagements linking one prominent family to another, so the rich could get richer.

"By the way, we got a call from the Hotel Galvez that may be worth checking into. That is, if you're not too busy." Was that a jab? My boss handed me a short scribbled note: A ghost sighting by a Galvez guest, on the fifth floor. Who really believed this malarkey?

I shoved it aside and began proofing Mrs. Harper's gossip column, typing it up as I went along, but the story kept coming back to haunt me, so to speak. Every so often, a tourist claimed to have seen ghosts wandering the halls of the Galvez or the Strand. Sure, I'd heard stories of ghostly Great Storm victims or jilted lovers popping up or phantom duels taking place in alleys. Yet I dismissed them as the fantasies of romantics with vivid imaginations or spiritualists with extremely poor eyesight.

Mrs. Harper waved me over with an encouraging smile. "I'm sure you've heard the rumors about the ghost bride haunting the Galvez. I thought the story might be amusing for our readers."

Spirits haunting hotel hallways were amusing? "Want me to follow up?"

"Seems to me you like chasing fairy tales and ghosts."

What? Did she know about our outing at the cemetery?

"Spiritualism is all the rage with the society set now," she added. "Why don't you investigate it in your free time, perhaps during your lunch break?"

What free time? "Will the paper cover my expenses?"

"We'll see." She fluttered her lashes so fast I knew she was annoyed. "Try to set up a meeting today, before she leaves town, and hear what she has to say. Could be a fun story for our readers."

Fun? To me, it was yet one more fluffy society story to entertain the bored old money and *nouveau riche* crowd. Clearly the story seemed too insignificant for Mrs. high and mighty Harper. No doubt it meant another fanciful trip into the occult, but I could avoid her scrutiny for a while.

"As you know, Jasmine, I can't guarantee it's anything we might print. Unless the guest is of interest? A bigwig from Austin or Dallas or Houston perhaps?"

A lush who got high from too many highballs? An oilman who saw demons after imbibing too much demon rum?

"Yes, ma'am," I mumbled, irritated. Why even bring up the subject if it wasn't going to get published? "I'll call the Hotel Galvez soon as possible."

"How about now? Time's a'wasting!" With that, she wheeled her chair around, blocking me out, and resumed typing.

When would I ever get a shot at a real news article? I sighed. Oh well, at least it was my chance to escape the office. Maybe afterwards, Nathan and I could sneak back to the cemetery, locate the fresh graves in daylight—and try to uncover a real story. Gangsters over ghosts any day.

In a way, I wanted to call Burton and describe our late-night adventures, but I needed privacy from the nosy staff and operators who listened in on conversations. Nor did I want a stern lecture from him, so I decided to wait to share our tales of the crypts.

After all, those poor dead souls weren't going to escape their confined coffins anytime soon.

CHAPTER NINE

Overwhelmed by the occult, I tried to put thoughts of ghosts and graveyards out of my mind while I typed up Mrs. Harper's latest column. Thank goodness Nathan stopped by my desk before noon. Boy, did I need a break from brides and burials. "Ready for lunch?"

"I may have to go on some wild ghost chase at the Galvez for you-know-who," I complained.

"Ghost chase, huh?"

"Haven't you heard about the ghost bride haunting the halls? If you give me a lift, we can eat at the hotel first."

Nathan whistled. "On whose dime? I can barely buy a soda pop on my paltry pay. Can the paper spring for lunch?"

At least Nathan was honest about his bribery. Still, his jalopy sure beat taking the ancient trolley on this cold December day.

"I'll see if I can get Mrs. Harper to pick up the tab."

"Good luck getting a cent out of her," he said. "Make it fast, please. I'm starving."

After he left, I called and arranged to meet Lily Leavenwood, since I couldn't exactly interview the ghost. She seemed reasonable enough on the phone and we made plans to meet for afternoon tea in the main lobby.

Miraculously I convinced Mrs. Harper to give me a few bucks from petty cash, and we left at 12:30 in Nathan's Tin Lizzie.

"Good news!" I told him. "Mrs. Harper forked over enough dough to get sandwiches for lunch."

"Big spender. I thought we could only afford to eat the crusts."

The icy breeze whistled through the windows of his rattletrap as I held tight to my cap and wrap. With my windblown hair and hat askew, I hoped I'd look presentable enough for the glorious Hotel Galvez guests and Lily Leavenworth by the time we arrived.

Frankly, I couldn't help but wonder: Was Lily a nutter or caught up in the spiritualist craze that enthralled the society set?

Naturally I'd heard about ghost sightings at the Galvez and on the Strand, though no one seemed to offer any proof or question their validity. Most folks seemed to accept, even relish, the rumors as part of Galveston's local charm. Some brave souls flocked to the haunted sites, searching for spirits, but they sure scared the hell out of most tourists.

At the Galvez, Nathan dropped off his keys with the valet, who sniffed at his old jalopy like it was a smelly kettle of fish. Nathan grinned and proceeded to take my arm as if we were the Moodys or Sealys in the flesh.

The Galvez lobby felt like a palace with its graceful arches, high ceilings and Roman-style columns. I popped into the luxurious ladies' lounge—the Hotel Galvez was far too sophisticated to simply call it a restroom—and freshened up. Nathan and I settled into a booth at the elegant restaurant facing the ocean, watching the well-heeled crowd prance around in their furs and finery.

A perky waitress took our order of soup and sandwiches. I asked Nathan to wait while I met with the hotel manager.

"I'll relax and enjoy the view," he agreed. "Better than staring at the backs of hacks all day."

I didn't recognize the hotel manager, a stiff and sullen sort who seemed reluctant to discuss the ghostly guest. After I introduced myself, I told him, "I've heard rumors that you might have an *apparition* on the fifth floor?"

"Oh, that old tale," he sniffed, his moustache twitching. "Why are you so interested? Well, let's talk in my office, not out here where we can be heard."

His corner office seemed as stuffy and gloomy as he appeared, with faded wallpaper and wilting flowers. I sat down in an old wood banker's chair and leaned forward, my notepad ready.

"Have you ever seen the ghost bride or spoken to Lily Leavenworth yet?"

"Not personally, but I *have* heard whisperings over the years. Tourists often ask me if the hotel is haunted." His back stiffened. "Honestly, I don't want our guests to know about this so-called ghost-sighting. They may be scared away for good! During off-season, we need all the visitors we can get."

"On the contrary," I protested. "I think ghosts may be a big draw for many people. The occult seems to be of special interest these days."

"You think so?" He perked up. "In that case, I'll tell you everything I know. Rumor has it, a young bride planned to be married to a ship captain here in the ballroom over two years ago. She counted the days until he was ready to come home. Right before the wedding, she got word he'd shipwrecked."

"How sad." Tears stung my eyes as I imagined the heartbroken young woman, waiting for a bridegroom who never appeared.

"What did she do?"

"She got dressed for her big day as if nothing happened, and naturally he never showed up. After waiting until dark on the beach, the story goes that she was so distraught, she flung herself into the ocean, wedding dress and all, and drowned. Her body was found on the beach the next day, in front of the hotel, her gown still intact."

"Oh no! How terrible." I blinked back tears and sniffed, not very professional. "What happened to the groom? Did they ever find his ship?"

"That's the worst part. Her fiancé appeared a week later, fit as a fiddle, ready to walk down the aisle. Luckily, after the boat capsized, he and his shipmates were rescued by a group of fishermen. Unfortunately, they'd gotten caught in a storm and it took days to make it back to Galveston. He was so upset by her death that he also tried to drown himself—but his family stopped him in time."

"Right in front of the hotel?" By now, I had the sniffles and dabbed my eyes, trying not to cry in front of this proper stranger. "How awful. Is he still living on the island?"

"I have no idea. Please tell me what our guest has to say before you print your article." His eyes narrowed in warning. "I do have a friendly relationship with your boss."

Mrs. Harper and her spies. I doubt the newshawks had to get their stories approved in advance by their sources.

"Of course. I'll keep you posted. Now I'm having lunch with a friend." I stood up, glad for an excuse to leave, and dried my eyes, hoping Nathan wasn't getting too impatient. He'd just taken a huge bite of his corned beef on rye when I sat next to him in the booth.

"Thanks for waiting. I see my delay didn't spoil your appetite."

He chewed for a few minutes before answering. "Not at all." Nothing interrupted Nathan's constant quest for food. He was worse than Golliwog, my adopted stray black cat.

"Have you ever heard the ghost story about the abandoned bride who drowned herself?"

Nathan shook his head, still munching.

I gave him a condensed version, adding: "I can imagine this blushing bride waiting at the altar for her groom who never appeared. She was devastated after she heard about his shipwreck. Wonder why she finally gave up hope and drowned herself?"

"Beats me," Nathan shrugged, still engrossed in his sandwich.

Finally I gave up trying to talk to Nathan and decided to save my energy for Lily Leavenwood. After lunch, I stopped in the ladies room, dabbing on fresh face paint and putting on gloves I kept in my purse, just in case.

In the lobby, I prepared for my interview with a list of easy questions. Sure, it was interesting to ponder the supernatural, but as a journalist, I didn't go along with superstitions or sixth-sense feelings without actual proof. I had to be able to see and talk to people to believe they were real.

Even photographs could be altered, like the Cottingley fairies that gripped the public's interest in 1917 and turned out to be a big hoax. The fairy-tale creatures were nothing more than whimsical paper cut-outs concocted by two young British girls to "prove" fairies existed.

Nathan happily sipped a Coca-Cola, eyeing the spoiled princesses planning their debutante parties and society matrons putting their final touches on upcoming Christmas galas and balls.

As I waited, loud voices sounded across the lobby and I looked up to see a roly-poly man in a pin-striped suit with a red freckled face, holding a cane, accompanied by one of his many minions: Ollie Quinn, Sammy's new boss—and leader of the Beach Gang.

CHAPTER TEN

Last time I saw Ollie Quinn was at this very hotel, while I was trying to escape the clutches of Colin Ferris, the once-shady gangster who turned out to be a good guy in the end. Frozen in place, I turned my face so he wouldn't recognize me. Not that I had a beef with the mobster, but I'd rather not consort with gang leaders in front of the oh-so-proper Galvez guests or the hotel manager who claimed to be buddies with my editor. Still, I was curious. Why was Quinn here? After all, he had his pick of speakeasies and nightclubs to frequent, including Sammy's new digs, the Hollywood Dinner Club.

I leaned back and overheard him demand a room for his timid guest, a mild milquetoast kind of fella in a houndstooth jacket and bright geometric tie, who nervously shuffled his feet next to the larger-than-life gangster.

"Only the best will do for my friend here, a room with a beach view," Quinn said, pounding the counter as well as the thin man's bony chest. The poor guy flinched and gasped for air. "He's a special guest here. Take good care of him."

With that, Quinn practically shoved the fella at the hapless hotel manager, who looked as if he'd also seen a ghost. Then Quinn proceeded to parade around the hotel, perhaps hoping he'd be recognized, no doubt wanting to see and be seen. I pretended to dig into my handbag for my lipstick, anything, to avoid eye contact with the mobster.

Curses. He towered over me, tipped his dark felt hat, a contrast to his strawberry-blond hair, studying me with a curious expression.

"Hello, little lady. Haven't we met before?" What now—should I play dumb or would that be an insult to the powerful mob boss, who virtually held Sammy's life in his hands? Yes, the Maceos were up-and-coming gangsters, but Ollie was king of the castle.

Better to be safe. I smiled and nodded. "Yes, I believe so. I was a friend of one of your..." What could I say? The word *goon* would be appropriate, but not appreciated. I continued: "...associates."

"You mean Colin? If I recall, he was sweet on you." Quinn folded his beefy arms across his barrel chest. "What's your name?"

"Jasmine Cross." I blanched. Why did he need to know?

He gave me the once-over. "By the way, how's your beau?"

Why bring up Agent Burton now? "He's fine. Why?"

"Please give him my regards." What did *that* mean—a threat or a warning? He tapped his cane in dismissal, and headed toward the check-in counter. In any other setting, our exchange may have seemed mild, even cordial—not a conversation between a big-time mobster and a society reporter. But since Quinn practically owned and controlled half of Galveston, his words took on a sinister air.

In the past, Quinn had a few run-ins with Burton, the town's sole Prohibition agent. Like Sammy, Burton kept his business mostly private—for my own protection, so they said. Still, I didn't want to be treated like a dumb Dora. I wanted to be near the action, separate rumors from facts, discover the truth, like a real journalist.

Finally Nathan figured out what was going on, and came rushing to my side. "Was that Ollie Quinn?" he asked breathlessly. "Did he threaten you? What did he want?"

"That's what I'd like to know."

Still dazed, I replayed the conversation in my mind. "What's strange is he asked about Burton and mentioned Colin Ferris, the long-gone gangster. Maybe it *was* a warning?"

Surely Quinn knew that Burton helped Sammy escape from the Downtown Gang. Hadn't he seen him working at the Hollywood?

In fact, Quinn co-owned the swanky nightclub with the Maceos. Perhaps his polite inquiry was a way of showing gratitude to Burton for helping Sammy.

I took one last glance at Quinn, now in deep discussion with his friend. The men crossed the lobby toward the elevator, led by the twitching hotel manager, their faces solemn, as if going to a wake.

"Miss Cross?" A trim, prim woman in her mid-thirties interrupted my thoughts, extending a gloved hand. "I'm Lily Leavenworth. Thanks for meeting me here." From outward appearances, she didn't seem to be a lunatic or a charlatan or a publicity-seeking spiritualist at all. In fact, she appeared to be perfectly sane and sensible.

"How about some high tea?" I asked the petite brunette.

"Perfect." She nodded as we made our way to the now-deserted restaurant. We found a private half-moon booth in the corner and, after making small talk, Mrs. Leavenworth began to relax.

She settled back in the booth, and removed her fine leather gloves. "I hope you don't think me foolish with my ghost story."

"Not at all, Mrs. Leavenworth. I find stories of the spiritual world fascinating." I smiled brightly, trying to convince her I was a believer. Yes, I was telling the truth—to me, they were interesting flights of fancy.

"Please call me Lily. May I call you Jasmine?"

"Feel free to call me Jazz. All my friends do."

"Seems we're both named after flowers. How delightful."

A plump waitress came by, with her fair hair in a bun and a distinct British accent, perhaps a Great War bride?

To splurge, I ordered high tea with the works: a hot pot of Earl Grey, finger sandwiches and scones. Why not, if the paper was picking up the tab?

With all the excitement of seeing Quinn, I realized I hadn't even eaten a bite at lunch. No doubt Nathan had polished off my plate.

After the waitress left, I asked Lily softly, "When did you first see this ghost?"

"Marilyn," Lily added, as if they were old friends. "Her name is Marilyn Foster. Marilyn began visiting me in my hotel room, late at night. She'd stand by the curtains, waiting for me to notice her. At first, I thought I was dreaming since she was dressed all in white, like a bride. In fact, I believe she wore a beautiful lace wedding gown with a veil and long train."

Had Lily also heard the rumors or was she telling the truth?

The waitress reappeared and set down a tray with a floral china teapot and matching cups, plus a tower of treats: finger sandwiches on the lower level and scones positioned prettily on a lace doily, next to a bowl of clotted cream.

She poured us two cups of tea, asking, "Milk or lemon?"

Definitely a war bride. Who else added milk to their tea except the British?

After she left, I asked, "Does Marilyn usually visit you at night?"

Lily nodded. "It's like our own private secret. She's so petite, she can hide almost anywhere in the room, behind the bed, the curtains, the furniture. As the week went by, she'd pop up in the most unexpected places, down the hall, behind a potted plant or column. Once I caught her by the grand piano in the lobby, playing *Someone to Watch Over Me*. No one else noticed her. Only me."

"You don't say." OK, I'd go along with her tall tale to keep her talking. I took a sip of tea, the steaming teacup warming my hands. "What did she want? Did she try to communicate with you?"

"Yes, later she seemed to seek me out during the day, whispering to me. At first I thought it was the wind, the windows rattling or the floorboards creaking. But then I realized she was trying to convey a message."

Lily sounded so sincere, so earnest, that I wanted to believe her.

"Really? What message?"

She looked around the lobby, clearly afraid of being overheard by the staff or guests. "Marilyn repeated one word, over and over." Her eyes wide, Lily paused and set down her teacup, placing her hand over her heart.

Now I was getting the jitters. "What word?" I leaned forward to hear, coaxing her to continue.

Her face paled, her hands shook. "Murder."

CHAPTER ELEVEN

"Murder? Are you sure?" Now I really had my doubts.

"Of course I'm sure." Frowning, Lily shifted in her chair and looked away. "You must think I'm a daft, addle-brained woman, but I know what I saw and heard. This poor girl wanted to tell me that she didn't drown—she was murdered." Lily spoke with such conviction I wanted to believe her story.

I sat there in stunned silence, analyzing her words, wondering if her story was legitimate. Lily didn't seem the type given to making up stories or lying to get attention. Perhaps she had an overactive imagination or a fondness for weed and demon rum?

"Does she have any idea who killed her?" I asked Lily, wondering how far she'd take this story.

"If so, she hasn't told me. Could be a stranger or a friend. I want to help her, but I don't know how."

"I wonder why she singled you out?"

"The bride, Marilyn, must sense I'm a kindred spirit." She looked out at the beach. "As a child, I was a daydreamer, always with my head in the clouds, as my parents used to say. I attended schools in Galveston, but my parents wanted to move as far away as possible after that dreadful hurricane—north, to Minnesota. Still I'm drawn here every year, to escape the cold winters there. My husband stays behind to take care of our children."

All I could say was: "Your family is from Galveston?"

"Yes, originally." Her face flushed, her voice dropped to a whisper. "Can I tell you a secret? My grandmother used to visit me too, in my bedroom, after she died in the Great Storm."

Taken aback, I tried to compose myself. This stranger just confessed that she saw ghosts on a regular basis. Was she really a spiritualist or delusional or simply screwy?

Lily's eyes misted. "She was a devoted elementary school teacher with young children, and drowned trying to save her students. Unlike most of the teachers, she didn't tie them to a rope, but let them swim away. The ones who survived still honor her to this day."

"Good for her. What a brave woman."

"Very brave. A suffragette as well. I'm her namesake."

"How nice." I smiled. "Will you be in town long?"

"A couple of weeks." She bit into her scone, regarding me. "Jasmine, in your article, please don't portray me as a spoiled society woman trying to seek the spotlight. To be honest, I'd rather you didn't mention my real name in print."

So the "fame and fortune" theory didn't apply to Lily at all.

"I understand. Let me check with my editor, but I'm sure that will be acceptable."

"Do you believe me?"

I nodded, hoping to win her trust. True, I believed Lily *thought* she saw a ghost. "Thanks for your time. I'll be in touch."

She shook my hand, and stood up to leave. "I hope so."

I sipped my tea, mulling over her words. Lily seemed to be telling the truth, or her version of the truth. Was this story worth pursuing or would I be a laughingstock if I turned in an article on a ghost bride?

Nathan saw his cue and sat down at the table. "Those sandwiches look tasty. Do you mind?" Seems he didn't care since he reached across the table and helped himself to the leftovers.

His mouth full, he asked, "So how'd it go with the ghost lady? Was she a nut job or just a ditzy dame?"

"I don't believe in ghosts, but she seemed so sincere that I don't doubt her word. I'm sure she saw something haunting the halls, but whether or not it was an actual spirit remains to be seen."

"Literally." He grinned. "Maybe she's had one too many spirits of her own. Haven't you ever read *A Christmas Carol*?"

"Of course. Burton and I plan to see the play next week at the Grand Old Opera House." I knew Burton was being a good sport since he considered the Dickens classic a fairy tale for children.

"Well, keep it in mind if you decide to write up the story. What if it was all one long dream?" he cracked. "Or maybe she imbibed some bad hooch."

"Lily? I suspect she doesn't drink anything stronger than Earl Grey. Who am I to doubt her word? What if she does have a sixth sense and can communicate with ghosts? Just because I've never seen one doesn't mean they don't exist."

"Don't tell the news guys. They'll think you're as batty as she is."

"So what?" I felt an obligation to Lily, to all of my subjects and sources who confided in me and trusted me with their stories, no matter how strange. "Finished yet? Let's go before Mr. Thomas thinks we skipped town."

Outside, a young valet in a knit cap drove up with Nathan's Tin Lizzie, sorely out of place among the Cadillacs and Bentleys. He handed the kid a quarter tip, saying, "Keep the change, old sport" like a proper gent, grinning at the boy's grateful expression.

At the office, I stopped by Mrs. Harper's desk and gave her an update on Lily's ghost bride story. "Lily thinks the woman was murdered, but is there any proof? If so, who are the suspects? What's the motive?"

Mrs. Harper raised her brows. "Sounds a bit lurid, if not far-fetched. I suppose it could appeal to our murder mystery readers. Go ahead and write up a short tidbit if you want. I'll try to fit it in."

Then I began having second thoughts. If Marilyn really was murdered, could her killer still be on the Island? "Do you think publishing the piece might put Lily in danger?" I asked. "Lily prefers to use a pseudonym to be safe."

"That may be best." My boss took off her spectacles and rubbed the bridge of her nose. "What about your Madame Farushka story? Have you made any progress? You should finish one project before starting a new one."

What story? Who cared about a fake gypsy spouting canned predictions and false fortunes?

"I didn't see much of an angle." I'd begun the story, but put it aside in my desultory way.

"Just because you weren't impressed doesn't mean she's a phony," she huffed. "I suggest you try a second reading before you draw any conclusions. Try to find some of her past customers and see if her predictions came true. You may be surprised."

Not the same old lecture. Did I really want to traipse around town, searching for Madame Farushka's fans—or rather, victims? In a word, no. I decided to present a new idea to my boss. "If you're interested, I may be able to combine both stories into one feature."

Skeptical, Mrs. Harper pursed her red lips. "Pray tell, how would you manage that small feat?"

"Why don't I arrange a séance with Lily and Madame Farushka?" I suggested. "She can try to contact the bride, find out if she was really murdered."

Was I a sucker to go along with this bunk? Still, writing one long article might save me from having to cover more supernatural stories. Despite my doubts, I wanted to trust Lily and learn the truth. Who knew where it could lead?

"A séance?" Mrs. Harper sat up, actually interested. "My dear, if you can convince Madame to pull it off, I may want to attend the séance myself."

Oh no, I groaned. A simple séance—or a three-ring circus?

CHAPTER TWELVE

Trying to keep an open mind, I called Madame Farushka and described Lily's sightings. "Lily is staying at the Hotel Galvez for only a few days and I'm on a tight deadline. Is it possible to hold the séance tonight?" I prodded the seer with politeness. After I'd spoken, I realized how unusual the request seemed. Some journalist I was, trying to track down imaginary ghosts for strangers.

"I'll need more than an eyewitness if I'm to conduct a proper séance," she harrumphed. "Can you bring a piece of clothing, perhaps a scarf, hat or even a purse that belonged to the spirit? And Miss Cross, we need only believers present if we are to speak to the deceased. A skeptic will only hamper the communication channels into the afterworld."

She was clairvoyant enough to know I wasn't a big fan of her touted talents. "I doubt we can find any of her possessions by then. Can you at least speak to the witness, Lily Leavenworth? Discover if her visions are real?"

"She saw the ghost at the Hotel Galvez?" She paused, perhaps realizing Lily was a potential golden goose. "I may have a better idea." Her voice lifted. "How about a Ouija board reading? I just bought a new one and this is a good opportunity to try it out, before it's tainted with..."

"Tainted? What do you mean by tainted?"

When she didn't reply, I gave in. "OK, that sounds fine for now. Let me try to arrange it with Lily. How about six o'clock?"

"I require five dollars for my time on such short notice."

Highway robbery! Of course there was a big fat fee. Would the great Madame Farushka work for any less?

Even Mrs. Harper rolled her eyes at the princely amount and handed over the cash grudgingly, afraid to challenge the fortune teller—rather, fortune hunter. Seems I was in the wrong business.

Despite Madame's high price, I was excited at the thought of witnessing an actual Ouija board demonstration with a willing victim. Amanda had wanted one for months, but my Aunt Eva refused to let such an "evil contraption" into her home. If I was a skeptic, Eva was a full-blown scoffer, who swore, "They're the work of the devil. A demon's device."

Sad to say, while Eva had progressed in many ways, she held fast to several old-fashioned and outmoded beliefs. Why not give it try? After all, even Sir Arthur Conan Doyle was a spiritualist.

Lily seemed happy to meet, glad we were taking her seriously. Nathan volunteered to be my escort and promised to sneak in a few shots of the whole experience. Even if Madame Farushka was a fake, she certainly was a publicity hound, artful at milking the public, and press, for money. Yes, I was curious, but I wanted to get this whole charade over with and chase real leads, not flim-flam fluff.

"Ready for a little spiritual ritual?" I asked Nathan as he plopped his camera equipment on my desk. "Let's get there early and help set the stage."

"Set the stage? Sounds very dramatic to me."

"I'm sure Madame Farushka will put on a performance to remember."

"Swell." He rolled his eyes. "I can't wait."

As we started to leave, Mrs. Page yelled, "Jasmine! Agent Burton is on the line!" Did she use a megaphone?

"Wait a minute." I ignored the staff's smug smiles, and retreated to a back office, away from eager eavesdroppers.

"There you are," my semi-official beau said. "I tried to call you last night, but you were out. Say, are you free this evening?"

How could I tell my practical Prohibition agent guy that I was attending a Ouija board reading that night?

"Wish I was, but I have an assignment."

"You're going out tonight—again?"

He sounded so forlorn that I wanted to cancel my plans and meet him for dinner, but we agreed to go out the next night. After we hung up, I rushed to the front door, searching for Nathan.

"He's in the lobby, waiting for you." Mrs. Page gave me a smirk, implying she thought I was two-timing faithful, cuckolded Burton.

I smirked back, grabbing my leather handbag and notebook, and pulling my felt cloche over my ears. December was one of the few months in South Texas that actually felt cold.

Tapping his watch, Nathan barged ahead and opened the door. "Hurry, we'll be late for your appointment with the gypsy. What's your story about anyway?"

"This is all Mrs. Harper's crazy idea, trying to titillate her society snobs." Why admit that the crazy idea was all mine?

In his Model T, Nathan asked, "You didn't say anything to Burton about the gravediggers, did you?"

"Why should I? He handles booze, not dead bodies." I shifted in the hard-as-bricks seat. "But if the gangs are fighting again, he needs to know, even if Chuck and Pete claim there's no turf war."

"I have a confession to make." He looked guilty. "I told the guys about the coffins, and we plan to dig up the graves tonight."

"What? Gee, thanks, Nathan." I bristled. "I wanted to scoop those dewdroppers!"

"You can't scoop anyone without facts. The sooner we dig up the bodies, the sooner we find out what happened. I'll be glad to take photos—the rest is up to you reporters." He eyed me. "Are you willing to grab a shovel and do it yourself?"

"No, thanks. What about getting permission? How will we explain the bodies to the cops or an M.E.? They'll think *we're* the grave robbers—or the killers!"

"No reason to get your hands dirty. You can stay in the car."

I could hear the disappointment in his voice, thinking I was as chicken as Pete and Chuck last night. I realized he was right: we had to dig up the coffins, now or never. If we waited too long, the thugs could move the coffins or the bodies. Either way, the victims' secrets could be buried forever.

"Maybe I can be our lookout," I suggested. "Better than staring down into a bloody coffin. Make that two bloody coffins."

"Too bad it's not Halloween." Nathan looked worried as he neared Madame Farushka's Victorian mansion. "Say, I don't have to participate in the séance, do I? I'd rather stay in the background, taking photos."

"This isn't a formal séance, only a Ouija board reading."

"What's a Ouija board?"

Did he live under Murdoch's Pier? I reminded myself that Nathan was a normal fella, not given to foolish fads or trends.

"It's a mystical board that communicates with spirits," I said.

"Oh yeah? I'll have to see this contraption to believe it."

"Be my guest."

We'd arrived a few minutes early, to allow Nathan time to set up his camera equipment. Madame Farushka, dressed like a Cleopatra clone with flowing scarves and arms of jangly bracelets and huge hoop earrings—probably real gold, with her fees—seemed to enjoy playing dress-up. With a dramatic flourish, she flung open the double stained-glass doors and led us down the dark hall past a beaded curtain entrance into her parlor, filled with massive carved Victorian furniture and ugly gargoyle bronzes.

A new Ouija board sat in the middle of a round oak table, with four chairs evenly spaced apart, a candelabra in the center. Madame rose to untie the thick silk cords and closed the heavy burgundy velvet curtains trimmed with long fringe, blocking out any twilight in the already-dark room.

Nervously I eyed the flickering candles. Sure, they helped set the supernatural mood, but to me they represented a fire hazard.

The flames cast an eerie glow: shadows and misshapen faces and figures of statues and religious icons seemed to magnify and flash like images in a fun-house mirror.

I got the shakes, feeling as if I'd stepped onto the set of *The Phantom of the Opera*. All we needed was an enormous swaying crystal chandelier to complete the Gothic scene.

Nathan scanned the room, giving me a dubious look that meant: Why waste our time with this hooey? Honestly, I wanted to find out if Madame was truly a visionary or a carnival barker in disguise.

"Nathan needs to take photos for the paper," I informed her. "Hope you don't mind."

"I prefer to keep my readings private, for obvious reasons," she huffed. "But if you insist..."

I showed her the bill I'd managed to seize from Mrs. Harper's claws. "I'm afraid I must."

Frowning, she grabbed the cash, giving Nathan the evil eye. Since she had the money in hand, she couldn't exactly object.

Lily arrived right on time, her pale face flushed with anticipation. "Thanks for seeing me on such short notice. I hope we can help end this girl's suffering once and for all." With a start, she noticed Nathan's camera and tapped his arm. "Please, I'd prefer it if you didn't include me in your photos. I'd rather not upset...the spirit."

He shrugged. "Yes, ma'am. The lighting is dark here anyway."

Lily briefly described her encounters with the ghost bride, Marilyn, but didn't mention murder. She glanced at the Ouija board, exclaiming, "I'm so excited. How exactly do these work?"

After Madame explained the rules—we must remain silent during the reading while she asked the questions—we solemnly took our seats, scooted our chairs closer and placed our fingers on the celluloid triangular-shaped planchette, or pointer. Then she chanted in low tones: "Oh, dear spirit, why do you haunt the Hotel Galvez? What unfinished business must you resolve?"

The planchette was still. No vibration, no movement. I stole a peek at Nathan, who tried not to laugh. The women seemed so intent on the Ouija board's powers that I felt guilty, and obediently shut my eyes. Madame again attempted to summon the bride. "Tell us, spirit, why did you seek out Lily? Do you have a message for her, for all of us? Why is your soul so troubled?"

Suddenly our fingers began to tremble and the planchette moved across the board as if a gust of wind pushed it: landing on the letter S. What did the S stand for? The planchette glided across the board. Next the letter H, then I and finally P, spelling out: S-H-I-P.

That made sense. After all, Marilyn's fiancé was a ship captain and she drowned after his ship was lost at sea. I began to breathe easy, opened my eyes, and gave Nathan a sly smile. So this wasn't very hard, I thought, ready to remove my hands from the planchette. Firmly Madame clamped her hand on mine, weighing it down.

OK, seems the so-called spirit wasn't finished yet. My fingers remained on the planchette for what seemed like ages when it started vibrating again, slowly moving to the letter M. Was it an M for Marilyn? Or marriage?

Madame Farushka's eyes were closed and she swayed back and forth to a silent rhythm. Tilting my head, I signaled Nathan to start taking photos. No one paid attention as he quietly moved around the dark room and took a few shots. His flash added to the atmosphere, the puffs of smoke creating a cloudy haze.

Once again, the planchette vibrated and kept sliding across the board. Wary, I watched Lily and Madame for any evidence of trickery or manipulation, but everything appeared above board, so to speak. Slowly the planchette picked up speed and floated across the Ouija's surface, spelling out a familiar, frightening word: M-U-R-D-E-R.

CHAPTER THIRTEEN

Murder!? Now I was really getting spooked. Hearsay was one thing, but to actually witness a Ouija board literally spell it out...Wait, was I falling for this hooey?

I eyed Madame and Lily across the table, searching for signs of trickery or deception. To my knowledge, the seer had no idea the ghost bride was allegedly murdered. Was it possible? Could people actually communicate with the dead via a board game?

Rattled, I stood up and turned on the lights, giving Nathan the cue to take a few more photos.

"Interesting," I told Lily. "That certainly supports your story."

"I knew Marilyn was telling the truth," Lily said with a satisfied smile. "Why else would she roam the Hotel Galvez? Who was she looking for—her killer or her lost love?"

"Or both?" I added. "What if they're one and the same?"

"What else do you know about this Marilyn woman?" Madame asked Lily, acting puzzled. Didn't the crystal ball give her any clues?

After Lily repeated her story, the mystic narrowed her eyes. "Now I understand. I thought she'd been left at the altar and that's why she drowned herself."

"What should we do next? Try to find her killer?" I suggested, semi-serious.

"That's an excellent idea," Lily nodded. "Then poor Marilyn can rest in peace. How do we proceed, Madame Farushka?"

"Given this new revelation, I feel a proper séance is in order. Can we locate her family or fiancé? Any personal items?" She stared at the Ouija board as if in a trance.

"They may have moved out of town and taken her belongings," I said, to dampen their spirits, so to speak. "Maybe they've accepted her death as fate."

"Nonsense! I'll make it my personal mission to help this poor soul." Standing up, Lily shook Madame's hand with vigor. "Thank you for confirming Marilyn's story, however dreadful. I appreciate your help."

"My pleasure," the seer gloated. "Glad I can be of service."

"I hope to see you soon with more information. And please call me Lily." She beamed at her.

Now they were on a first-name basis? Lily touched her hat brim and strode to the door, waving at a private car waiting in front. Courtesy of the Galvez? Still dazed, we followed her outside and Nathan helped her down the wide stairs. Turning, she fluttered a hand as she descended the steep steps.

"Thanks for everything, Jasmine. You too, Nathan. I'll be in touch soon."

Great, I groaned. Now what had I gotten myself into?

Skeptical, I approached Madame in the hall, wanting to shake her and find out if she'd secretly manipulated the Ouija pointer. "How accurate are these things? Do people truly believe a board game can communicate with spirits?"

"Believe me, Miss Cross, this is not a game." She gave me a chilling stare and tied her scarf, defiant. "This poor soul is in distress and it's up to us to relieve her burden."

"You don't really believe any of that hocus-pocus, do you?" Nathan asked when we got into his Model T.

"All I know is that the board spelled out murder."

"Maybe they deliberately pushed that pointy thing toward those letters," he scoffed.

"Honestly, it seemed to float across the board on its own. What if the bride *was* murdered? The idea of trying to solve an old case sounds intriguing."

"Might be all a waste of time."

"True, but Lily seems so intent on helping solve the ghost bride's mystery. She's convinced she was murdered. I wonder why?"

"May be better to let sleeping dogs, and bodies, lie," he cracked. "Speaking of, are you ready to visit the cemetery?"

"You guys still want to risk digging up two rotting corpses?"

"How else can we solve this crime?" He held up his hands like a goal post. "If not, say the word and I'll take you home."

Staged or not, that Ouija board reading made my pulse race. Honestly, I wasn't ready to sit by the fire, reading with my Aunt Eva.

"And miss all the fun?" I put on a brave face. "What are we waiting for?"

At the cemetery, Nathan parked near the same secluded spot, rummaged around the trunk and handed me some old clothes plus a pair of big, dirty sneakers resembling clown shoes. Quickly I changed while he pulled out his trusty, rusty shovel and looked for the fellas.

"No sign of Chuck or Pete. Maybe they stood us up again?"

"What a surprise. Still want to go through with it?" I asked, hoping he'd change his mind about this morbid plan.

But no, he charged ahead, holding his shovel. The moon shone bright as we tiptoed amongst the tombstones, looking for the fresh graves. I shivered as the wind howled and shrieked, sounding like a woman's cry for help.

Bare trees resembled spindly Medusas, sharp branches outstretched like dozens of thin arms. Sharp twigs scratched my cheek, and I pushed them away, my face stinging, blood on my fingers. I wandered off toward a huge mausoleum covered by shrubbery and vines. Then I spotted the rum bottle still on the grave.

"Looks like the gravesite is intact." Now I wished I'd mentioned our plans to Burton—or was it better to keep him out of this latest gang bloodshed?

As I walked by the majestic tomb, I heard murmurs, voices, singing or chanting. Not again. I froze like a graveyard statue. Robbers or gangsters?

"Wait. I hear something." A flash of white darted among the shadows and I stopped in my tracks. What was it? A ghost? No, it couldn't be a ghost. Maybe I got confused, thinking of the ghost bride. Ghosts didn't exist, did they? Was my mind playing tricks on me—or was I going batty?

Then I saw another streak of white, and another. I blanched and gripped Nathan's arm. "Did you see that?"

"What? Where?" he whispered.

The moon sliced a spot near the clearing and I crept closer to the noise.

"Ghosts. I swear, I see ghosts." I blinked at the white flowing images, rubbing my eyes, pointing at the apparitions. Did ghosts really haunt cemeteries? Was I hallucinating? Had Madame put a spooky spell on us? The voices grew louder as we got closer and hid behind an ornate tomb.

Silhouetted against the night sky, I saw ghosts, all right: the distinctive white robes and pointed hoods of the Ku Klux Klan.

CHAPTER FOURTEEN

"The Klan?" I gasped, covering my mouth. "What in hell is the KKK doing here?" With their long flowing white robes and masked hoods, they appeared like a mirage in the night. I'd seen photos and heard about their evil deeds, but to actually see them up close made my heart thud.

I peeked through the trees at the handful of Klansmen in white outfits forming a half circle. Doing what, exactly? The cemetery certainly seemed to be a popular meeting spot, especially for lowlifes and criminals. What were they waiting for—more men or reinforcements?

"This must be one of their clandestine meeting places," I said to Nathan. "Wonder why they picked this spot?"

"Strange. Usually the KKK likes to make a spectacle of themselves and parade around town pretending they're war heroes."

I shuddered. "Why do these palookas think they're better than anyone else? Why are they even here?"

"These monsters are everywhere," Nathan pointed out. "They're just more visible in small towns."

Hiding behind headstones, we strained to hear the Klansmen, but the whistling wind drowned out their words. Hard to see or hear in the dark with the dense shrubbery and huge mausoleums blocking our view. Were they connected to the grave robbers or the gravediggers we saw?

"What's going on?" I whispered to Nathan.

When we heard a motor, we slowly moved forward. Had Chuck and Pete finally arrived? How could we warn them in time?

But no, it was a flatbed truck that brazenly backed into the driveway by the front. More coffins?

The Klansmen spread out and began removing crates from the truck onto a wheelbarrow, like an assembly line. Clearly this operation had been organized in advance, with no one around to intervene. Then again, did anyone ever try to stop the KKK?

After they loaded up the wheelbarrow, a Klansman pushed it toward a grand mausoleum big enough for an Army brigade. The mausoleum had to be at least one-hundred years old, bolted and locked. Two Klansmen managed to unlock the doors, allowing the rest to load the crates inside for safekeeping. How did they break the locks? What was so valuable that it warranted such secrecy? Guns, weapons, ammunition? Were they planning an attack?

Then the Klansman steering the wheelbarrow stuck something and lost his balance, while a few crates tumbled out, splitting open.

"Damn it!" Cursing, he bent over to inspect the damage, then held up an item for inspection, the glass gleaming in the moonlight.

No doubt about it—a bottle of booze.

Dumbstruck, Nathan and I stared at the bottle, our eyes and mouths wide open. Since when had the KKK become a bunch of bootleggers? So this is where they hid their stash—in an old forgotten mausoleum. I nudged Nathan. "You think they're part of a local gang or acting on their own?"

"Who knows? Let's wait and see."

"Count me out. You know what they do to certain people."

"They won't touch us."

"Wanna bet? If they find us here spying on them, they'll probably kill us first, ask questions later." Trembling, I backed away and stepped on a branch that cracked with a loud snap. The murmurs subsided and all was still for a minute. Oh no, they heard us!

A beam of light flashed, waving wildly in our direction, criss-crossing the ground. "Who goes there?" I heard a deep voice call out.

Nathan and I pressed against the stone mausoleum, frozen in place, still as the concrete angels guarding the tombstones.

"Must be some animal. The rodents like to come out at night."

"Yeah, like us," laughed one man.

A few spoke with a deep drawl, perhaps Cajun, from Louisiana? Was this a new underground gang, an offshoot of the KKK, trying to weasel their way into Galveston, like Frank Nitti and Al Capone?

Soon the men resumed their task of moving crates to the mausoleum. "Let's scram!" I told Nathan. "I've had enough scares for one night."

Carefully I made my way across the graveyard, using the moonlight to guide the way, only stopping long enough to wait for Nathan. Looking down Broadway, I noticed a car slow down as it approached the cemetery, its headlights flashing in the dark. Was that a signal or a warning?

"Let's skedaddle!" I motioned toward the street. "May be more Klansmen." Anxious, I made a beeline for Nathan's Model T, glancing behind me to see if we were being followed.

That's when I tripped and fell over something long and hard and solid: a pair of legs. What in hell?

The body of a man, dressed in a nice suit, was slumped against a tall headstone with a cross on top, his head down as if taking a nap. A bright silk tie circled his neck, tied to the cross, like a noose.

CHAPTER FIFTEEN

My heartbeat came straight from Poe's *Telltale Heart*.

I stared in shock, unable to move or breathe: he was a white middle-aged man, well-dressed, his eyes wide open.

I couldn't help myself, I let out a blood-curdling scream.

I'm surprised I didn't wake the dead.

"Run!" I pointed to the battered body on the ground. Nathan pulled me up and we made a dash toward his car.

This time I didn't bother to look back, racing helter-skelter across the cemetery, my feet pounding the ground, not caring whose graves or ghosts I trampled. I knew if we got caught, we'd be joining the victim tied to the cross on the headstone.

Beams of light bounced on the ground and I turned to see a few Klansmen running after us, their robes flowing eerily behind them like giant cranes taking flight. "Hurry!" Nathan ran alongside me, flung open the Model T doors and jumped inside.

"Hit the gas!" I screamed, shielding my face. Nathan maneuvered the car out onto Broadway, blending in with the few cars on the road. I checked the mirrors, but luckily there were no signs of the Klansmen.

"Close call." Nathan turned off on a side street and we didn't speak for a few minutes, catching our breaths.

"Did you see the body?" I gasped. "I thought we were goners, just like the corpse."

Then we began talking at once, trying to piece together the night's events: Was the victim in the KKK? Who was he—and why was he tied to a headstone? Finally we said in unison: "What do we do now?"

We knew the where and how, but still needed to fill in the who, what, when and why? Was it another gang slaying? The way the man was positioned on the grave seemed to be a message, a clear warning.

My first thought was to stop by the Hollywood, but they'd turn us away if showed up at the swanky club dressed like hobos.

"What about calling Burton?" I suggested. "Who else can help us this time of night?"

"Good idea." Nathan nodded. "Safer at the police station than a KKK meeting."

"Can't figure out why the victim was tied to a headstone," I said. "He looked like an average Joe to me."

"Those average Joes are the ones you have to watch out for."

As we neared the police station, I started having second thoughts, especially since I'd been avoiding Burton all week. "Please drop me off at the boarding house first, OK?"

"Nothing doing. Burton is your beau and you're the one who stumbled on the body. Too bad I didn't get a good look at him."

Nathan sped up and headed downtown while I replayed the night's strange turn of events. All I wanted to do was spend a few minutes poking around the cemetery, looking for evidence of a crime, not get hunted down by madmen in white robes.

"You go on inside. I need to take off these old clothes."

"What should I tell Agent Burton?"

How could we walk in so late dressed like bums and explain the KKK, the dead body, the cemetery—well, everything?

"Tell him we need to speak in private. One crisis at a time."

Showing up here unannounced tonight would be enough of a shock for Burton. I snuck a peek in the mirror, hoping I hadn't smeared mud all over my face and frock. Nervous, I wiped my face, pulled out an enameled tango compact from my handbag, and reapplied fresh lipstick and rouge, as if it mattered in the dark.

Nathan seemed amused. "Really? Now?"

I realized how ridiculous it looked. "You catch more bees with honey..."

"OK, *honey*." He shook his head, baffled, and went in to the police station.

I struggled to pull the shirt over my head, but my arms got stuck. As I tried to wriggle free, I heard a familiar voice.

"Need some help, doll?"

Of all the luck. Why did Burton have to see me tangled up in these dirty duds? "What in hell are you two doing here at this hour? Are you in some kind of trouble?" His expression showed relief and bewilderment. "You look like you've been digging ditches."

I smoothed out the shirt and fluffed my hair to distract from my sloppy appearance. "You could call it an emergency." My voice caught. "I stumbled over a dead body...literally."

"Where?" Burton's jaw tightened.

"The Broadway cemetery," I admitted. "There was a man tied to a headstone."

"A headstone?" Stomping around the car, Burton yanked open my door and motioned for us to get into his fancy Roadster. Of course Prohibition agents had to look the part, to blend in with wealthy gangsters and bootleggers. "We can't talk out here."

After we got settled, he turned toward me, his long fingers tapping the steering wheel with impatience. "OK, tell me what happened—from the top. What were you kids doing hanging around a graveyard tonight?"

Kids? Was he really that upset—or mad at me personally?

I let out a breath. "We heard rumors of grave robbers stealing jewelry off a corpse..."

"You two think you're cops now? Better stick to your day jobs. How'd you find the body?"

I began babbling the whole story, from the gravediggers last night to the KKK and the body tied to a headstone tonight. So much for keeping quiet.

"I wonder if the two events are related?" Burton seemed surprised. "Why don't you show me where you found the poor sap?"

"Are you sure it's safe? The KKK may still be there."

"I doubt it. If the Klan wants to be seen, they make their presence known. They've probably disbanded by now."

"Boy, I hope so," Nathan piped up from the back seat.

"Maybe the victim witnessed something the Klansmen didn't want him to see?" Burton said, hands kneading the steering wheel as he drove. "Wrong place, wrong time."

"Seemed deliberate to me," I said. "The way he was positioned against the headstone, like it was planned, premeditated."

"Did you see his face at all?" Burton asked. "You didn't recognize him from the papers or anywhere else?"

"Maybe. A businessman in a nice suit, choked by his own tie."

"Did you find his wallet or any form of ID?"

"Uh, no." I glanced out the window, feeling stupid. "The last thing I wanted to do was pat down a dead man or search his pockets with the KKK breathing down our necks. I was too busy being scared to death."

"Not a good idea with killer Klansmen on your tail," Nathan added. "No time to waste."

"We were running for our lives. We wanted to get help—namely you." I flashed Burton my best smile, but he stared ahead. Oh well. The tension in the air was thick as bricks.

"You didn't notice anything else, any blood, a weapon, signs of a struggle?" Burton seemed impatient.

"Hard to see in the dark. I know better than to touch a corpse or a crime scene. I just wanted to get the hell out of there."

"Too bad." His face fell. "I doubt we can remove the body without an M.E. on site. Show me his location and we'll go from there." Good thing Nathan didn't mention his brilliant plan to dig up the first two coffins—with or without Chuck and Pete.

"Wonder why the KKK picked that spot?"

"Privacy. Wish I could bust those guys for bootlegging and murder, but we'll need proof. The victim may have been dumped off before by a different gang."

His matter-of-fact tone gave me chills. Burton parked on Broadway and opened the car door for me, gallant even at a murder scene. "Try to stay quiet and out of sight," he warned.

"I'm no dumb Dora." I glared at him.

Inside the entrance, we looked for signs of the KKK but all seemed silent. I jumped when a seagull swooped across the sky—or was it a bat? The moonlight cast a soft glow while I circled the area, feeling queasy as I studied the grounds, looking for fresh footprints, clues, anything amiss. Wasn't this a rather morbid way to spend an evening, especially with my beau?

"All these crypts look the same to me," Nathan griped.

"I expected gangsters to be sloppy, careless, especially late at night," I said. "I thought they'd leave traces behind, some evidence, like gloves or a shovel."

Stepping on sunken graves, I prayed I wouldn't disturb the spirits. The whole evening felt like a dream, or rather a nightmare, surrealistic and spooky, as if I were a disembodied presence caught in the otherworld.

Burton pulled out a flashlight and we combed the area, the light flickering over the graves. I remembered seeing a full shrub and tall tree by the clearing, but nothing looked familiar.

Disoriented, I walked around in circles, shaking my head. "Nathan, do you remember where we found the man?"

He shrugged. "If you've seen one grave, you've seen them all."

Big help he was. Finally I spotted the ornate headstone, the cross illuminated by a slant of moonlight. "Here's the spot!"

Then I stopped dead in my tracks: the body had disappeared.

CHAPTER SIXTEEN

"Where's the body?" Confused, I studied the gravesite, circling around the tombstone. "Where is it? What happened?"

"What in hell?" Nathan said.

"Are you sure this is the right spot?" Burton asked calmly.

"Yes, I'm sure...I think." I looked over to Nathan for confirmation. "But what happened to the corpse?"

"You're positive you saw a body tied to this headstone?" Burton raised his brows. "You weren't..."

"Hallucinating? Making it all up? Tipsy? Why would I bother to concoct a dead body out of thin air?" I flung out my hands, annoyed. Was Burton questioning me, my eyesight—my sanity?

"Maybe he wasn't quite dead yet," Burton suggested. "He may have passed out and you assumed he was dead."

"You think he just got up and walked away?" I stared at him, indignant. Yet to be fair, he hadn't seen the sad sack, the way his head hung low over his collar, his eerie stare. "I highly doubt he was in any shape to stand up and leave. And I screamed so loudly, I'm sure it stopped traffic."

"You can say that again," Nathan nodded. "That's when the Klan came after us like goblins, and we took off running."

"Nathan, what did you see?" Burton asked.

"We saw a man tied by the throat to this headstone, like a hangman's noose," he nodded. "Just like Jazz said. I didn't stop to check, but he appeared to be strangled."

Burton crouched down, shining his flashlight on the ground, searching for evidence. "I think the tie wrapped around his neck was a warning, a threat, a message from the gangs: Don't be a squealer."

"You mean like a snitch?" I asked.

Burton nodded. "A rat. A stool pigeon. All those gang terms for a double-crosser. Once we find out who the victim was, we'll know who he fingered." Yes, I'd heard all those words before—directed at my brother Sammy, when the gangs tried to frame him for murder.

"Now you're starting to sound like a gangster," I told Burton.

"When you deal with the criminal element, it's bound to rub off." He shrugged. "Sorry, but I can't really investigate a murder without a corpse."

"He was there, I promise!" I raised my voice, frustrated. "Why would I drag you out here in the middle of the night—for fun?"

"Hey, I'm as surprised as you are. But until we have a body..."

"Why would they move him?" I broke in.

"Probably because they heard you scream bloody murder," Nathan said.

"Maybe he's still in the cemetery. They could have just dumped him on another grave, somewhere less conspicuous." Then I had an idea, and did a 360-degree spin, looking around.

"What if the poor stiff was one of the guys inside the coffins? If so, why pull him out and put him on display?"

"That's a new tactic." Nathan grimaced. "To bury a body, then dig him up again."

"Here's a possibility. Maybe they hid this guy in the same coffin?" I suggested. "The deaths may all be connected since they showed up here around the same time."

"While we're here, why not dig up the coffins and check?" Nathan said, as if suggesting we play a game of cards.

"Not on your life. That's illegal." Burton's face twisted. "I really can't condone digging up graves without permission. We can wait till morning to notify the proper authorities and get some help."

"By then, it may be too late," I pointed out. "The KKK could come back and remove the body. Again."

"Hell, I'll dig up the coffins by myself," Nathan said. "There's got to be a shovel on the grounds. You can look the other way."

"Fine, you go ahead," Burton worked his jaw. "Break the law. While you're busy, Jazz, can you show me the mausoleum with the crates of liquor? That's my department, not Homicide."

Like Burton said, he was only a lowly Prohibition agent, assigned to investigate booze, not murder.

"I think Nathan wants to be a photojournalist," I explained as we walked. "His pal Mack is giving him big ideas."

"Fine, but it's not safe to take flash pictures here at night."

True. While we headed toward the tomb, we searched the grounds for the body or leftover liquor bottles or any possible evidence. No luck. As we crept closer, I pointed at the massive mausoleum. "That's the one."

Up close, the imposing tomb resembled a Gothic monstrosity with its elaborate spindles and gargoyles guarding the entrance, like a mini-Notre Dame. "See the wheelbarrow tracks leading here?"

"One wheelbarrow for a tomb full of liquor?"

"Must be the good stuff. Sammy said his customers pay top dollar for real rum or pure whiskey. He should know how much top-grade liquor costs."

"Quality over quantity. Still, I've never heard of the KKK involved in the rum-running racket." He tugged at the heavy chain locking the massive double doors. "I wonder how they got inside? This chain must be over a hundred years old."

"Looks like the chain worn by Ebenezer Scrooge's ghost," I said, reminding him of *A Christmas Carol.*

"I'll say." Burton studied the lock, then handed me the flashlight. "Got any hair pins?" I undid my messy 'do and held out a couple of bobby pins, watching while he tried to pick the lock. Nothing seemed to work.

Owls hooted in the dark and I thought I saw a few bats darting at jerky angles between the trees. Vampire bats?

Sliding the chain through his fingers, Burton fingered the links one by one. "Aha! Wait here while I get my tools from the car."

"Alone?" I shivered. "Forget it, I'm tagging along."

We crept back to his Roadster, parked between lights to be safe. As he rummaged around for his tools, I noticed he had a shovel in the trunk.

"That's a lot of gadgets," I said. "Were you a Boy Scout?"

"Matter of fact, I became an Eagle Scout," he boasted. "I always carry extra tools in my trunk for raids or emergencies. Tools of the Prohibition trade—to break into clubs, not crypts."

"What about bringing that shovel? Nathan may need our help."

Burton handed me the shovel. "Feel free to carry it yourself."

We crept back to the mausoleum, our hands full, and listened for voices, but the area seemed quiet.

"I need some help here." Burton gave me a flashlight. I tried to steady my shaking hands as I held the light, watching him manipulate the chain. "You've heard of the weakest link? Instead of breaking open the lock, they managed to twist open the link, then forced it closed again. No need to cut it and alert them that we were here."

Burton tugged at the chain and pulled apart a rusty link with his pliers, then yanked the chain out from the heavy door handles, worn with age. "Open sesame!" he exclaimed, like a victory cry. Then he yanked open the mausoleum entrance, the heavy doors creaking in protest, showing their age.

I focused the flashlight inside the dark tomb and saw stacks of crates lining the walls, so deep and high it was hard to move. Apparently the KKK had been storing crates of booze inside the crypt for a while. The Klansmen had left in a hurry since a couple of whiskey bottles lay on their side.

"The boys will be impressed with this haul." Burton let out a whistle. "No doubt, the KKK has entered the booze business."

CHAPTER SEVENTEEN

"Looks like they robbed a whiskey distillery," I told Burton in amazement. "There has to be at least fifty crates in there." I pointed at the loose bottles on top. "Did they mean to leave this whiskey here or was that an oversight?"

"Who knows?" Burton shrugged. "For now, I'll take a bottle with me, see if I can ID the bootleggers or gang who sell this brand." He rubbed his chin, as if considering his options. "Tomorrow we'll remove these crates before the KKK returns and takes this stash too." He ran the chain through the door handles, and picked up the pliers. "Hold this for me while I fix the link."

While he worked, I marveled at his ingenuity. From all appearances, the mausoleum seemed untouched. No telltale signs of breaking or entering.

After he'd "locked" the double doors, I wondered, "What will you tell Chief Jones about the KKK? You won't mention our names, will you?"

"Of course not. I'll just say I got a head's up from a solid source. Don't worry, no need to get you involved."

"That's a relief." I heaved a sigh.

"All I need are a few trusted men who can help load up the liquor. Rumor is, cops with sticky fingers use the booze to trade for favors or they sell crates to their gangster pals. Wish I could catch them in the act."

He'd warned me about crooked cops, but the local gangs were so powerful, both politicians and policemen tended to look the other way when it came to demon rum—still, they drew the line at murder.

Even Sammy had trouble distinguishing between the good and bad officers and officials in town.

To the public, Prohibition was an inconvenience, a worthless law to be ignored. But to bootleggers exploiting the Volstead Act, selling illegal booze offered a lucrative, if dangerous, get-rich-quick venture. Mobsters with third-grade educations and street smarts became millionaires selling hooch to thirsty and otherwise law-abiding citizens.

"What about the victim? What if we can't find him?"

"I'll try to discreetly ask around, check for any missing persons cases," Burton said. "I can hardly report a murder without a body, can I? Homicide would laugh me right out of the station."

"Speaking of bodies, we need to see if Nathan's made any progress. I hate to leave him alone in case the Klansmen come back."

We spied Nathan hunched over the gravesite, covered in mud, scowling. Despite the morbid scene, Burton and I burst out laughing.

"You look like one of the *Katzenjammer Kids* or the Grim Reaper," I teased him.

"Well, if I had some help, this might go faster," Nathan griped.

Burton looked upward, muttering, "God help me...if we don't get struck down by lightning..." That was as religious as I'd ever seen Burton, who continued to complain and curse under his breath.

Removing his jacket, he said, "Jazz, hand me your shirt, uh, Nathan's shirt." He slipped it on, picked up his shovel and began digging with Nathan. Like a rubber-necker, I had to watch, alternately repulsed and fascinated.

Halloween had always been my favorite holiday as a child. Like an actor, I enjoyed the chance to dress up in various costumes and play different characters, a fun way to indulge my sense of drama and theatrics. But this was a real-life murder, or two, and digging up coffins constituted a serious and scary crime.

"How will I explain this mud to the fellas at the police station?" Burton complained, wiping his face. "Hope these coffins aren't buried too deep."

I felt like we were in an Edgar Alan Poe story, waiting for the horrific ending. Any ravens around?

When I heard the shovels strike the first coffin, I turned my back. "I can't look!" I hid my face. "How will you ID the bodies?"

"Depends on the shape they're in," Burton said. "Impossible if they're mutilated or riddled with bullets unless they have some ID."

Did he have to be so graphic? "Then what?" I shuddered.

"First we'll have to get official permission to dig them up."

"We'll just call this a look-see," Nathan said, reaching down. "Ready for the big opening?"

Even under the direst circumstances, Nathan always had a joke or two handy. Mack must have taught him to distance himself from the gore and reality of a crime scene, a tactic I had yet to learn.

"Jazz, let us know if anyone shows up, OK?" Burton motioned toward the entrance. "If they find us digging up graves, they'll shoot first, ask questions later."

"Hurry, before they accuse *you* of being grave robbers!"

I began to panic, wanting this whole nightmare to be over. Cautiously I backed away, watching the street, heart hammering so hard, my chest hurt. Finally I heard the coffin creak open and clasped my hand over my mouth, half-expecting Dracula to pop out. The Gothic Galveston graveyard setting sure seemed ideal for vampires and witches.

"Holy hell!" Nathan exclaimed.

"Well, I'll be damned," Burton said.

"What? Who is it? Anyone we know—knew?" I cringed.

"Jazz, come take a look. You've got to see it to believe it."

"Why? What is it? Are you razzing me?" I whimpered, starting to shake. Nathan was known for his childish pranks and I was in no mood for tricks.

"Don't worry, Jazz. No dead bodies in here." Burton waved me over. Frightened, I dragged my feet toward the fresh graves, my hands half-covering my eyes, and peered into the coffin.

Burton gave a low whistle. "There's enough rum in here to stock a speakeasy."

CHAPTER EIGHTEEN

"You're telling me!" I gasped.

Agent Burton wasn't kidding: the coffins were filled to the brim with bottles of rum, neat and tight as a box of Tootsie Rolls. How could they cram so many bottles into one small coffin?

"You think the second coffin is full of rum too?" I wondered. "Should we open it to make sure?"

"I'd bet on it," Burton nodded. "But let's not stick around to find out. Come on, Nathan, let's cover up these coffins and scram."

"Hey, don't we need some bottles for evidence?" Nathan reached in and tossed out two bottles. "Don't I deserve a reward for all my hard work?"

Burton shook his head at Nathan, then grabbed a bottle and handed it to me. After they closed the coffin and packed down the dirt, he said, "Thanks for insisting we dig up those coffins. Who knew they'd be full of booze?"

"Lucky for you." Nathan flushed with pride. "I always trust my gut." True, his gut served him well—and vice versa.

"Gotta hand it to you two hooligans, you helped me locate not one, but two major stashes of hooch. Wait till my boss gets wind of this haul."

"Attaboy!" I praised him, patting his back. "You mean the big cheese in D.C., right?"

"Both bosses. I still need to figure out who stashed the booze— the KKK or local rum-runners skimming off the load? What are the odds two different gangs chose this cemetery to store their stash?"

Burton examined the bottle. "I know Johnny Jack and his gang favor this particular brand of rum."

"I wonder if it's part of the haul the Coast Guard confiscated?"

"Good question. I'll try to find out, discreetly of course."

I tugged on his arm. "For now, how about we hit the road?"

"I vote for that," Nathan said, sprinting away.

Burton and I raced to his Roadster but before we got in, he rummaged in his trunk, pulled out two worn Army blankets and carefully placed them over our seats. The wool felt coarse and scratchy, but it did the trick.

On the ride home, Burton seemed upset. "How come I didn't know the KKK is getting into the booze business?" He pounded the steering wheel. "I wonder if two different gangs are involved, hiding two types of liquor?"

"Looked like two separate operations to me," I said.

"Jazz, don't you dare go there alone at night again," he scolded. "You and Nathan could be in grave danger."

"Grave danger?" Nathan piped up. "Good one."

Burton stifled a smile. "Cut it out. When you get mixed up with gangsters and Klansmen...If they ever caught you spying on them, trust me, you two wouldn't stand a chance."

"I've taken my share of KKK photos," Nathan said soberly. "Not only burning crosses, but burning bodies, too—all Negroes, from what we can tell."

Glad our editor had the good sense not to print such sensational photographs in a family newspaper.

"I've seen their handiwork." Burton nodded. "These cretins think they're superior beings, but in reality they're cruel, ignorant barbarians. Pure evil."

"You said it." I squeezed Burton's hand in appreciation.

"I feel like I should start clapping or something," Nathan said.

"Thanks." Burton's face flushed. "I'd better alert the chief about these new bootleggers tomorrow."

"Are you going to mention the dead man?" I asked.

"Not until we find a corpse. The victim has to turn up somewhere," Burton said. "They must have heard you scream and hid the body."

I got goose bumps. "I wonder if the killer was watching us the whole time? He probably wasn't counting on having an audience."

"All I saw were a bunch of cowards in sheets pretending to be ghosts," Nathan said. "Doesn't seem like a KKK killing to me. For one thing, he's the wrong color."

"Maybe they witnessed the murder?" I said.

"Whoever it was, you'd better keep out of sight a while," Burton warned, "or one of you could be his next victim."

What a thought.

At the police station, Burton got out of his Roadster and handed Nathan his shirt. "Jazz, how about a ride home? We need to talk."

Talk? Swell. From his somber tone, that could mean anything: a lecture on the dangers of trespassing on graves at night? Or did he want to discuss our "future" or supposed engagement or whatever we called our relationship? For now, beau was sufficient.

Nathan walked over to my side after Burton left. "What a night! Too bad Chuck and Pete missed all the fun."

"Fun? I'd compare it to a roller-coaster ride!"

After Nathan drove off, I waited a few minutes, tempted to join Burton in the station, but resisted the urge.

"What happened?" I asked when he appeared.

He started his Roadster, giving me a sideways glance. "I reported the booze, saying I got an anonymous tip. I didn't dare bring up the body or mention the mausoleum."

"Did they buy it?"

"Hope so. We plan to unload the crates tomorrow morning and store them for safekeeping."

"The sooner, the better. Any talk of gang slayings or turf wars?"

"Not yet. I'll keep my eyes and ears open, try to nose around," Burton said. "I figure if I stay out of their business, they'll stay out of the Prohibition game."

"Be careful or they could stab you in the back."

"I'll say. We need to find out if the KKK is operating independently or with another gang."

Burton eyed me. "You don't want to get caught in the crossfire. Call me if you insist on going back there so I can come with you."

At first I was touched, then I thought: Did Nellie Bly's beau tag along on her assignments? Did she need an escort during her trips to Europe and Mexico—or her undercover investigation into New York's insane asylum? No. She risked everything, even her life, to become a world-class journalist.

"Thanks, but I can handle this on my own."

Burton shook his head, frustrated. "I don't understand you, Jazz. I considered us a team, but now you treat me like the enemy."

"You don't expect me to follow you around during raids or booze busts, do you? What kind of reporter would I be if I always asked for your help?"

He shifted in his seat. "You think I'm interfering with your job."

"I appreciate your concern, but I don't need a chaperone."

His face fell. "That's what you think of me? Damn it, Jazz. I'm not trying to stifle your *budding* career. Didn't *you* ask for *my* help?"

"Who else could I call so late at night?" I blurted out, then realized how thoughtless that sounded, too late.

Burton jerked to a stop in front of the boarding house, staring into space. "I see. I'm supposed to be at your beck and call whenever you need me, but I should keep my distance. Is that right?"

"That's not what I meant..." I fumbled for words.

Despite my attraction to Burton, I wasn't ready to "settle down"—or settle for less—to feel trapped or suffocated like so many married women I knew.

Burton seemed to read my mind and looked down, picking the dried mud off his fingers. I kissed him on the cheek and jumped out of his car before he could walk me to the door.

"Thanks for your help, James. See you soon." Until I could sort out my feelings, I preferred to keep him at arm's length—literally.

Stone-faced, he stared ahead, then sped off in the dark, without looking back. Once again, I'd stuck my foot in my big mouth, and possibly ruined our once-romantic relationship.

CHAPTER NINETEEN

Like an omen, my black stray cat Golliwogg, or Golly for short, greeted me on the steps of the *Gazette* the next day. When I stopped to pet her silky fur, she purred and circled my ankles.

Bleary-eyed from lack of sleep, I faithfully typed up Mrs. Harper's tedious tidbits. I tried to eavesdrop on the reporters, hoping they'd mention a murder or at least a missing gangster.

Nathan stopped by and set down a cup of black coffee that looked like mud. "Hey, what did Burton say after I left? Did he put the cuffs on you for trampling graves—or just for fun?"

I ignored his innuendo. "He's supposed to go back today with a team after he gets permission from his boss to search the cemetery."

Chuck and Pete stumbled in and rushed to their desks, acting unusually quiet.

"Say, where were you lollygaggers last night?" Nathan called out.

"Boy, am I glad to see you two today," Pete said, wide-eyed. "We had every intention of meeting you last night. But when we drove by the cemetery, I swear there was a KKK meeting going on."

Nathan played dumb. "What happened?"

"A bunch of Klansmen getting out of their trucks and putting on their hoods. Now I'm not afraid of the Klan, but I didn't want to be around if they got rowdy. Who knows what they'll do when they're drunk and stupid."

As if the Klan needed an excuse.

"So you were there." Nathan balled his fists. "Admit it, you're both big cowards."

"Did it ever occur to you that we might need help?" I frowned.

"You mean you stuck around while the Klansmen were there?" Chuck gave me the once-over. "Boy, you're gutsier than I thought, for a girl."

That was a back-handed compliment coming from him.

"We didn't have much choice."

Chuck leaned over my desk. "So did you see any lynchings? Did they burn any crosses? Tar and feather anyone?"

Disgusted, I made a face. "No, thank God. Luckily they seemed to be holding a regular meeting, nothing unusual."

Pete studied our expressions, moving closer. "Are you sure? You two look guilty as hell. What happened?"

"Nothing, I promise." Nathan shook his head. "You think we'd be standing here today if they caught us watching them? We'd be skinned alive."

"Heck, they wouldn't touch you. You're as white as their robes."

Mr. Thomas came out of his office, puffing on a cigar. "Break it up, all of you. This is an office, not a speakeasy."

Nathan and I stifled our smiles and looked away, hoping Chuck and Pete didn't notice. Briefly I wondered if Burton had managed to load up all the booze by now. Did he find any more surprises?

Reluctantly, I returned to my stack of papers, and pored over the society column: Did anyone really care that Debutante Deborah had just returned from a whirlwind trip to Paris and bought all the latest fashions from Elsa Schiaparelli and Jeanne Lanvin and even met Coco Chanel? Of course I wouldn't mind meeting Miss Gabrielle Chanel, but who could afford to pay thousands for a frock or outfit you only wore once, no matter how chic?

To be honest, I was jealous of the Moodys and Sealys and all the rich ladies of luxury who could afford such extravagances. I wanted to be an eyewitness to the news, travel to London and Paris and Rome, see the sights and yes, visit the famous fashion houses I only read about in magazines. I didn't want to just read or write about Europe's latest news or trends in the paper, third-hand, like a long-distance window shopper.

Traveling to Europe was my dream. Better yet, I longed to be a foreign correspondent like Nellie Bly and embark on endless adventures that provided material for my column.

Oh, yes, in my mind's eye, I'd already been promoted as a columnist for *The New York Times*, able to write on whatever exciting topic struck my fancy. I continued daydreaming until a familiar voice disrupted my reverie. "Jasmine, it's a call for you! A man—but it's not your Agent Burton!"

The newsroom twittered while, blushing, I made my way to an empty back office where I could speak in peace. Who on earth would call me here, now? My mind raced: The hotel manager? Ollie Quinn? Dear God, not the cops or the coroner!

What a surprise to hear Sammy's voice.

"Sorry to bother you at work, but can you come to the club right away? I can't explain over the phone."

Rare that my brother ever called me at work, asking for help.

"Sure, I'll ask Nathan to give me a ride soon as possible."

He hesitated. "Can you bring Burton instead? I need his advice."

Even rarer that Sammy wanted Burton's assistance.

I lowered my voice, cupping the mouthpiece, knowing the switchboard spies could hear every word.

"What's wrong? What's the matter?"

"Remember that fella we discussed the other night?" Sammy paused. "He showed up here late last night. You and Burton might want to see him."

"Really? Why me and Burton? Does he want police protection?"

"You'll find out soon enough. Hurry, come quick."

The line went dead.

I knew he couldn't elaborate with the operators and possibly the Maceos listening in on his phone calls. Somehow I had to figure out a way to convince Burton to go with me to the Hollywood after our spat last night.

Fingering my long pearls, I hovered over the phone, trying to get up the nerve to call Burton. No doubt Mrs. Page would accuse me of being a big flirt. Then her loud voice boomed across the newsroom.

"Jazz, another call. This time it *is* Agent Burton!" She raised her brows at me, giving me a smug look, like I was some floozy.

"Miss Cross? Agent Burton here." Cold and all-business. "You recall those *packages* we discussed? Our department was supposed to pick them up this morning."

I was caught off-guard, still considering Sammy's request.

"Packages? Oh, you mean...yes, I bet the cops were surprised."

"They were surprised, all right." Burton paused and cleared his throat. "Turns out they weren't where we left them last night."

"What happened?" I started to panic. What could be safer than a locked mausoleum?

"Evidently they disappeared. Vanished into thin air."

"What—are you serious? All the crates? Even the...rest?"

I didn't want to say the word *coffins* out loud. "Everything?"

"Everything."

CHAPTER TWENTY

My heart seized. So the Klansmen *were* watching us at the cemetery last night. "Can we meet in person?" I asked Burton. "Sammy just called and asked us to come by the club."

"Now? Did he say why?"

"I think he has a visitor." I gave Mrs. Page a "I know you're eavesdropping" look across the newsroom. "When can you stop by?"

"I'm on my way."

After I told Mrs. Harper that Agent Burton needed me on "police business," she seemed incredulous. "Why in the world does he need *your* help?" How could I tell her that my outlaw brother was in dire straits?

"I think he wants to meet for lunch, to make up after our fight last night. He thought that might get my attention."

Mrs. Harper gave me a smug smile. "Men! They're so crafty sometimes. Well, have a nice time and you can finish your work later." Fooled again!

When Agent Burton made an appearance, hat in hand, the newsroom twittered with excitement, but he ignored the nosy reporters and the two swooning females. The way they reacted, you'd think I was going to the prom all over again with our neighbors standing on the porch to watch the spectacle.

In his Roadster, parked conspicuously out in front, Burton said slyly, "Seems you do need me to chaperone you, after all."

"Sometimes." I blushed, and reached out to take his hand. "I'm sorry we fought last night. I didn't mean to sound so high-hat."

"That's OK." Then he winked and everything was forgotten, at least for now. "So what's all the mystery? What's so urgent?"

I shrugged. "I'm as surprised as you are. I think some witness stopped by the club. He's going to testify against Johnny Jack at the grand jury hearing."

Burton's head snapped to attention. "That's supposed to be hush-hush. How did you know?"

"I do work at a newspaper. Reporters hear things."

"Yes, but it's meant to be a secret, that's why he's being summoned before a grand jury. No one is supposed to know, particularly the press."

"Ollie Quinn and the Maceos must be in cahoots since they found the witness," I added. Burton gave me a look of reprimand. "Don't worry. Mum's the word."

"So what do they want with me?"

"Information? Police protection—maybe a bodyguard?"

Burton headed down Beach Boulevard, the fastest route to the Hollywood. The cool breeze felt soft on my face, rippling through my hair. I enjoyed watching the foamy waves crash against the beach, dreamy and desolate in the foggy gray air. I loved the beach in winter, so mysterious and soothing. The stark monochromatic setting seemed apropos after our night at the cemetery.

"Tell me what happened today." I hated to bring up a sore subject, but I was dying of curiosity. "All the bottles were gone?"

"Every last one. The crates of booze had completely disappeared without a trace. I felt like a damn fool. I'd gathered a squad of men, cops I trusted, but the whole mausoleum had been cleared out. To say I was a laughingstock is an understatement."

My heart sank. "What about the coffins?"

"All gone. I was hoping to save face by at least showing them the coffins full of rum but the graves were empty. Oh, I did find a silver dollar for our trouble." He forced a half-hearted smile. "Actually I'm grateful you wanted me to tag along today. Anything to get out of the station, away from those babbling baboons."

I sucked in my breath. "Why not tell Jones you were there with two *Gazette* staffers? We could back up your story, tell them the truth. After all, it's my fault you got involved."

"Not yet. But I may take you up on your offer later, if I'm forced to reveal my sources. Hate to drag your good names down with mine. Even the captain got mad, said it cut into our budget and he might take it out of my paycheck." Burton scowled, his grip tightening on the steering wheel.

"I'm so sorry, James. Let me know how I can help."

"No one can help me. I don't know why I do this damn job anyway. The pay is lousy, I have to risk my life every day—and for what? No one appreciates all the work I do. Even the cops try to sabotage me. I show up at a bar for a raid, and the place is cleared out, clean as a whistle. Wonder who tipped them off?"

"You mean today?" My mind started racing, wondering if dirty cops were involved in today's sabotage. "You think it may be an inside job?"

"I wouldn't be surprised. I get threats all the time from gangsters and bootleggers, even civilians blame me for Prohibition. Hard to tell the good guys from the crooks these days. Hell, I didn't make the rules. I just do my best to enforce them."

I listened to his tirade with sympathy. No matter how frustrated and discouraged I felt at the paper, at least my life wasn't on the line every day.

"You do make a difference. You're saving lives all over Galveston County. It's a shame people don't show their gratitude."

"Thanks, Jazz. I know you're trying to cheer me up. Don't tell anyone about my rant, OK?" He looked sheepish as he pulled up to the Hollywood.

At the front entrance, Burton flashed his badge. "I'm here to see Sammy Cook," he informed the valet at the door, who clearly recognized him.

The valet looked more like a bouncer with his heavy, muscular build. Crossing his beefy arms, he planted himself in front of us like a massive tree trunk.

"Did you hear me?" Burton raised his voice. "Let us in. Pronto."

"No need to make a scene." I nudged him, embarrassed.

"Say, we're here to see Sammy at his request," I told the valet. "We're good friends. Tell him Jasmine is here."

"Let them in, Rocco." Sammy pushed the baby grand aside and shook Burton's hand. "Thanks for coming so fast."

"How are you? Jazz said you wanted us to meet someone?"

Sammy nodded. "He's in the back. Right this way."

No small talk, no pleasantries. The Hollywood seemed bare, even eerie without the usual swell of glitzy crowds and staff and jazz bands. Were the Maceos here? I felt like a trespasser, peeking behind the scenes of a popular play.

Silently Sammy led us through the ritzy nightclub, breezing past the rattan chairs and potted palms until we reached the kitchen, sparse with only a handful of workers. He held open the back door of the kitchen, leading out to the back parking lot.

"Now you can see my problem."

A businessman in a nice suit lay crumpled in a heap, his face bloated and pale, his shirt collar unbuttoned, missing a tie.

CHAPTER TWENTY-ONE

"That's him!" I stepped back in shock. "The dead man tied to the headstone."

"So that's the victim you mentioned." Burton acted apologetic. "In the flesh."

"What happened?" I turned to Sammy. "How'd he get here?"

"That's what I'd like to know." He frowned, his eyes narrowed. "I have no idea how anyone got past the Maceos' men."

"Do you know who he is?"

"Sure, I know the sap. Mick O'Brien, a bootlegger from Kemah. He was supposed to testify in front of the grand jury," Sammy said. "He had so much dirt on Johnny Jack, there's no question they'd go ahead with a trial."

"Seems he's been dead less than a day." Burton bent down by the body to get a better look. "I don't recognize the stiff. This is out of my jurisdiction. I'd better alert Homicide at the station, tell them we need a coroner."

"Hell, no," Sammy snapped. "We've got to move the body before the Maceos show up and blame *me* for knocking him off."

"Not a good idea." Burton stood up suddenly. "You could be charged with illegal tampering, removing evidence from a crime scene, interfering with a murder investigation, desecrating a corpse...among other things."

"What could be worse than murder?" Sammy's eyes flashed.

"Why'd they drop him *here*?" I asked. "They could've left him at any Beach Gang speakeasy, say, the Surf Club or on the beach."

"Johnny Jack wants to frame me, get me in hot water with the Maceos. They've done it before, you know."

"Don't remind me," I sighed, recalling the ice man murder. "But why would the Maceos accuse *you*, especially without proof?"

"Not the Maceos, but their men." Sammy scowled. "They know I was in the Downtown Gang and some wiseguys think I'm still in cahoots with Johnny Jack. They accuse me of being a double-crosser, an inside man, deliberately trying to sabotage the case."

Burton nodded. "Without a solid witness, the grand jury won't recommend prosecution, so there's no trial. The case disappears."

"Don't these thugs know how loyal you are?" I protested. "You risked your life to join the Beach Gang."

"They're jealous of my position here, think I didn't work hard enough to get this job." Sammy lit up a cigarette. "Let's face it, they don't trust me."

"Gangsters don't trust anyone in their line of work, especially outsiders," Burton pointed out. "With good reason."

I flashed Burton a look of irritation. Was he implying that Sammy was untrustworthy or dishonest?"

"Jazz, you saw the body. You know I'm on the level. I can't sit around here like a sap so I can be charged with murder!" Sammy griped to Burton.

A young Negro worker holding a broom opened the back door, took one look at the body, yelped and rushed back inside.

"Time's wasting," Sammy said. "We can't leave him here all day. How about you take him down to the police station?"

"Nothing doing." Burton shook his head. "How would I explain this stiff in my car? I picked him up in a parking lot for fun?"

"Tell them you found him at the cemetery," I said. "Partly true."

"They may still try to pin the murder on us. Dirty cops can plant evidence or remove anything incriminating, depending on whose side they're on—or who's paying the most."

"So what do you suggest?" I asked, getting worried.

"I think the hospital morgue is the best idea. He needs to be examined by a coroner, to determine the actual time and cause of death." Burton pointed to Sammy's Roadster, a new model that was his pride and joy. "You take him in *your* car."

"Fine." Sammy bristled. "Let's get out of here and pronto. Big Sam and Papa Rose could show up any minute. Jazz, be on the look-out for a new Rolls-Royce while I go inside."

Boy, being a gangster sure paid off.

While we waited for Sammy, Burton and I traded anxious looks. "Sure he's the same guy?" he asked me.

"Of course I'm sure. Who forgets a dead body?"

Sweating, Sammy returned with a worn throw rug and mopped his forehead with a hanky. "Ollie Quinn sure went to a lot of trouble to track down this witness. When they find out he's dead, no telling what they'll do."

"Ollie Quinn?" I repeated, dread sinking in. "I knew the guy looked familiar. I saw him with Quinn at the Hotel Galvez recently, when they were checking in."

"Positive?" Burton's head snapped around. "Why didn't you mention this before?"

"I didn't realize it was the same fella until Sammy mentioned Quinn," I said, defensive. "He's so bloated and pale, I didn't really recognize him."

"Dead people don't tend to look their best," said Burton dryly.

"True, but I'd remember him anywhere." I watched them roll the victim onto the rug and wrap him up like a pig in a blanket. As they positioned the body in the back seat, I recalled Horace, the blotto banker, getting a sick sense of déjà vu.

"Did you find out anything from Quinn?" Burton asked.

"I couldn't exactly interview him in the hotel lobby," I said, miffed. Now it was *my* fault the fella was killed? "How was I to know he'd show up dead here?"

CHAPTER TWENTY-TWO

Agent Burton tailed Sammy closely down Seawall Boulevard, cursing under his breath. "Damn it, why'd I let Sammy talk me into this mess? I'm not even a homicide cop, so why am I getting involved in a murder?"

"Because you care about justice, even if it's not your department," I placated him.

"What can I say to the hospital staff or to the cops? If I admit the victim was found at the Hollywood Dinner Club, that'll implicate the whole Beach Gang, including the Maceos and Ollie Quinn, not just Sammy."

He was right. "Wish you could tell them the truth, that he was at the Broadway Cemetery and you got tipped off."

"They won't believe it. Why call *me*, a Prohibition agent, about a murder? Why wouldn't they call the cops first? Sounds suspicious."

"I doubt the staff will question you on the spot. Maybe later."

"Yeah, right. They'll probably consider me a suspect."

I had an idea. "Why not say you found him at a speakeasy, but don't name the place? Tell them you want to keep it quiet so it won't start a turf war."

"You think that'll keep the cops and gangs off my back?" He followed Sammy down Broadway, heading toward Big Red.

"Why not? Worth a shot."

By now it was almost noon and traffic was building up along the grand avenue, graced with the red brick Bishop's Palace and Moody Mansion, famous for their ornate Victorian architecture. Short palms dotted the median, the locals' attempts to replace the tall trees destroyed by the 1900 Storm.

Suddenly Burton sped up and signaled to Sammy, calling out over the traffic and pointing to me: "I'll meet you at Big Red. Need to drop off Jazz."

Sammy nodded and kept going down Broadway, while Burton made a sharp turn on 25th Street toward the *Gazette*.

"Say, what's the big idea?" I pouted, feeling left out. "I wanted to come along. After all, Nathan and I found the body first."

"Forget it. I don't want to get you involved in a murder case. If we need you, I'll be in touch."

"Do you trust Sammy?" I asked.

"You tell me. He's *your* brother. I'm sure I'll hear about it if he dumps off the body on the Downtown Gang's turf, or worse, in the ocean. For now, Sealy Hospital is his safest bet."

"You're right. What's one more dead body in a morgue?" I said, half-joking. "Promise you'll fill me in later?"

"Better yet, how about a ride home after work?"

"Sounds swell." At the *Gazette*, Burton dropped me off in front. Just as well. I didn't want any more snide remarks from those nosy blowhards. Guess I'd have to sit on pins and needles all day.

Mrs. Harper sat up expectantly when I walked in the door, like my mother did after my high school dates. Half the staff was gone, probably to drown their sorrows and savings at the nearest gin mill. Several juice joints, including the Oasis, stayed open all day and night to serve round-the-clock workers. Very convenient if you wanted to get zozzled.

"How was your rendezvous with Agent Burton? Were you able to help solve a case— or was it a *crime of passion?*" Her eyes twinkled at her own innuendo, as if we'd had a romantic romp on the beach or a petting party in his Roadster.

In my opinion, my boss missed her calling as a steamy romance writer. For now, she seemed keen to concoct her own fantasies—with me as the lovestruck heroine and James as the bodice-ripping hero. Should I be flattered?

"Still an ongoing investigation." I tried to keep my face blank. "Nothing significant."

She practically winked at me. "If you say so. For now, I have plenty to keep you busy all day. Check on your desk."

Distracted, I proofed some copy and did a quick write-up about yet another engagement between the scion of a moneyed old guard family and a *nouveau riche* bride with a sizable dowry. I heard marrying old and new money across continents was all the rage in merry old England now. Wealthy American brides often wed titled Englishmen, bailing out their bankrupt families—trading fortunes for status and fancy castles, not to mention their husband's aristocratic accents.

I kept glancing at Mrs. Page, willing the phone to ring, hoping the fellas made it safely to the hospital, praying Sammy hadn't taken any last-minute detours. Wish I could have tagged along, but Burton was right. Did I really need to get caught up in a murder case now?

When Mrs. Page yelled across the room, "Jasmine, there's a call for you!" I almost fell out of my chair.

"Who is it?" I mouthed to her, trying to prepare myself for the worst, but she shrugged.

"Miss Cross?" A quiet female voice asked.

I couldn't place the voice until Lily Leavenworth repeated her name twice. "I've got good news, Miss Cross. Now Madame Farushka can conduct a proper séance!"

"What do you mean? How? She said..."

"Yes, I know—she needed an article of clothing or personal item from the ghost bride. Well, guess what? She gave me her purse!"

Startled, I asked, "*Who* gave you whose purse?"

"Marilyn, of course. When I told her what I needed, she left a purse for me on my vanity—a nice tooled leather handbag."

Glad she couldn't see my jaw drop open. "Really? Are you sure it's hers?" I hated to squelch her enthusiasm, but I was getting suspicious. Could Lily really communicate with ghosts? "Did you find anything personal inside, any type of ID?"

"Only a few things, but I know it's Marilyn's purse," she insisted. "I believe her."

Sad to say, I began to suspect both Lily and the ghost bride were very possibly purse snatchers or petty thieves. She must have sensed my skepticism because she added, "Let's show Madame Farushka the handbag and see for ourselves. I'm leaving Galveston soon and it's all I have from Marilyn for now."

"Fine." I nodded at the phone. "I'll call right away and make an appointment."

"I can do it myself," Lily offered. "I don't get many chances to talk to a real diviner. I may have more questions for her."

A diviner or a diva? "Of course." Maybe Madame Farushka and Lily were both fakes and con artists—if so, they deserved each other. "I can't make it this evening, maybe tomorrow?"

"You don't have to attend the séance if you don't believe in spirits," she pouted.

I felt relieved, but remembered my assignment: a supernatural article to satisfy Mrs. Harper and her society matrons. "I'd love to go," I fibbed. "I've always wanted to see what a séance is like. Please keep me posted."

I updated Mrs. Harper, secretly hoping Madame was too busy to see us on short notice. Lily called an hour later to notify me that the meeting had been arranged for six o'clock tomorrow night.

What else did they discuss, I wondered? I made a note to ask Nathan for a ride, hoping he could take photos.

Tell the truth, I considered séances all hocus-pocus, mostly magic tricks and misdirection. Still, I was curious to see what all the fuss was about. If stories about the occult made our readers happy, who was I to complain? Besides, a trip to a spiritualist sounded much more entertaining than facing mob bosses and dead bodies.

CHAPTER TWENTY-THREE

An hour later, Mrs. Page called out my name again as if everyone in the newsroom needed a hearing aid: "Jasmine—Agent Burton on the phone!"

"Boy, the Fed must be sweet on you!" Pete said, while Chuck made smooching noises. Such juveniles.

"Go back to your playpens," I retorted. "It's almost nap time."

Not very clever, but it was the best I could do in a pinch. Anxious, I picked up a phone in the back, and heard Burton's somber tone.

"Are you ready for our outing tonight? I can swing by after work in about an hour."

"Outing?" My heart dropped and my first thought was of Sammy. "What happened at the hospital? Is Sammy OK?"

"Fine for now. If he was in trouble, I wouldn't tell you over the phone. Why don't we talk to him tonight at the club?" Burton didn't call it a date. Obviously he'd noticed my ambivalent attitude.

Luckily, I'd worn an outfit that could pass for evening attire. With a touch-up of kohl eyeliner, lipstick and rouge, I hoped the Hollywood brass would grant me entrée—if Sammy still had a job.

Swell, now I had a whole hour to fret about Sammy and Burton. I dashed into the toilet stall that passed for a makeshift ladies' room to reapply my face paint. Taking a few deep breaths, I sat on a rickety old chair and tried not to pass out from worry. Who'd killed the victim, then tried to frame Sammy?

At my desk, I distracted myself with proofreading and edits, wondering: what did Burton want to discuss with Sammy tonight?

Agent Burton showed up right on time, and I didn't bother explaining anything to my boss, who only gave us a coy smile and nodded her approval.

My face lit up when I saw him, looking like a rogue in a snazzy suit and tie, his boater hat tilted to the side. Naturally, all the newsmen craned their necks to stare like a gaggle of gossip mongers. I flashed a smug smile as I gathered my handbag and stuffed work papers into my new red satchel, a recent splurge from Eiband's.

Outside, the cool air felt fresh and frosty and I stopped to take a deep breath. Burton opened the car door and I jumped in, saying, "Don't keep me in suspense. What happened at the hospital?"

"Good news. Sammy showed up as promised and the medics helped us load the body onto the gurney, no questions asked. Then he took off like a bandit the moment we got inside."

I squirmed in my seat. "Can you blame him? He's afraid the cops will try to pin the murder on him. Did he say anything else?"

"Before he left, Sammy told me more about O'Brien. Seems he was a driver for the bootleggers who supplied the Downtown Gang. He'd pick up the cargo on the beach or docks, and deliver the booze to all the gang's speakeasies."

"You don't say. I may have seen him at the Oasis, but didn't notice him." I frowned, wishing I'd paid more attention. "So he wasn't a top gun, just a delivery guy."

"According to Sammy, he was an important witness because he kept organized lists of all his deliveries. Records of the gangs, bars, even barkeeps who received the orders—dates, places, names—a written account."

"Why would he risk his life to testify against Johnny Jack? He must have been desperate."

"Apparently they treated him like a slave. Johnny Jack only paid him half the time, and squelched any chance he had of moving up in the gang," Burton said.

"The stiff got stiffed." I nodded. "What a lousy job, trying to make a living delivering the wrong kind of merchandise."

"When Ollie came calling with a big fat offer in exchange for his testimony, O'Brien was ready for revenge. For a small-time crook, giving up the goods meant easy money. Too bad he left behind a wife and five kids."

"How sad. Maybe the Beach Gang can help out the family. No sense in making them suffer any more."

I hoped Sammy was still in the Maceos' good graces after this fiasco. The brothers were known as generous donors to charities, in a sense paying back the locals for their loyalty and support.

"What did you tell the staff about finding the body?"

"Nothing. I just flashed my badge and told them we had a corpse to examine. They assumed I was a homicide cop, not a treasury agent."

"That's a relief. What did the M.E. say? Was he suspicious?"

"Hold your horses, Jazz." Burton gave me a half-grin. "The coroner thinks the victim was dead before you found him at the cemetery. Appears to be strangulation by hand. Lots of bruises around his neck. The tie was wrapped around his neck for effect."

"Wonder why he was tied to the cross—atonement for his sins?" Shuddering, I thought it over. "So you don't think he witnessed the KKK loading up the crates of liquor?"

"Not that night anyway." Burton shrugged. "Like I said, we assume he was deliberately placed there as a warning, a threat to anyone who tries to snitch on Johnny Jack. Certainly narrows down the list of suspects to the Downtown Gang, not the KKK."

"I wonder if it's that simple. Maybe the victim saw the grave robbers digging up jewels or watched the gangsters burying coffins full of booze?" I suggested. "Maybe he stumbled onto the crime scene— like I stumbled over his dead body." I knew I was grasping at straw theories, but I was trying to keep Sammy's name in the clear.

"Guess that's possible. Your theory gives us a new angle on this murder." Burton grinned, scratching his chin stubble. "Jazz, have you ever thought of writing pulp fiction? I hear they pay a penny a word."

"Really? That's a lot more than I make at the paper." Then a light bulb went off. "Maybe I'll give it a try?"

CHAPTER TWENTY-FOUR

At the Hollywood, I breathed a sigh of relief when I saw Sammy manning the door in his usual spot. Still, I could tell he was nervous, the way he kept running his fingers through his unruly dark hair, tugging on his tuxedo. The place was hopping tonight, full of slinky dames and their dapper dates.

"What brings you two here? Am I under arrest?" He pretended to joke, watching Burton's reaction.

"Can we get a quiet table so we can talk?" Burton asked.

"How about somewhere noisy?" Sammy suggested. "Lots of eyes and ears in this place. The band is tuning up now so you can get a ringside seat."

"Swell," I said, pleased that our mission could turn into a pleasant evening. "How are things going with...your bosses?"

"Right this way," he said, turning his back. He led us to a private table near a potted palm, the fronds half-blocking our spot, like camouflage. A six-piece jazz band warmed up their instruments, trying out different tunes.

"How about a sidecar and a Dubonnet?" Sammy asked.

"Sure, one of each." I smiled at him, but he avoided my gaze.

What was going on? I knew Sammy was on edge and probably under scrutiny, yet I almost felt snubbed. No doubt he was nervous since he'd ditched Burton at the hospital after he found the body.

When he left, I tried to lighten the mood. "Guess what?" I told Burton. "I'm going to a séance tomorrow evening."

"A séance? Why do you want to conjure up dead spirits?"

"Remember the ghost bride story I'm working on?" I briefly described Lily's encounters with Marilyn's ghost and my attempt to appease Mrs. Harper. "I want to combine the fortune teller piece with the ghost bride article so that's one less society story to write."

"Do you really believe in that mumbo-jumbo?"

"Not really, but the séance might be interesting." I lowered my voice. "Lily thinks the ghost bride didn't drown by accident—she was murdered."

"Haven't you had enough sensationalism for now?"

"Beats writing about society dames and debs who get to travel the world on their parents' dime."

"Do I detect a note of jealousy?"

"Not just a note, but a whole symphony." I forced a smile. "Speaking of, I think the band is about to start."

"Just imagine, Jazz. You and I will have grand adventures in New York—and beyond." He took my hand and squeezed it lightly.

"Europe?" I perked up. "I've always wanted to see Western Europe... Venice, London, Paris, Rome and Barcelona. Not to mention the pyramids of Egypt."

"Is that all?" He smiled. "What about Vienna, Madrid, Munich, the Bavarian Alps and Geneva—heck, all of Switzerland?"

He ticked off the great cities like he'd just returned from a Grand Tour.

"Yes, I'd love to see all those places!" I clapped my hands like a child at the circus. "When can we go?" Was I so easily persuaded?

"Soon, I hope. Till then, we'll make our mark here. First we have to help Sammy get out of this mess."

Back to reality. I saw Sammy heading our way, struggling with a cocktail tray. Since when did the busy Hollywood maître d' serve drinks to patrons?

"Here you go." He carefully set down the drinks and a plate of crusty bread and pesto. "Here's a starter for my favorite customers."

To my surprise, he pulled up a chair and scooted in between us, resting his elbows on our rattan chairs. Luckily, the band started playing *Side by Side*, drowning out our conversation.

"What happened after I left Big Red?" Sammy asked Burton. "Sorry I had to take off so fast but I couldn't risk getting caught, not with Johnny Jack on my back." After Burton briefly filled him in, Sammy let out a low whistle. "I saw the bruises on the victim's neck, but you never know with gangsters. Some guys like to torture their victims slowly until their heads explode."

What a picture. "Please, not before dinner—or anytime."

"Sorry, sis," he said, but he didn't seem sorry at all. "Can I make it up to you? How about lasagna or chicken marsala or veal piccata? On the house. It's the least I can do for helping me today."

"Thanks, but I can pick up the check." Burton tried to sound gracious, but I think he felt awkward.

After Sammy took our order, I leaned forward.

"Sammy sure is acting strange, offering to treat us to dinner and drinks. He's definitely avoiding something."

"You'd think he'd be glad the victim is out of his way."

Was that all? When he returned, I asked, "What did the Maceos have to say about..." I motioned to the back lot. "The visitor?"

Sammy's face fell. "I think these wiseguys planted ideas in their heads. Now they want to test my loyalty to the gang."

"What do you mean?" I prodded. "They know you had nothing to do with O'Brien's death, right?"

Sammy shrugged and started toying with his fancy gold watch, winding the stem over and over, adjusting the band. A Rolex? How could he afford such a luxury? Seems he had to keep up appearances for the Hollywood's spiffy crowd. Only the best for the Maceos.

"I'd better go check on your dinners," Sammy said, standing up. When he returned with our plates, he had a faraway look in his eyes. Sure, the food looked good, but I'd lost my appetite.

"Sammy, be honest," I prodded. "How does the Beach Gang expect you to prove your loyalty?"

"Simple." He waited until the orchestra started *Ain't She Sweet* before answering. "Ollie wants me to find a new witness to testify against Johnny Jack. A fella who can stand up in court, someone with credibility, a long history with the gang. They want the grand jury proceedings to go on as if nothing happened."

I was surprised. "Can you just substitute one witness for another without presenting them in advance?"

"You can add a new witness if it's not too late. No one is supposed to know their identity beforehand. That's the purpose of a grand jury—secrecy."

"Tough job." Burton let out a low whistle. "I don't know many thugs willing to risk their necks to put Johnny Jack behind bars. He's in and out of prison so fast, they may as well install a revolving door in his jail cell."

"Exactly." Sammy nodded. "If I can't find a new witness soon, then I'm through."

My heart sank. "You mean you're kicked out of the Hollywood, and the Beach Gang? Then you'll be a sitting duck for the Downtown Gang."

"Looks that way." He lit a fag and blew smoke rings in the air.

"Don't you know anyone willing to do you a favor?" I asked. "What about Dino or Frank—can they ask around?"

"I couldn't do that to my friends." He frowned. "I do have one other option though."

"What's that?" I asked, guessing the answer.

"Me. I could be the new witness."

CHAPTER TWENTY-FIVE

"No!" I yelped, so upset that I almost jumped out of my chair.

A few diners turned to stare while I composed myself.

"Please don't get involved, Sammy. That's nuts. Surely there's a better way to convict Johnny Jack. You'd be offering yourself up to his goons on a silver platter, asking to be killed."

"Says who? This whole grand jury thing is supposed to be hush-hush, right? Johnny may not even realize I turned him in until he's locked up for good."

Burton and I traded wary looks, and I poked his ribs, hoping he'd talk some sense into Sammy.

"Do you really think that's such a smart idea?" Burton finally spoke up. "You saw what happened to the last snitch."

"I can't think of any other way out." Sammy puffed on his cigarette. "Believe me, I know how Johnny Jack's system works. You can bet this case will go to trial. Remember when he expected me to collect rent by any means necessary? Hell, I may even have records stashed away at the Oasis. Enough to put him behind bars—for life."

"Sammy, you can't go through with this," I pleaded. "I lost you for all those years, and now... now... you're willing to sacrifice yourself—for a *gangster*?" Frustrated, I turned to Burton. "Is there any way he can give a private deposition? Can you arrange for him to talk to a judge or someone without revealing his identity? What if he taped his testimony instead of appearing in person?"

Clearly, I knew next to nothing about the legal system.

Burton shrugged. "I'm no lawyer, but I'll see what I can do."

"Thanks, pal." Sammy looked hopeful for the first time that day.

Just as I was beginning to relax, a dark shadow appeared and we looked up to see Sam Maceo, the suave owner of the Hollywood. Startled, Sammy leapt to his feet, towering over his debonair boss.

"Good evening, Agent Burton." Smiling, Maceo shook his hand with vigor. "Jasmine, is it? Nice to see you again." He lightly tapped my shoulder.

What? Big boss Sam Maceo remembered my name? What else did he know about me?

"Thanks, happy to be here," I managed to squeak out.

That was one of Big Sam's many charms. Smooth as a silk tie, he made you feel like a special guest, the only person in the room.

Then he faced Burton, touching the brim of his hat, almost a salute. "Agent Burton, I'll never forget what you did for me that night during the bathing beauties performance. Too bad we couldn't make the charges against Johnny Jack stick."

"Unfortunately Mr. Nounes is a slippery devil," Burton agreed.

"Devil is right. But we have other plans for Nounes, don't we?" Maceo gave Sammy a pointed look.

Was that a not-so-veiled threat to pressure Sammy, or was he indirectly asking for Burton's blessing?

"I hope you two enjoy your evening." Maceo patted our backs. "Did Sammy mention that your drinks and dinner are on the house?"

"Yes, and I really appreciate the gesture, but I can pay my way," Burton said with a proud smile.

"Please accept my gratitude and my hospitality."

Big Sam practically bowed before us, showing just the right amount of courtesy and humility.

Maceo was smart, all right. Technically, drinking was legal in the U.S.—as long as he wasn't caught buying, selling, manufacturing or transporting liquor under the Volstead Act.

Not that Galveston cops or locals paid much attention to Prohibition laws. Burton usually played along, but he targeted those bootleggers who sold tainted booze and barkeeps who took advantage of customers' weaknesses, collecting their cash and letting them get bamboozled.

A young waiter with wavy auburn hair in a black suit and bow tie approached Sam Maceo, looking anxious.

"Excuse me, sir, you're wanted up front. A dame claims she knows you and Sammy and insists on seeing you. I told her you're busy, but she won't take no for an answer."

"Who is she?" Maceo asked the flustered fella, who shrugged.

"Don't worry, boss. I'll take care of it." Sammy started to head for the front entrance, then stopped in his tracks.

We all turned to stare at the beautiful blonde in a long flowing gown and fringed shawl with her tall, dark and quite handsome escort striding toward our table. I did a double-take: *Amanda?*

I knew Amanda had a flair for the dramatic, but no one expected this scenario, least of all Sammy, who looked dazed and angry and jealous, all at once.

"There you are!" Amanda fingered Sammy's boutonniere while her date watched with a smirk, amused. "I've been looking for you."

When she spotted me at the table, her mouth gaped open.

"Jazz? What are you doing here?"

Stunned, I rushed to greet her, and gave her escort the once-over. "I can ask you the same thing."

"Just painting the town scarlet with my date, Marco." Who was Marco? She flashed a brazen smile, giving Sammy the brush-off. "Everyone knows the Hollywood Dinner Club is the place to see and be seen in Galveston."

The buzz in the dining room died down as the crowd turned to watch the love triangle play out. Sam Maceo motioned to the band, and they broke into a loud rendition of: *Yes, Sir, That's My Baby.* Coincidence?

"Get your mitts off my girl." Sammy charged at Marco, yanking his arm away from Amanda's small waist.

"*Your* girl?" She huffed, hands on her hips. "I haven't seen you in ages. Since when do I belong to *you?*"

Sammy grabbed her by the wrist and pulled her aside, hissing, "What's the big idea, showing up here with this lounge lizard?"

"Who're you calling a lounge lizard?" Marco stepped between the two, breathing hard.

In a flash, Sammy grabbed the goon by the collar with one hand and shoved his face with his other, sending him crashing to the floor.

"Stop it, Sammy!" Amanda cried out, rushing to help Marco.

Marco scrambled to his feet and lunged at Sammy, arms flailing, taking punches at his face and gut.

"How do you like this, pretty boy?" he taunted Sammy. "You won't be so pretty after I get through with you!"

Like a pro, Sammy dodged and ducked and landed a blow to Marco's jaw that made him reel back in pain. Naturally, I was cheering for Sammy, hoping he'd knock out the gate-crasher.

"What should we do?" I asked Burton, who stood by watching in silence, probably wondering if he should intervene.

"That's up to the Maceos to decide."

He knew better than to get involved in this romantic drama.

Sam Maceo tilted his head and, like a phantom, Rose Maceo appeared out of the woodwork. No secret Papa Rose worked behind the scenes to keep their operation running smoothly, using force as needed and not-so-friendly persuasion.

Stomping across the tiled floor, Rose took his cue and grabbed both men by the arms, eyes blazing, shaking them like rag dolls.

"What's the ruckus?" he yelled. "Take it outside, you hotheads."

Ever the diplomat, Sam Maceo instructed the band to keep playing. Sidling up to Sammy, he said, "Better yet, take the night off, buster. You need to cool down before you come back to work."

Rose motioned for the bouncer, a big, burly brute. "Give 'em the bum's rush!" Maceo growled, pointing to the door. They paraded the men through the club like hooligans caught stealing moonshine.

Clearly the Maceos didn't want any disruptions in their *haute* hotspot, a sanctuary for the *nouveau riche* and beautiful and hopeful social climbers.

Anxious, Amanda clutched my arm as we followed the men out the door. "Jeepers, all this fuss over me?"

To our dismay, they continued duking it out in the parking lot like a street brawl. Papa Rose stood there watching, his right hand tapping his jacket pocket, and I knew he wasn't pledging allegiance to any flag. Finally he threw his hands up, turned on his heel and stomped back inside the club.

Frankly, I worried this showdown might make things worse with the Maceos, but Sammy obviously felt he had to defend his honor and "his girl" by pummeling Marco to a pulp.

We winced as the guys slugged it out, pushing and shoving, and calling each other names you wouldn't repeat in polite company.

They sure were putting on a good show for the sake of Amanda, the staff and the hoity-toity crowd. Marco's threats sounded even worse in Italian, curses I'd heard yelled out at the Oasis, usually accompanied by a rude gesture or two. I stole a glance at Amanda who watched the fight in awe, a satisfied smile on her face.

No surprise—she loved being the center of male attention.

Then I heard Burton's booming voice behind me: "Cut it out, wiseguys. I can arrest you both on drunk-and-disorderly conduct, not to mention public intoxication and defacing public property."

The pair stopped with their fists in mid-air to stare at him.

"What?" Sammy looked puzzled. "We haven't broken anything."

"Not yet," Burton warned. "Come on, let's shake hands and call it a night. We'll take Amanda home. Keep her away from you two loose cannons."

The men retreated to opposite sides of the parking lot and Marco started his car, a fancy gold Bentley. I worried they might chase each other along Seawall Boulevard, playing a dangerous game of cat and mouse—or worse.

"Should we follow them home?" I asked Burton. "I don't trust this Marco character."

"Might be a good idea, considering the circumstances."

"Relax, he's harmless," Amanda said. "Marco seemed more interested in meeting Sam Maceo than romancing me. Story of my life. Boy, do I have lousy luck with men."

"You've always been attracted to bad boys," I pointed out.

"They've always been attracted to me," she sulked. "Tell me, how can I ever find any nice guys if all I ever do is work at a cheap five-and-dime diner?"

"I'll go say a few words to Sammy, try to detain him a bit, so your Marco can get a head start," Burton said.

"He's not my Marco. I barely know the fella. Do we have to leave now?" Amanda whined. "Can't I at least get a cocktail before we go? I got all dolled up for nothing."

Tempted, I nudged Burton. "Why not? I'd like to stay a while."

"OK, you girls go on inside." Burton nodded. "Besides, I still need to talk to Big Sam."

"Swell." Amanda's angelic face lit up and she happily entered the club, prancing like a coquettish chorus girl. A few couples applauded when we reappeared, as if we'd put on a paid performance.

Glancing around, I hoped there weren't any reporters or gossip columnists in the crowd, but most journalists knew better than to get on the Maceos' bad side.

I could see the headlines now: "Fists fly at the Hollywood while Sam Maceo gives the bad guys the boot."

Just the kind of scuttlebutt my nosy boss would include in her daily gossip column, also known as the society section.

CHAPTER TWENTY-SIX

As we returned to our table, Sam Maceo rushed over to pull out a chair for Amanda. "Glad you ladies could join us." He smiled at her appreciatively, his chocolate eyes taking in her form-fitting frock.

"I can see why you have so many suitors fighting over you. You're such a lovely lady."

Amanda returned the smile, blushing like a Southern belle, and held out her hand, nails carefully manicured with pearly pink polish. Like a sport, he kissed her hand, always a gentleman.

"Such a pleasure to be here," she cooed. "I'm just a lowly waitress at Star Diner so it's a real treat to see such a glamorous nightclub." Her blue eyes widened in awe as she looked around in admiration. "Why, this place reminds me of a palace!"

To me, it looked more like a fancy Spanish hacienda or a tropical nightclub in Havana or L.A.—not that I'd ever been.

"We aim to please." Big Sam's dark eyes twinkled. "Well, doll, if you ever need a job, you know where to find me. We could always use a pretty hostess out in front." He slipped Amanda his business card, circled his phone number and winked. "Just don't let Sammy distract you or get in the way."

"Why thank you, kind sir," she beamed. "I might take you up on your offer."

After he left, Amanda squealed in delight. "Jeepers! Sam Maceo offered me a job, a real job. Who knows? Maybe I could end up performing a dance routine here, or singing with the band."

Leave it to Amanda to turn a modest job into a whole career. Still, the prospect was interesting. Surely after the fireworks tonight, Maceo figured out that Sammy and Amanda were once an item.

"How exciting!" I smiled at her eager expression. "But do you really want to work here—with Sammy as the maître d'? Wouldn't it be...uncomfortable?"

"Sure, at first, but I'd meet a hell of a lot more big spenders here than at Star Diner. I'm lucky if I make a dollar a day there."

"Why not talk to Sammy and get his take?" I suggested. With his hot temper and her flirtatious personality, I could imagine this scenario playing out every night. What was Big Sam really up to? Was he trying to keep my brother on his toes—or off-balance?

"Why bother?" She huffed. "Sammy obviously doesn't consult me about his every move. I don't need to ask for his approval."

"True," I agreed. "But working together every night might get rather awkward."

"So what? Let him get hot under the collar. Serves him right for ignoring me."

Then Burton reappeared, saying, "Don't worry, I gave Sammy a talking-to, told him not to throw his life away over one misunderstanding." He gave Amanda a pointed look and her face flushed before she looked away.

A cocktail waitress set down a bottle of rosé nestled in a silver ice bucket in the center of our table. "Compliments of Sam Maceo."

With a flourish, she proceeded to uncork the wine and fill three glasses. "How lovely." I smiled. "Please give him our thanks."

We sipped our wine, watching a few couples dressed to the nines in beaded gowns and tuxedos dance the tango, foxtrot and cha-cha.

I was only dressed to the fives, but I caught Burton's eye to see if he was game. Instead, he stood up, looking uneasy. "Excuse me, ladies, while I speak to Big Sam."

About the dead body he dropped off at the morgue?

"Good, that means more wine for us." Amanda grinned and leaned forward. "Now that the guys are gone, we can have a good girl talk. Burton can be a bit of a wet blanket, don't you think?"

"Goes with the territory." I nodded. "He has to keep up the image of an upright Prohibition agent in public, especially in a swanky nightclub like the Hollywood. You know how Galveston's elite likes to gossip."

"And how! I've heard quite a few juicy rumors at the Star diner that I couldn't even tell my deaf grandmother."

"You don't say. I'm all ears!" I made a mental note to ask her questions back at the boarding house. Gee, maybe my nosy boss was rubbing off on me.

She lowered her voice. "So do you think Sammy was jealous?"

"I'll say! After tonight, you know he still cares for you. He's just busy and...preoccupied."

Amanda's face puckered. "What do you mean, preoccupied? With a dame?"

"That's a load of hooey. Let's just say he's got a lot on his mind." How could I tell her the truth, under the circumstances? Amanda was a great gal and an even better pal, but she often couldn't keep her trap shut. To change the subject, I said, "Tell me where you met this Marco fella. He sure is easy on the eyes."

"So you noticed?" she teased me. "I met Marco at the diner, where else? Said he'd just moved to Galveston, looking for work. He told me he hails from New Orleans, but his family is originally from Italy—Sicily, like the Maceos." She took a sip of wine. "I'll bet that's why he was so keen on meeting Big Sam, to get a job. Too bad he didn't make a great first impression. Lucky for me, I ended up getting the job offer!"

"He wanted to work *here*?" A warning bell went off in my mind.

"Why not? Since he's new in town, Marco asked if I'd show him the sights, specifically the Hollywood. When I said I could get him in, that's all he could talk about. He insisted he'd give me a good time."

"Amanda, you know nothing about this wiseguy!" I scolded her like a prissy old bluenose. "How do you know he's above board?"

No telling what this Marco character had in mind.

"Who else am I gonna meet at that stinking greasy spoon? Not everyone can date such a fine upstanding young gent as your good-looking Agent Burton."

"Did someone mention me?" Burton stood behind my chair, rubbing my shoulders. "If you're finished, ladies, we can leave now."

"We're not finished at all," Amanda said, gulping down her wine. "Can we at least take the bottle with us?"

"How about our dinners, too?" I added. "Hate to let all this delicious food go to waste."

"Sure, I'll ask the kitchen to wrap it all up. Then we really must be on our way."

The urgency in his voice made me wonder what he and Big Sam had discussed. The victim, the grand jury, Sammy?

On the drive home, we were mostly quiet though I was dying to pry. Of course, I knew Burton wouldn't answer any questions with Amanda around. I had to admit, I was miffed at Amanda for her impulsive behavior, creating such a scene.

"Gosh, I hope Sammy isn't in too much trouble," she piped up from the back seat. "I didn't mean to cause a big scandal. I was just trying to get Sammy's attention..."

Finally I couldn't hold my temper or my tongue.

"Well, it worked. What were you thinking, bringing a date to the Hollywood Club?" I lashed out. "Don't you realize Sammy might get fired after you pulled that stunt?"

"Fired—because of me?" She genuinely seemed surprised. "I'm sure there are worse reasons to be fired than slugging some guy."

"Believe me, you don't know the half of it," I scolded. "He's already on thin ice."

"Guess I wasn't thinking," Amanda admitted. "I didn't do it on purpose. Well, yes, I suppose I did. I didn't mean to cause any problems for Sammy. I just miss him, that's all. And you're so busy with work and all these late-night shenanigans, I hardly get to see you either, Jazz."

"I second that motion," Burton added. "What's the point of hanging out at the Broadway cemetery and going to fortune tellers and all that baloney?"

Now they were ganging up on me? "If I hadn't found that body, then one more murder might go unresolved."

Amanda leaned forward, her hands grasping our seats, her face suddenly pale. "What murder? What body?"

CHAPTER TWENTY-SEVEN

"Never mind," I stammered, my face flaming while Burton gave me a warning look. "It's still under investigation."

"Yes, it's a private case," Burton said. "We can't reveal any details to the public."

"For your information, I'm not the *public*," Amanda said hotly, throwing her shawl around her shoulders like a prima donna. "I'm your friend, or so I thought."

Burton braked in front of the boarding house and Amanda jumped out without uttering a word, rare for her. She held tight to the wine bottle wrapped in a paper bag, and flounced up the walkway in a huff.

"What business did you have telling Amanda about the victim?"

"I didn't exactly tell her...it just slipped out. Sorry, my mistake."

"Well, make sure you don't let it *slip out* at work or those nosy reporters could splash it all over the paper."

Another lecture from Burton?

"Don't worry, I don't share private information with those bozos." I let out a sigh. "So what did you talk about with Big Sam? Does he really expect Sammy to testify against Johnny Jack?"

"I'd better keep this matter under wraps until we get more facts," Burton said coldly, as if reading a formal statement at a press conference. "I need to make sure you don't blab to the reporters or anyone else."

"*Blab*? Are you calling me a blabbermouth?" I fumed. "You know that Amanda is my best friend. I didn't exactly call Mack about Johnny Jack and give him a hot tip. Don't you trust me by now?"

With that, I slammed the door and raced down the walkway, not bothering to look back as I heard Burton race off down the street. Damn it, in my haste, I'd forgotten the lasagna.

Inside the boarding house, I knocked on Amanda's door, trying to make up. All she said was: "Go away!"

Great, I groaned. Now everyone I knew was mad at me.

At the *Gazette* the next morning, I fed Golliwogg some ham scraps I'd saved from home. All day, I tried to prop up my head while I skimmed the stack of papers on my desk. For once, I was glad to spend time on routine activities like filing and reading the daily gossip section. Temples pounding, I tried to edit Mrs. Harper's column but the words were a blur. Did the wine give me a headache?

Still tired, I poured myself a cup of coffee with extra sugar and milk and tried again. Suddenly I sat up—a white embossed invitation in particular stood out to me: On December 13th, the Moodys were throwing a holiday party for Lily Leavenworth, featuring Madame Farushka as the main attraction. Even the prim and proper Moodys were caught up in this mania? My boss wasn't kidding about the society crowd going gaga over the faux fortune teller.

Perhaps that's why Lily wanted to speak to Madame directly, to make arrangements for the party. With a start, I remembered the séance that evening and Lily's quest to help the ghost bride.

Lately my life seemed to be one long melodrama, with nonstop daily crises. Still I had to get used to constant change and embrace unexpected challenges if ever I wanted to become a real reporter like Nellie Bly.

To prepare for the séance, I walked downstairs to the morgue and looked up the ghost bride and her engagement photos. I figured anyone who could afford to get married at the Hotel Galvez would certainly post their pictures in both the *Galveston Daily News* and the *Galveston Gazette*.

The morgue held the damp, moldy air of an underground basement full of old books, papers and magazines that had survived several storms, stored for ages without proper ventilation.

Quickly I searched the racks for the years 1924-1925, and heaved the cumbersome newspapers to a desk in the back corner.

Scouring the aging papers, I came across a December, 1924 engagement announcement with photos and a short blurb. Interesting that the engagement notices read like short profiles without a byline.

The fiancé, Charles Howard, was a fisherman and boat captain, born and raised in Galveston. I studied his photo and rugged, weather-beaten features—an attractive 30-ish young man with unruly blond hair. Did he still live on the Island, I wondered?

Sadly, I spotted the would-be bride and her obituary in a paper from June 1925. I examined Marilyn Foster's photo, a pretty young thing with long wavy black hair in a traditional ruffled dress. Who knew what she might have achieved had she lived?

Yes, the coroner, whose name seemed familiar, ruled her death a suicide by drowning. An off-duty policeman discovered her body on the beach that evening and assumed she'd taken her life.

Did everyone believe this vibrant young woman was so distraught at being "left at the altar" that she killed herself? Frankly, I doubted the police force had conducted a proper investigation or questioned the coroner's findings.

Was her death considered at all suspicious or did the cops just want to close the books and move on? I considered contacting the coroner or the off-duty officer, or both, myself. To throw them off, I'd try to sneak in questions about recent gang killings, namely O'Brien, the would-be witness.

I contemplated asking James for his help with police reports, then thought twice. He'd probably tell me to mind my own business and concentrate on society news, just like my boss. Even if he agreed, I knew it would open up a Pandora's box of trouble.

After replacing the newspapers on their racks, I returned to my desk and proofed a few society pieces until my boss left for lunch. Then I looked up the fiancé in the phone book and, lo and behold, he was still living in Galveston, at a boarding house by the Seawall, a convenient residence for a fisherman. I jotted down the pertinent names and information, and stuffed the notebook into my handbag.

Then a thought crossed my mind: How could a simple fisherman and his future wife afford a wedding at the elegant and *expensive* Hotel Galvez? Did her family have money—or did they splurge on a fancy wedding to impress their friends?

Sure, I could call the fiancé, but what would I say? 'I'm so sorry your sweetheart died on your wedding day and by the way, we're investigating her suicide as a possible murder? Know anyone who wanted to bump her off—and why?'

My eyes welled as I imagined the innocent bride waiting at the altar for her beloved groom who she thought was lost at sea.

Sadly, the love story reminded me a bit of Romeo and Juliet, set on a Galveston beach.

CHAPTER TWENTY-EIGHT

"What's wrong? You look like you've seen a ghost...a ghost bride, I mean," Nathan cracked when he stopped by my desk.

Did he know I was down in the morgue, researching her death?

"Nathan—just the person I wanted to see. Remember we have to cover the séance with Lily this evening?"

"Oh, boy. I've been dreading it all week."

"Why?" I faked a smile. "It'll be fun."

"Fun? Conjuring up dead brides?" He made a face. "Say, what happened with Burton yesterday? What was so urgent?"

I pulled Nathan aside to give him a brief update away from the newsboys. "Guess who showed up uninvited to the Hollywood Dinner Club? Our missing victim."

"Out of the blue?" He looked surprised. "Sounds like the gang is targeting the Maceos and your pal Sammy. Since he's unavailable, will they cancel the hearing or find a new witness?" Nathan could be our next Mack, he was so good at asking questions, and just as persistent.

"No idea. In any case, please don't say anything—to anyone."

"Mum's the word. Don't wanna see Sammy go down in flames. Besides, I owe him for all that delicious pasta."

Seems the quickest way to his heart was via his stomach. How in heck did he keep his boyish figure with his insatiable appetite?

"Jazz!" Mrs. Page yelled, "Agent Burton on the line. Urgent!"

"Seems he can't get enough of you, can he?" Nathan teased me.

I rushed to the phone, wondering what was wrong. "I need you to come down to the police station—now," he said. "Sammy's been taken in for questioning in the murder of Mick O'Brien."

"Why? Sammy had nothing to do with it!"

"Yes, but the police chief wants to hear it from you."

"You told him I found the body?"

"I had to." Burton paused. "Johnny Jack is going around telling everyone that Sammy got him off the hook and took care of the prime witness. From the way he's bragging, you'd think Sammy *had* bumped off O'Brien as a favor."

"What?" I was floored. "How dare he! Why would the cops believe a mob boss like Johnny Jack over Sammy? Everyone knows he'd say or do anything to clear his name."

Burton lowered his voice, sounding sympathetic. "Let's face it, Jazz, Sammy doesn't have the best track record. You and I both know he's not a killer, we just need to prove he's innocent."

"Why don't I ask Nathan to come along?" I said, glad I'd filled him in. "He was there when we first found the body and can corroborate my story."

"Good idea. Sammy needs all the help he can get now."

I found Nathan in the break room, munching on a sandwich. Corn beef came first, before any crisis.

"Burton needs us down at the police station," I blurted out. "Let's hurry—it's an emergency."

"But I'm eating lunch!" he protested.

"Take it with you. Sammy's in trouble." I left a note on Mrs. Harper's desk and we rushed outside before the newsboys caught wind of our exit.

In his car, I explained the situation to Nathan, who seemed unfazed. "I'll do the best I can," he said, between bites. "But I've never testified under oath."

"This is more informal, like a deposition, not a trial. We need to explain exactly why we were at the cemetery that night. Always best to tell the truth. Number one rule of journalism."

"Got it—stick to the facts. Besides, we did nothing wrong."

"Should we mention the KKK? That might throw suspicion off Sammy. But I suspect some cops are also Klansmen."

"I wouldn't be surprised. If we point fingers, they may retaliate." Nathan thought it over as he drove to the station. "Let's leave out that part for now."

Burton waited for us outside, hands in his pockets, his breath coming out in frosty puffs. "Where's Sammy?" I asked. "Is he OK?"

"No need to panic, Jazz. They've got him in a holding cell. Don't worry, I'm keeping an eye on him in case Johnny Jack's buddies try anything." He nodded at Nathan. "Thanks for coming."

"Anything to help our pal Sammy."

As we entered the station, Burton clutched my arm, purposely holding me back. "Calm down, Jazz. You can't let on how well you know Sammy. You and Nathan need to present a united front. Just be honest and state the facts. Don't get overly emotional or excited."

"What?" I bristled. "Are you implying that I'm some sort of hysterical dame who can't keep her facts straight?"

"Jazz, you know what I mean. In front of the police chief, you need to be calm and collected. The more rational and reasonable you both sound, the better for Sammy's defense."

"Defense? He's not the one who's guilty. Johnny Jack was behind this murder. I'll bet his thugs killed the witness!"

"That may be true, but it's not your job to find suspects. And whatever you do, for your own safety, don't bring up the KKK."

"I know, you're right." I took a few deep breaths, realizing he was only trying to help. "Don't forget, I've been here before—and so has Sammy."

"One more thing. Since the victim was a witness for a grand jury, you won't only be talking to the police chief. We want to keep things on the level."

"Who else will be there?" Nathan asked.

"You'll see." Burton gave me a cryptic smile.

"We'll keep this private, right?" I wanted his word.

"Of course," he nodded. "For Sammy's sake, as well as yours."

In a way, the police station reminded me of the newspaper, full of men and cigarette smoke and desks lined up like a classroom—except for the jail cells in full view of everyone, not to mention the graphic WANTED posters covering the walls. In fact, the *Gazette* had reported on most of the criminals on public display—probably half in Huntsville prison, half still on the lam.

My heart sank when I saw Sammy sitting in the cell, elbows on his knees, hands clasped, defeated. How many times would he have to defend himself to the cops?

A couple of jokers wolf-whistled as we walked in, and Nathan cracked, "Sorry, fellas, not my type."

The cops snickered and Sammy glanced at us with gratitude, locking eyes with me, giving me a hopeful nod. He stood up as we approached and began to pace around the tiny eight-by-eight cell like a trapped tiger. Sadly, I was reminded of the last time he was here, when he was framed for murder the first time.

My mind flashed back a few years, when my dad told me to: "Take care of Sammy," as if I were the big sister, not ten years younger. To this day, I tried to honor my promise, yet it often proved difficult to keep my wayward brother out of trouble, and out of jail.

Tell the truth, I never considered Sammy to be a gangster, not officially. Sure, I knew owning a speakeasy during Prohibition was technically breaking the law, but he also operated the Oasis as a casual restaurant.

In my opinion, Sammy could do no wrong, and I wanted to pretend he was infallible, honest and trustworthy—which he was—yet I knew he was no Boy Scout. I didn't even want to contemplate the dark deeds he may have committed in his past.

Burton led us down a narrow hallway and I recognized the dank, dimly-lit cubbyhole, smelling of cigarettes and sweat. A few spots stained the walls—blood?—and initials were carved on the worn oak desk. Knives were allowed inside? I hated to think what else they did in the interrogation room—torture suspects?

"Wait here while I get the officers."

Why did I feel like I was the one on trial?

Trying to still my shaky hands, I fished in my purse and pulled out my triple vanity. I checked my makeup, then applied fresh rouge and lipstick, anything to keep my mind off the investigation.

"Really, Jazz? Do you have a secret crush on the police chief?"

"You're a riot." I suppressed a smile. Nathan always managed to make light of a serious situation.

"Look, we've got Burton on our side. Everything will be fine."

"Says you." I chewed on my lip, ruining my fresh lipstick. "Even if they let Sammy go, what will happen afterwards?"

"Let's help them nail the real killer."

I jumped when the door opened and looked up to see Agent Burton, followed by Chief Jones and my aunt's old beau in limbo, Sheriff Sanders.

CHAPTER TWENTY-NINE

"What are you doing here?" Sheriff Sanders and I said at once, staring in surprise.

"I came in town to provide security for the grand jury proceedings," Sanders said. He looked thinner, pale, his eyes sunken as if he hadn't been sleeping well. "They wanted someone who knew the principal parties. Then after the witness was murdered, I got orders to come here right away."

Burton hesitated at the door before Chief Jones dismissed him.

"How do you two know each other?" Jones asked Sanders.

I couldn't wait to hear his explanation.

"I was...uh...seeing her aunt last time I was in town." He turned to me, his face pink. "Too bad I had to leave just as we were getting to know each other. A fine gal."

Yeah, right. "Seems to me you've recovered nicely."

"I'm planning to visit Eva right after we get done here." Sanders looked sheepish. "Don't tell her, OK? I want it to be a surprise."

Chief Jones cleared his throat. "Now that we've gotten the pleasantries out of the way, can you tell me about finding the victim, Miss Cross and..." He glanced at Nathan. "What's your name, son?"

"Nathan Cooper. *Gazette* photographer." He reached out his hand, but Jones ignored it and instead studied some papers.

"According to Agent Burton, you found the body tied to a headstone at Broadway Cemetery?"

"Right. I first saw him at the graveyard, not the Hollywood Dinner Club."

"I see." Jones eyed Nathan. "Can you confirm that, son?"

"Yes, sir. I was there when she found the body."

"What were you doing at the cemetery in the first place?" Sanders acted concerned. "Does Eva know what you've been up to?"

"Trying to follow a lead. We heard rumors of grave robbers..."

"We've heard those same rumors," Jones interrupted. "Did you see anything suspicious?"

"Yes, we did," I began, eager to cast suspicion on the Klan and away from Sammy, then remembered James' warning.

Nathan kicked my leg under the table to shut me up. "We did see a couple of gravediggers," he nodded. "Burying coffins."

"Coffins? You mean the ones supposedly full of rum? Boy, Burton led us on some wild goose chase." Jones smiled to himself. "So you didn't actually see them steal anything from a grave?"

"No, sir. That's why we went back the second night. When we found..." How much could I say without making fools of ourselves or Agent Burton after that huge haul of hooch disappeared?

Jones glanced at Sanders, looking amused. "See any ghosts?"

Was that a reference to the KKK, I wondered? "No, sir. I don't believe in ghosts." I didn't dare mention the bootlegging Klansmen we witnessed stashing booze in the mausoleum. For all I knew, Chief Jones was the Grand Dragon of Galveston County.

Jones narrowed his eyes. "Does your editor know you've been sneaking around cemeteries at night? In case you weren't aware, Bill Thomas and I go way back. We attended Ball High together."

Was this a lecture from my father, beyond the grave?

"As I said, we were following up on a lead..."

"I thought you were a society reporter, Miss Cross. What does that have to do with grave robbers?"

"I heard they were taking jewelry from one of Galveston's wealthiest families, who still have relatives on the Island. Don't they have a right to know?" I let out a slow breath. "By the way, I don't plan on being a society reporter all my life."

Jones leaned forward, steely blue eyes like an arrow.

"Miss Cross, we'd rather you didn't pursue this particular lead at this time until we can investigate the matter ourselves."

Which lead? Was this a friendly bit of advice or a warning?

"For your own protection," Sheriff Sanders chimed in.

"Back to the case at hand. You believe someone else murdered the victim, then dumped him off at the Hollywood Dinner Club to send a message? Possibly to frame your friend, Sammy Cook?"

"Yes, that's exactly right. Ask the morgue if you're unsure about the time of death." Damn, why did I have to mention the morgue? "Why would Sammy murder a witness in Johnny Jack's case, then deposit him in plain sight where he works? He's not stupid."

Sanders nodded. "You think the Downtown Gang set him up?"

"Of course, who else? Sammy was trying to get away from the gang, not help Johnny Jack escape a probable jail sentence. He's not a killer or a snitch or a double-crosser or a rat or whatever else Nounes' gang makes up about him." I paused after my rant. "I'll bet one of his goons killed the victim, not Sammy."

Jones tapped his fingers on his desk. "You seem to know a lot about Sammy Cook and the local gangs, Miss Cross. Where do you get this information? Anything you'd like to add?"

Great, what now? Nathan flashed me a "Watch your step" look.

"Reporters are privy to all sorts of scoops. By the way, Sammy worked for my father and my dad was a good judge of character. He's always been on the up and up and I trust him completely."

They looked wary, so I added, "Ask Agent Burton how Sammy risked his life last summer to take down a dangerous bootlegger, Black Jack. Remember the con artists passing off poisoned hooch as pure liquor? Sammy confronted the thugs and helped Burton shut down his whole operation."

Jones nodded. "Of course we're grateful for his help in the past." He put on his politician's pose and stood up to signal an end to our discussion. "I understand your loyalty to Mr. Cook, and we appreciate your candor, Miss Cross. Please don't be alarmed if we decide to keep your friend here overnight to see what Nounes' next move might be."

"Overnight?" I jumped up. "But that makes Sammy seem guilty! The Maceos and everyone else will assume he *did* kill the witness to bail out Johnny Jack."

Taken aback, Chief Jones glared at me, flung open the door and stomped out, speechless. Guess I'd never make it as a lawyer or a liar since I blurted out every single thought in my head.

Sanders put on his cowboy hat, and showed us the door. "Honestly, Jasmine, if your friend Sammy wants to stay alive, jail may be the safest place for him tonight."

CHAPTER THIRTY

My head was reeling like a roulette wheel when I left the room. What just happened? The police seemed to believe my story, that the Downtown Gang had framed Sammy, yet they wanted to keep him locked up—for his own protection? How safe was he surrounded by crooked cops who also snitched to Johnny Jack? Agent Burton didn't know exactly who was on the take, but he'd made it his mission to reveal the dirty cops on the gangs' payroll.

"Sorry about all the questions, but we have to cover our bases." Sanders followed me down the hall, then asked shyly, "How's Eva?"

"You should know if you'd called her every week like you promised," I snapped, still upset.

He seemed embarrassed. "I try my best, but Houston is a big city, full of criminals and killers. On my pay, I can barely afford long-distance calls."

"Galveston has its share of crime, as you know."

"A promotion sounded good at the time. They promised me more pay, more control over my cases." He heaved a sigh. "Wish I'd never left. I'll make it up to Eva, I swear. I'm heading there now."

"Good to hear." I finally released a smile. "Promise you won't tell her I'm kinda involved in a murder case."

"Deal." He patted my back. "If Eva doesn't kick me out first."

"Don't forget, we have a séance to attend," Nathan told me.

"A séance, huh?" Sanders frowned.

I checked my watch. "I almost forgot! Sheriff, would you mind telling Eva I'm working late? Please don't mention the séance."

"I doubt she'd approve. She's not the superstitious sort."

"Neither am I, but this is an assignment. Maybe I'll see you and Eva at the boarding house later?"

"Hope so, *if* she finds it in her heart to forgive me." Sanders hung his head, looking so sad I wanted to believe him. "For now, be careful, all of you."

I stopped by Sammy's cell and his face fell when he saw my expression.

"How'd it go in there? Did you tell them I'm not guilty?"

"Of course. You have no motive for killing O'Brien. Besides, there's no proof."

"So what's the beef?"

I looked away. "Chief Jones wants to keep you here overnight, for your own safety."

"Great, that's all I need." Sammy stared up at the water-stained ceiling as if searching for stars. "First I get kicked out of the Hollywood, then I don't show up for work. Hell, the Maceos will fire me if I skip two nights in a row."

"Better to be fired and alive..." I eyed him.

"I'm safer at the Hollywood than I am here," he muttered.

"I'm sure you can make a phone call. You're not a prisoner."

"Oh yeah? If you're stuck in jail overnight, I'd say that makes you a prisoner."

Sammy had a point. I beckoned to Burton, who was talking to a cop across the room. "Everything all right?" Burton asked.

"The cops want to keep me locked up tonight," Sammy griped. "For my own good, they claim. You think this dump is secure?"

"Maybe there's someplace else you can stay?" Burton said. "You could bunk with me, but I doubt that will help your situation any."

I gave Burton a grateful smile. "How about staying at the boarding house? There's always room for you. You can keep an eye on Eva and Sheriff Sanders, make sure there's no hanky-panky."

"Sanders? No, thanks." Sammy grimaced. "It's too dangerous. I'd rather not get you all involved."

"What? Walt and Eva are back together? Who said romance is dead?" Burton grinned. "Say, Jazz, want a ride back to the paper?"

"Wish I could, but Nathan and I are going to a séance tonight."

"A séance? Do you have to go?" Burton seemed miffed.

"Remember, my assignment?" I tapped Sammy's arm. "Instead, why don't you give this guy a ride back to the Hollywood? If you want, he can ride in the back like a suspect."

"More like my chauffeur." Sammy's eyes lit up. "How about it, Fed? I can go out in handcuffs for show. Can't stand another minute in this hellhole."

"Let me talk to the captain first, try to pull some strings." Burton let out a snort. "Only string I have left is probably a noose."

"Good luck." I turned to Sammy. "Can you try to stop by the boarding house after work? Amanda would love to see you..."

"What am I going to do about that ditzy dame?" He threw his hands in the air. "Why'd she have to show up with that good-for-nothing bastard?"

"You know Amanda, always wanting, needing, attention."

"I'll say." Sammy nodded, acting exasperated.

When Burton returned, he gave a thumb's up. "Chief says it's fine if we're not held responsible. Technically we can't hold you without any formal charges."

"That's 'cause I've done nothing wrong." Sammy tugged on the bars, clearly impatient. "Come on, Fed, get me outta here."

"Thanks, James." I squeezed his hand, repeating my father's words: "Take good care of Sammy."

"Between us," Burton said, "I think the chief was relieved to get Sammy off his hands. He doesn't need any more trouble from Johnny Jack and his gang."

After leaving the police station, Nathan and I headed straight for Madame Farushka's mansion, nestled amidst the rows of stately Victorian homes that hadn't been ravaged by time or hurricanes. Sadly several of Galveston's most beautiful buildings had been destroyed during the Great Storm of 1900 and the not-so-great storms since then.

"Sure you don't want to stop by work first, check in with Mrs. Harper?" Nathan asked.

"No, thanks. She'll only ask me snoopy questions about Agent Burton. Then the newshounds will start razzing me again."

Frustrated, I shook my head. "The guys refuse to take me seriously. They think I'm trying to invade their territory, break into their all-male clubhouse."

"You may be right," Nathan agreed as he turned down the seer's street. "Gotta admit, I think Mack is partly to blame."

"He still fantasizes about the Victorian era, when men kept women locked up in the kitchen or in the attic." I thought of Mr. Rochester's mad wife in *Jane Eyre*. "But that didn't stop Nelly Bly from travelling the world."

"Who?" Nathan stopped in front of the imposing mansion.

"My idol."

After he parked, I waited while he fiddled with his camera equipment, then helped carry his flash pan up the grand stairs.

That's when the doors opened and we brushed by an older fella in a heavy trench coat, head down, a meaty hand on his wool cap.

"Excuse me," the man said in a familiar voice as he bustled down the stairs.

Our heads spun around like tops. Nathan called after his retreating bulk, "Mack? Is that you?"

CHAPTER THIRTY-ONE

Speaking of the devil..."Are you here to see Madame Farushka?" I asked Mack, incredulous.

"Betting on the ponies?" Nathan joked. "Hoping you'll get lucky? Never thought of using a fortune teller to predict the races."

Mack's face flushed beet-red and I noticed he'd grown a bushy beard. A disguise?

"I could ask you both the same question," he bristled.

"I'm working on a story for Mrs. Harper. How about you?"

"I'm chasing a lead," he snapped, avoiding my gaze.

Mack never struck me as the type to believe in fairy tales or rumors or gossip, only hard facts. So what kind of information could Madame offer up? A scandal involving her rich clients? What was he *really* doing here?

"A society story?" Nathan seemed skeptical.

"Let's just say Madame Farushka is privy to all sorts of information." He turned to go, reaching in his pockets for knit gloves. "You can read all about it in the *Daily News*."

So that's how Mack was getting his leads—she was a news source? I bet she required a pretty penny for her services—or rather a shiny silver dollar as her choice of payment. If so, where was Mack getting the money? Perhaps freelancing for the *Daily News* paid better than I thought.

Nathan motioned for me to wait while he walked with Mack down the stairs, their backs turned. Curious, I craned my neck to eavesdrop. "Everything OK, old sport? When will you start batting for our team again?"

"Whenever that goody-two-shoes Thomas gives me a second chance. I'm hoping to impress him with my *Daily News* stories."

"Well, why don't you just get a job there?" Nathan asked.

"Freelancing suits me fine, better than being broke."

Then he caught me eavesdropping, adding loudly, "This time I'll be on my best behavior, Miss Cross, I promise. Franny, I mean Frances, taught me a thing or two about dames."

Franny? Madame Farushka actually had a first name? And Mack, of all people, knew it?

"Oh yeah?" Nathan grinned. "Got a thing for fortune tellers?"

"You've got it all wrong." Mack looked down. "Nothing like that." He opened his mouth to continue, when a taxi pulled up and he hurried down the street, hands in his pockets. "See you later," he said over his shoulder.

Right on time. Lily Leavenworth stepped out in a handsome ivory wool suit, holding a large train case.

"Good to see you," she said to Nathan, who took her hand and helped her cross the curb. She smiled at me and patted her case. Like a gentleman, Nathan picked up her bag and helped her up the stairs. "Have you talked to Madame Farushka yet? I'm ready to get started."

"Nice to see you again. You brought the bag?"

"I've got everything right here."

Madame Farushka greeted us with a big smile as if expecting a social call, not clients. Had Mack put the smile on her face?

"How do you know Mack Brown?" I blurted out as I entered.

"Who?" Madame Farushka looked startled, blinking rapidly.

Was she playing dumb? "The gentleman who just left."

"Oh, is that his real name? I should have known he'd give me a phony name." As phony-baloney as she was a seer. If she was so smart, why didn't she conjure up his actual name?

"We met through mutual friends," she said curtly. Hard to imagine a world where Mack and Madame Franny even had mutual friends. Then again, he *had* just darkened her doorstep minutes ago. "Shall we retire to the parlor?"

Like a picky society hostess, Madame led us to the same table as before and indicated our seats, placing us by Lily so that Nathan and I faced each other.

"Is it OK if I take a few photos?" he asked.

"I doubt the spirit world would approve," she frowned. "These séances are best left secret, a private exchange between the participants and the past."

Nathan looked at me helplessly, his hands out, like "What now?"

"That was part of our agreement," I reminded her. Did her meeting with Mack rattle her, especially since we knew him and his actual name? Couldn't her super powers deduct his real reasons for meeting her here?

"Why don't we only take photos of you, without the rest of us in the photo?" I appealed to her ego. "You'll be the main feature and you can show the world—or at least Galveston—how you conduct your magic."

She considered that for a moment and then gave a nod. "That will be fine. I've made a promise to keep my clients' identities a secret. To that end, I want to respect everyone's privacy and protect their good names."

Even scoundrels like Mack?

"Fine. Our readers will be intrigued! And the story will help publicize your business."

Madame gave a smug smile. "How nice. But I'm already so busy...My schedule is quite full."

While Nathan took several dramatic shots of Madame hamming it up, I made a few suggestions, asking her to pull out her crystal ball, her Tarot cards. I even offered to pose with the Ouija board and asked Nathan to take photos with my back to the camera, my cloche pulled tight, my face turned away from the flash so I'd blend into the background. While we posed, I saw Lily rifle through the tooled leather handbag she brought, a rather simple number with a hand strap on the back.

To me, Lily wasn't acting like a total stranger, but more like a dear friend. I prodded, "Did you happen to know Marilyn, perhaps in school?" She ignored my question and instead moved her chair closer to the table.

Madame dimmed the lights and asked everyone to take their places, like a director setting the stage. Without a word, Lily placed the handbag on the table and pushed it toward the seer.

"My goodness, does this belong to the ghost bride?" Madame seemed impressed, praising an obedient pupil. "Please share with us your findings."

One by one, Lily showed us the contents of the purse, placing them on the table. We watched as she pulled out the items, caressing them with her fingers as carefully as a blind woman. She described each object in great detail: a celluloid comb and brush set, a coin purse, a dainty silk hanky, a postcard from the ghost bride's fiancé. The way she acted, you'd think each item held private memories. Her enthusiastic performance reminded me of our weekly school displays of "Show and Tell."

"Marilyn's brush still has a few dark hairs. See? And these are tickets to a vaudeville show at Martini Theatre," Lily told us, passing around the objects. I smiled to myself, wondering if it was the same devious troupe Burton and I had recently seen, but was no longer in business, thanks to our teamwork.

Madame shut her eyes and stroked each item as if willing it to speak, chanting while rocking back and forth in her large velvet chair. An incense burner shaped like a pharaoh glowed on the credenza, emitting a sharp smell of sandalwood and a small cloud of smoke over the room.

"Please close your eyes and hold hands while we concentrate our energy on Marilyn," she chanted. I didn't know if the rules for conducting a séance were the same as for a Ouija board reading, so to be safe, I kept quiet and shut my eyes, briefly. Wasn't Madame supposed to be conjuring up Marilyn's spirit, and actually speaking *to* her—or was Marilyn supposed to communicate *through* Madame?

Then the seer let out a low moan as she started shuddering, almost convulsing, gripping our hands tightly. Nathan stared at me, eyes wide, glancing around the table, mouthing: *Get me out of here!*

CHAPTER THIRTY-TWO

"Marilyn, is that you?" Lily broke the silence. "What happened to you that day, Marilyn?"

No response. Madame stopped shuddering, and the candles flickered ominously, casting long dark shadows on the ceiling. The sandalwood smell seemed almost suffocating. I glanced around, looking for signs of trickery: windows flying open, tables levitating, phantom images suddenly materializing. Nothing. By all appearances, we could have been a prayer group or friends at a tea party.

Lily didn't give up. "Marilyn, I should have been by your side to protect you. I'm so sorry I wasn't there for you. Why did you run off so suddenly?"

My ears pricked up. Was Lily actually at Marilyn's wedding? If so, they were closer friends than I thought!

Madame started to tremble again and Lily continued to speak to her as if Marilyn really was present. Spellbound, I watched and listened in fascination.

"Marilyn, you looked so pretty that day, with your long gown and flowers in your hair. I know your wedding should have been the happiest day of your life. I'm so sorry it had to end that way."

Tears began to roll down her cheeks and my heart turned over, knowing she was feeling genuine grief. Whether or not this whole experience was a sham, to Lily this was a real chance to reconnect with a lost friend.

Then a strange, disembodied voice emanated from Madame Farushka: "Help! Help me...can't breathe. I'm drowning...so much water. Rough hands...choking me."

Everyone's eyes flew open. I admit, I was getting the screaming meemies. Lily jumped out of her chair, breaking the circle. "I knew it! Marilyn would never take her own life! Why would she, when she had so much to live for?"

Madame stared at her, still in a trance, then seemed to shake off the spirit. She gently asked Lily, "You seem to know a lot about Marilyn Foster. Did you perhaps know her in life as well?"

Lily smoothed out her skirt and looked down, wringing her hands. She closed her eyes and was silent a few moments. Finally she let out a deep breath. "You might as well know the truth. My maiden name is Foster. Marilyn was my sister."

Suddenly it all made sense. Had Lily concocted the ghost bride sightings to get attention? "No wonder you're so upset," I said to console her. "Your poor sister. I'm so sorry for your loss."

Her eyes began to water. "My family is Christian, you understand. We're God-fearing, church-going people. We don't believe in taking our own lives. Marilyn always had faith. She always thought that she and Charles were meant to be together. I think she would have waited for him forever."

How romantic—and sad.

No one spoke for a few minutes until Madame said, "I'm sure it was difficult for you to grieve for so long. What brought you back to Galveston now?"

Lily's pale cheeks flamed pink. "To be honest, I read an item in the paper that Charles was engaged again. I had to find out if it was true. Had he gotten over my sister so easily, and did he mean to go through with it?"

Did she plan to stop the wedding?

"Maybe he was lonely," Nathan said. "That's a long time to be on your own."

"I doubt he was alone for long," Lily fumed. "How dare he marry someone else when he's the one who killed my sister!"

"What?" I sat up straighter, asking Lily, "Do you know for a fact that Marilyn's fiancé killed her? Why didn't you say so sooner?"

"Honestly, I don't mean Charles choked her with his bare hands, but I suspect he's to blame. That's why I'm here." Lily lifted her chin, defiant. "To prove she was murdered."

She rummaged in her purse and unfolded a newspaper clipping, wrinkled and torn, then held it up—the same grainy photo I'd seen in the *Gazette*. "See how happy they were? She was so sweet, so trusting, so naïve . Why would he have her killed?"

"Let me see that." Madame squinted at the clipping, and her eyes appeared to widen in recognition. "He doesn't look like a killer to me. He seems familiar, but it's hard to tell from an old newspaper photo. Does he still go by the same name, Charles Howard?"

Lily looked startled. "Yes, why wouldn't he?"

"If Charles is indeed guilty of murder, wouldn't he try to leave town, or at least change his name and perhaps his appearance?"

Good job, I thought, impressed with her line of questioning.

"I doubt he did the deed, but maybe one of his partners did."

"Partners?" I frowned. A fancy word for a fisherman. "I thought he owned a boat, caught fish for a living."

Lily lowered her voice and looked around the room as if the spirits were watching. "I have a feeling that fresh fish wasn't the only cargo he had on board."

I wasn't surprised. "You think Charles is a rum-runner?"

"I have my suspicions. How else could they afford that fancy wedding at the Galvez? The wedding that never took place."

My thoughts exactly. Now the pieces were adding up.

Lily let out a bitter sigh. "Did I mention the costly honeymoon to France, paid for in advance? My husband and I could have gone in their place, but naturally we were too upset. What a waste. My family had to pick up the whole tab and what did we get in return? A dead bride and a missing groom."

"The problem is trying to prove a murder years later," I said.

"Do you have any proof or eyewitnesses?" Madame probed.

Loudly, I scraped back my chair, hoping Lily would get the hint and stop sharing private information. "That's where we come in."

To be honest, I worried Madame was an opportunist who sold secrets to the highest bidder. After all, she was privy to the secrets of Galveston's elite, who hid more than skeletons in their cloistered closets and triple armoires. Even Mack solicited her services.

Had Lily already revealed too much? Sure, Madame had the society crowd eating out of her palm reader's hand, but did they really know her well enough to trust her?

A crash that sounded like glass breaking came from the parlor and we all jumped up, startled. "Marilyn, is that you?" Lily asked. "Do you have something to tell me in private?"

Unfazed, Madame remained seated as we all bolted out the parlor door to find that a crystal vase had indeed crashed to the floor, glittering pieces of sharp shards strewn all over, water seeping into the wooden slats and Persian carpet. Papers littered the floor, desk drawers were opened, mail lay scattered on the rug. Clearly the culprit was searching for something, but what?

Nathan and I raced to the front entrance, the double doors left ajar. Who was eavesdropping—a would-be robber or one of her clients? Had he overheard or found anything important?

We rushed down the front stairs to get a glimpse of the intruder, but all I saw was his back: a tall, lean man with dark hair in a nice suit racing down the street, apparently young by his agility. Then he hopped into a car and when he pulled away, I noticed it was a gold Bentley. Where had I seen that gold Bentley before?

Then it struck me: the Hollywood Dinner Club, the night that Sammy got into a fistfight. Could he be the same fella, Amanda's fake beau? If so, what did he want? Was he spying on us—or Madame Farushka?

"Should we call the police?" I asked Madame Farushka, who stood by the door, looking out onto the street.

For a moment, I saw distress cross her calm features, then she replied, "That won't be necessary."

"Are you sure?" Nathan asked. "Will you be safe here?"

"I'll be fine, thank you."

"Well, that certainly was exciting," Lily said, her face bright.

"Which part—the séance or the break-in?" Nathan asked.

"Both." Lily smiled. I sensed that a great weight had been lifted. Sharing her burden seemed to help relieve her pain.

I turned to Madame Farushka, asking, "Were you expecting a visitor? Do you have any idea who that was?"

She nodded, her smile mysterious. "Yes, I do," was all she said.

"Was anything taken?" I asked, looking around at the disarray, but she didn't bother to check. In fact, she seemed unperturbed, acting as if she'd expected the intruder.

"Let us help you clean up," I offered, and bent down to pick up a few pieces of shattered crystal with my hanky.

"There's no need. I'll have my girl clean up. No harm done."

"Are you positive we can't help?" Lily asked.

"My maid will be here shortly." Madame seemed strangely calm for a woman who'd just had a possible robbery. Wasn't she worried the culprit might return? Why didn't she want to call the cops?

I resisted the urge to grab a mop and bucket and start tidying the parlor. "If you're OK, I think we have enough for a decent article. I'm sorry but we'd better skedaddle so I can make my deadline."

"And I've got photos to develop," Nathan chimed in. "Gotta shake a leg!"

"Must you be leaving so soon?" Madame loomed over us, her bracelets jingling on her wrists. "Lily, I hope this session has brought you some peace."

"I admit it's opened up a whole Pandora's box of questions," Lily said. "Now I remember incidents and things that I've chosen to forget or blocked out from memory over the years."

"Would you like to stay a while to discuss these fears?" Madame asked Lily. She was a crafty one, all right—either she wanted a bigger payoff or she'd taken a particular interest in Lily and her late sister. Question was, why?

"I'm afraid dredging up old memories has taken its toll on me," Lily said with a sigh. "I want nothing more than a cup of hot tea and a nap at the hotel."

After her revelation, I hoped she'd want to share more stories with me at the Galvez restaurant.

Madame shook our hands and stood by the door. "I hope to see you all again soon. Lily, I'm certain your sister has many secrets to tell. Perhaps she can give you a clue in our next session?"

Next session? Boy, she sure was milking this fat cow—and how.

Lily clasped Madame's hand warmly. "I look forward to seeing you at the Moodys' party this weekend. Should be enjoyable."

"Yes, thank you for thinking of me," Madame told her.

So why weren't we invited to this snooty shindig? Maybe Mrs. Harper and I could finagle a way to go since fancy parties were my boss's specialty. Perhaps I could spy on the crowd, see who might have been connected to Lily's sister and her fiancé.

No secret that the society set often hired bootleggers to supply their parties and stock their pantries—but it was common knowledge that the Moodys refused to imbibe.

"Can we give you a lift back to the hotel?" I asked Lily, knowing Nathan wouldn't mind.

Lily looked up and down the street in dismay, knowing she'd have to wait a while for a taxi. "Yes, I'd be delighted," she said politely, though her sour expression revealed the opposite. Seems Nathan's old jalopy wasn't up to her high-society standards.

Nathan held the door open for us and we stood on the front steps, shivering.

"Wait here while I put up my equipment," he said, lugging his camera to his car. When Nathan returned, he helped Lily down the stairs while I held back. I had to ask Madame one more question.

"Excuse me, how long have you been seeing Mack Brown? Do you meet on a regular basis?"

She crossed her arms, irritated. "Why do you want to know?"

"We're good friends," I fibbed. "He's been on leave from the paper for a few months now and I was worried about him."

"He's a troubled soul. I've been giving him spiritual guidance for a few months now."

Spiritual guidance? Is that what she called their *rendezvous?*

Outside, I stopped Nathan after he helped Lily into his Model T.

"Say, what's going on with Mack and Madame Farushka?"

"Beats me. What an odd couple those two make."

"How about we make a detour to Mack's part of town after we drop off Lily? Doesn't it seem dicey that this thug shows up here right after Mack leaves?" I gave him a grin. "I'd love to put Mack in the hot seat for once!"

CHAPTER THIRTY-THREE

"That was interesting," I said to Lily in the car. "Was that your first séance? Now I know why you're so determined to solve Marilyn's murder."

"I assumed they'd laugh or try to harm me if they knew I was the least bit suspicious," she said. "I had to play the naïve socialite so I could try to investigate her murder right under their noses."

"Who's *they*? Who do you suspect?" I asked.

"That's what I want to find out. Why do you think I called the paper? I need some real journalists to help me find her killer."

"Thanks for the vote of confidence." I beamed. "We'll try our best to help you."

Nathan gave me a wary look as he parked in front of the Hotel Galvez and waited while Lily and I entered the lobby. Posh guests bustled in and out wearing heavy fur coats though it was only about 50 degrees outside—any excuse to show off their minks and sables.

Shivering, I pulled my wool coat tighter, and put on a pair of worn mittens Eva knitted for me years ago. We made our way to a quiet corner, out of earshot.

"How I can get in touch with your sister's fiancé, Charles Howard? Does he still live on the Island?"

"He moved away for a while but he's back now. When I came in town, I called and left messages, but he never replied. I suppose he doesn't want to relive the past." She sighed. "I know he was madly in love with Marilyn and felt guilty about her death."

"Guilty? Why did he feel guilty?" I prodded.

"Charles blamed himself for her drowning—her death—since he was away at sea. He wanted to take one last job before their wedding, to help pay for their honeymoon and put money down on a house. Or so he said."

"I'm sure he meant well," I consoled her. "He never would have left if he'd known his ship would capsize and he'd miss the wedding. And Marilyn..."

Lily's eyes welled up. "They loved each other so much."

Then I had a brainstorm. "Say, suppose I can arrange an interview with Charles and his bride-to-be about his upcoming nuptials for the society section? He has no reason to turn me down since he doesn't know that we're connected."

"It's worth a try," Lily agreed. "To be honest, I'm very curious about his fiancée."

"If I can talk to him privately and ask the right questions, maybe I can get him to open up about Marilyn's death." I paused, trying to find the right words. "Why do you suspect Charles if they truly loved each other?"

"I'm so confused, I don't know what to think." She pulled out a hanky and dabbed her eyes. "When I asked the local police about domestic murders, they said nine times out of ten the spouse is guilty, whether it's male or female. I hate to think the worst of Charles because we all loved him and welcomed him into our family.

"But with those odds, chances are he planned the whole murder and made it look like she drowned to cover his tracks." Lily sighed. "Maybe he had us all fooled."

As a journalist, I had to think in terms of logic and actual evidence, not hunches or suspicions. "But why do you blame him if there's no actual proof? Was he acting strange or distant? Did they have any serious quarrels or problems? This is only speculation on your part, right?"

Lily nodded. "I should give him the benefit of the doubt, but who else could it be? Who else would want Marilyn dead? What motive could anyone possibly have to kill such a sweet young girl?"

"Good question. Maybe Marilyn got involved in something that got out of hand, a situation she couldn't control."

"Wish I knew more about my baby sister." Her brows furrowed. "What about your Madame Farushka article?"

"I may take a different slant if my boss approves," I told her. "To be safe, I won't mention any names or specific cases."

"I wonder if you *should* highlight this case?" Lily said. "So that the guilty party, the killer, might make a mistake and show his face?"

"Are you sure that's a good idea? After the break-in today, I'm wondering if Madame Farushka is in any danger."

"I hope not. She has lots of friends in this town."

"And I suspect a few enemies as well."

"You may be right." Lily set down her train case and scribbled notes on a pad. "Here you go. Please let me know what you find out." As she turned to go inside, she asked, "Will we see you at the Moodys' party?"

"If we can finagle an invitation."

"I'll be glad to ask the Moodys if I can add your names to the list. I assumed you were already invited."

"How nice of you." Then I had an idea. "Say, why don't you give me one of your sister's things? Perhaps I can show it to Charles, see how he reacts."

Lily hesitated, then rummaged in her purse. "Why not? Here's a postcard he sent her from Cuba. That should jog his memory."

"Cuba? Sounds fishy to me."

"Fishy is right. You'd think Madame would figure it out, that he was doing more than catching fish."

"Perhaps she's not as a clairvoyant as we think." I tucked the postcard into my handbag. "I'll return it to you after I meet with Charles, maybe at the party?"

"I hope to see you there." She shook my hand. "Good luck. With everything."

After she left, I got to Nathan's car in time to see him arguing with an older valet who fancied himself a British butler. "I'm sorry, sir, but you must remove your *vehicle* at once." He sniffed, emphasizing the word vehicle as if it were a dead rodent. "We have guests who are checking in and out and the driveway must be clear."

I flashed the valet a sweet smile, pulled out a dime and tipped him, hoping he was insulted.

"Mustn't be late, Poindexter," I said loudly. "The Moodys are expecting us. The mansion isn't far from here."

Nathan started the Model T. "Yes, my dear. Can't keep the Colonel waiting." We drove off, laughing.

"Did you see the shocked look on his face?" I asked.

"Poindexter? Of all the corny names."

"Sorry." I grinned. "Say, does Mack live nearby? Let's ask him a few questions, find out why he's canoodling with Franny."

"I wouldn't use the word canoodle... but yes, he's only a few blocks away. I wouldn't mind talking to him myself, if he'll give me a straight answer." Nathan shifted his eyes at me and I got the hint.

"OK, I'll wait in the car. You don't even have to mention my name. Just tell me everything he says."

"Will do, boss." He eyed me. "So what did you gals gab about?"

"I think she wants us to attend the Moodys' party this weekend," I said. "Madame Farushka is the featured entertainment."

"You don't say. So you weren't joking about the Moodys. What's the occasion?"

"Their annual Christmas celebration, and a going-away party for Lily. You're invited too, if you're interested."

"Swell. I can't wait." He rolled his eyes. "You're the society reporter, not me. I'm more of the fishing on the pier or lounging on the beach type fella. Besides, I don't have any fancy duds to wear."

"I've seen you all spruced up before. You've got plenty of duds—what about the bathing beauties performance? You sure looked spiffy then."

"Aw, shucks, missy, those are kind words for a simple fella," he joked, turning down J Street. "Let me warn you, Mack's shack is a far cry from the Moody Mansion. Since his wife died, he's let the place go to seed."

"Sorry to hear that. Guess he's getting on in years. Doesn't he have any family who can help?"

"Not that I know of. He seems estranged—from everyone."

"Everyone except Madame Farushka," I teased.

"She's not a bad looker for an older broad." Nathan slowed the car down as he approached, pointing out the run-down wood-frame house with its overgrown lawn and half-dead bushes.

By now it was after 8 p.m. and quite dark, save for a lone lamp post in Mack's front yard. A Bentley was parked in the driveway behind an old Ford, with a driver waiting in front, idling his motor.

A Bentley? I craned my neck to see: was it gold or was that the reflection of the lamp lights?

"Wait a minute," Nathan said as we drove by. "Looks like Mack's got company."

"Get a load of that car. Who's the big cheese?" I wondered. "Why's he here with Mack?"

Nathan seemed worried. "Maybe some high-roller who came to collect his due."

"You think it's the same goon we saw at Madame's mansion? Can't be just a coincidence that first we see Mack, then this wiseguy, at her place on the same day?"

"That's some coincidence," Nathan agreed.

I started to panic: Had he seen us at Madame's place? How many gangsters owned gold Bentleys in Galveston?

"Should we wait out here or hit the road?"

"I don't want to park in front like we're spies," Nathan said. "Mack will recognize my car."

"Let's circle the neighborhood and maybe we can catch them as they leave," I suggested.

"Good idea." Nathan drove around the block and dimmed his lights as he passed by Mack's house once again. By now Mack stood on the front walkway with his guest and a young fella who looked familiar. Under the street lamps, I could make out the distinct figure of a tall thug with only one arm: Johnny Jack's own one-armed bandit and right-hand man, George Musey.

CHAPTER THIRTY-FOUR

"Do you see what I see?" I gulped, wishing we were singing Christmas carols instead of spying on Mack.

"Isn't that George Musey?" Nathan hissed. "How in the hell does Mack know Musey? What's he doing—making house calls?"

"Who knows?" I slid down in my seat. "For now, we'd better scram before they spot us watching. Come on, let's hurry!"

The car sputtered as he tried to floor the gas pedal, resulting in a loud squeal and the noisy put-put-put of his engine. Both goons snapped their heads to stare while we careened around the corner, going a speedy 25 miles an hour, fast for the decrepit Model T.

"Think they saw us?" Nathan peered anxiously into the rearview mirror, turning off a side street.

"They spotted the car, all right." I glanced behind us. "Thank God we got a head start. What do you think they want with Mack?"

"I'll bet his gambling habit got him into trouble. Mack probably lost a few poker games at the Kit Kat or High-Hat clubs and owes the Downtown Gang a pile of money."

"Wonder if Musey came to collect?" I wondered. "Mack knows better than to muck around with the gangs."

"He used to go to the Kit Kat or Grotto to get information on the sly, but stuck around for the cards. All these speakeasies have one-armed bandits in the back where rummies can lose a pile of coins. Doesn't sound like much, but it adds up."

"I'll say." I nodded. "For a while, Sammy was in charge of collections for Johnny Jack. Maybe Musey is teaching the driver, this young stooge, how to pick up cash."

"You've heard the rumors about George Musey, right? I hear he's gotten even meaner since his arm was shot off."

I nodded. "He and Burton had a few words this summer and he scared me to death."

"An ugly mug like his would scare anyone. What happened?"

"Tell the truth, I suspect he followed us that night. He marched up to our table and threatened Burton in front of all the diners."

"In public? He's got some balls."

"Believe me, he was even scarier then, with two good arms."

Just as we started to relax, a pair of headlights beamed behind our car, illuminating the dashboard. Nathan slowed down and made a sharp turn to the right, but the car also turned right.

"This joker is sticking to my bumper like glue," Nathan grumbled. "I'll try to lose him."

I turned around to look, but the bright headlights blinded me.

Nathan headed toward the Seawall and tried to blend in with the traffic, but the car kept following us. "You think it's Musey and his lackey?" I asked.

"I wouldn't be surprised," Nathan said through gritted teeth. "What do they want with us? We're harmless."

"I've got something to tell you..." I began. "Speaking of one-armed bandits, did you know Burton was the one who shot off Musey's arm? Think he recognized me?"

"Are you razzing me? Burton did the honors? No wonder Musey is such a heartless son of a bitch." He eyed me. "You mean they're after you, not me?"

"Me? Maybe it has to do with Madame's intruder today."

Suddenly, the car sped up and moved to my right. No doubt, it was the same gold Bentley I'd seen outside of Madame's mansion. Oh no—so what did Musey and Mack and Madame Farushka all have in common?

Squinting in the dark, I got a good look at the driver, handsome in a lounge lizard way with the dark hair and pencil-thin moustache. Where had I seen him before? Then it hit me: in the dim lights, the thug looked a lot like Marco, Amanda's escort at the Hollywood Dinner Club—definitely off-limits to the Downtown Gang.

My heart sank. No wonder that grifter was so interested in taking her out on the town after she mentioned she knew the Maceos. Seated next to him, waving with his one good arm, was Nounes' right-hand man, George Musey.

Without warning, the car moved sideways, forcing Nathan's car into oncoming traffic like a deadly game of chicken.

"Watch out!" I screamed.

Luckily, Nathan flashed his lights so the other cars changed lanes and got out of the way. Nathan weaved across the road, trying to loop away from the top-of-the-line Bentley, but it bore down on us like a bulldozer. Then the car slowed way down and we thought we'd lost them, for now.

"Whew, that was close," Nathan said, wiping his brow though it was close to 40 degrees.

Without warning, the Bentley reappeared again, this time on the left, and tried to shove the Model T toward the Seawall and onto the granite rocks below. Nathan slammed on his brakes and spun the car around in a half-circle while the Bentley purred on ahead.

"Look out!" I yelped as a car swerved to avoid us, narrowly missing a truck in the next lane.

"Those bastards!" Nathan sputtered. "What are they trying to do—kill us?"

My breath came out in spurts. "I think they're trying to warn us. What if we saw something we weren't supposed to see?"

"The KKK? A meeting with Mack?" Nathan frowned. "Mack talks and acts tough, but the old soldier is getting on in years. He's all bark and no bite."

"Sure about that? Look who just paid him a visit." I turned to Nathan. "Say, I have an idea, if you're game. Let's follow them!"

"Are you screwy?"

"I don't mean tail them or try to run them off the road. We can keep a safe distance, find out where they're going."

Nathan shook his head at me in dismay. "If they kill me, then you can visit Madame Farushka later and try to summon my ghost."

"Very funny." I made a face. "Why don't we just drive down the Seawall like tourists and look for fancy Bentleys?"

He mulled it over a minute, then shrugged. "Why not? The worst they can do is shoot at us, right?"

Nathan sped up until the Bentley was in our sights, then lagged behind as we watched it slow down and park in front of Murdoch's. Where were they going—Gaido's? Though the seafood restaurant was officially neutral and not affiliated with any gang, Sammy told me that several Downtown Gang members had adopted it as their favorite meeting place, off the turf, as they said. I made a mental note to visit Gaido's soon—with or without Burton.

Nathan followed their lead and parked several yards down the Seawall, between the Victorian street lamps. I saw the young goon help George Musey out of the car, but he shrugged him off, slapping him away with his one good arm.

I felt a tinge of guilt about that night, but knew Burton had shot the gangster in self-defense. If the tables were turned and Musey had taken a shot, I doubted Burton would still be alive.

The ornate Victorian-style lamps illuminated the gangsters while they headed up the steps. While we watched, I saw a lone figure walk down the steps to greet them. If I wasn't mistaken, the dapper man in a bowler's hat looked an awful lot like Johnny Jack.

CHAPTER THIRTY-FIVE

After our close call on the Seawall, I didn't want to stick around to find out if it *was* the mob boss.

"Seen enough?" Nathan said, starting his car. "I've had my fill of ghosts and gangsters for one night. I'm taking you home, missy."

Missy? I'd never seen Nathan so rattled. "Sorry, I didn't mean to get us into hot water. I had no idea that Mack knew George Musey."

He was silent, then spoke up. "I aim to go back there and get to the bottom of this mess. Mack sure has a lot of explaining to do."

Apparently Nathan was more upset by Mack's meeting with Musey than our near-brush with death.

"I'm sure there's a logical reason," I replied. "Musey's probably giving him information for his next article. After all, they can't be seen together in public."

"Musey wouldn't give him dirt on the gangs for free." Nathan snorted. "What's the payoff?"

"Good question. Let me know what you find out."

At the boarding house, I saw Sheriff Sanders' car parked in front, glad he was true to his word. I could only imagine the surprise on Eva's face when he showed up after all these months.

"Want to come inside?" I asked Nathan on the porch. The stained-glass door was slightly open and I peered inside: Aunt Eva and the sheriff were in the parlor, sitting awfully close together on the velvet settee. Too close. Had she forgiven him so easily?

"No, thanks," Nathan said. "You've gotten me in enough trouble for one night."

"Trouble? I just wanted to talk to Mack..."

"Right, and look what happened." He waved as he hurried down the walkway. "See you tomorrow!"

"Jazz, is that you and Agent Burton?" Aunt Eva called out.

"No, it's Nathan. We had an assignment so he drove me home."

"What kind of assignment?" she asked, but I didn't respond.

Sheriff Sanders stood up and nodded at me politely. "Nice to see you again, Jasmine."

Eva paused and looked at both of us suspiciously, question marks in her eyes. "Again? Walt, when did you see Jasmine today?"

He started stuttering, his face redder than usual. "Well, uh, we asked her down to the police station to clear up a little matter."

"A little matter—down at *the police station?*" Eva appeared aghast. "Tell me, if it's such a *little matter*, why did you need my niece—a society reporter—to help the police? And why were *you* involved if it's such a *little matter?*"

She repeated the phrase so many times in her schoolmarmish tone that I expected Sheriff Sanders to run away like a scared tomcat. Personally, I wanted to scream. I didn't need a lecture from my overprotective aunt now, not after tonight.

"I witnessed a traffic accident, that's all," I fibbed. No need to worry my aunt over dead bodies and graveside murders and Sammy's stay in jail, however brief.

Sanders looked grateful as he added, "My car was also involved in the fender-bender." His florid face flushed beet-red. "I was in such a hurry to see you, I'm afraid I drove too fast."

Boy, not only was he a sweet talker, he was a good liar as well.

Eva blushed, clearly pleased. "Oh, Walt! Are you all right?"

"I am now," he beamed, giving her a squeeze.

"Jazz, why didn't you tell me Walt was in town?" she scolded.

"Why, sugar plum, I wanted to surprise you!" He cut in.

Sugar plum? So he changed his sweet nothings to fit the season.

"You know, I almost didn't let you in," she frowned, hands on hips. "But those flowers sure were convincing, not to mention pretty." She turned to show me a huge bouquet of peony-pink roses on display in a crystal vase, maybe two dozen in all.

"Not half as pretty as you," Walt replied smoothly.

Oh, brother, I had to go upstairs before all these bonbons made me upchuck. I just hoped he didn't spend the night at the boarding house or it could get really awkward, especially if Sammy showed up. My brother tended to go his own way, ignoring offers of help, even from his own family.

"Let me get you a piece of hot apple pie and ice cream," Eva said to her wayward beau. "Do you want a piece, Jazz?" Guess I was forgiven since she was back to calling me Jazz again.

"Maybe later, Eva. By the way, is Amanda home?"

"Not yet, but she called and told me she's leaving work early. Said she's not feeling well."

After Eva retreated to the kitchen, I took Sheriff Sanders aside, motioning him outside onto the front porch.

"Fast thinking," he said. "I hate to disturb Eva with the details of my job. She's so delicate."

"Eva is tougher than you think. She volunteered during the Great War at John Sealy Hospital, without any formal training or experience. I'd have fainted dead away at the first sight of blood."

"You don't say." He nodded with admiration. "What a gal."

"She sure is, and don't you forget it." I gave him the once-over since he was still on shaky ground. "Say, are there any updates on the Nounes case?"

"Nothing new," he said. "Something on your mind?"

"Just wondering if a new witness has come forward." I hesitated. "What if they can't find a witness—will the case be dropped?"

"For now. At least it may be postponed until a witness is located." He studied me under the porch lights. "Why?"

"Just curious. Heard anything about George Musey lately? If this case against Nounes is dismissed, are there any charges pending against Musey?"

"Not yet." He rubbed his jowls and I noticed he'd lost weight, perhaps to impress and entice Aunt Eva? "Why do you ask?"

I lowered my voice. "We saw Musey and his goon meeting someone tonight."

"Who saw him—you and that young fella, Nathan?"

"Yes, they followed us down the Seawall and almost ran us off the road."

"Deliberately? Sure it was Musey? Did you get a plate?"

"No, it was too dark but I got a good look at his gold Bentley."

"Sounds like Musey, all right. Sneaks up on you and hits you from behind."

"If it wasn't for Nathan's quick thinking, we could've skidded off the Seawall and crashed onto the boulders."

"Be careful, Jasmine." Sanders frowned. "Musey is dangerous. We don't want you involved in any accidents."

That's when I saw Amanda trudging up the walkway, carrying a few bags. Goodies from the diner, I hoped?

"Who had an accident?" she asked, worried.

"Just a close call." I eyed Sanders, who got the hint.

"I'd better go inside. Can't keep my gal waiting."

His gal? What would Eva think?

Amanda and I shook our heads, thinking: Here we go again.

"What happened? Are you OK?" she asked.

How could I break the news to her nicely—that not only was her new squeeze a thug, he might be Musey's new flunky. I didn't have the heart to tell her the truth. What could I say? Oh, by the way, Musey and your new beau tried to kill us tonight, but luckily Nathan saved the day.

Finally I admitted: "I think George Musey and his driver tried to run me and Nathan off the road."

"Musey, the Downtown Gang leader? Why would they even follow you?" Her blue eyes widened in alarm.

Now what? "I suspect he thought we were spying on him."

"Why would you spy on Musey?"

"Long story." I decided to drop the matter until I had more information. How could I accuse her would-be beau without any proof? Still I had a sickening feeling that Amanda was getting in way over her head.

CHAPTER THIRTY-SIX

That evening, Amanda and I stayed up late talking like old times, almost. After she kept babbling about poor tips and pushy customers, I finally blurted out: "Are you still seeing that fella from the Hollywood? What was his name again?"

"You mean Marco? No, why? Did Sammy say anything?"

My heart sank. "Sammy's so busy with his own problems. Did you happen to catch his last name?"

"I think he said Polo, Marco Polo."

"Like the explorer?" A fake gangster moniker if I'd ever heard one. "You think that's his real name?"

"No." Amanda blinked. "Boy, do I feel like a dumb Dora."

"Not dumb at all. Just trusting. Too bad the Maceos had to give the guys the bum's rush."

"I shoulda been more careful, but I wanted Sammy to eat his heart out."

"Well, it worked. I've never seen Sammy so jealous. Say, the fella didn't try anything, did he?"

"Thank goodness he kept his hands to himself. Honestly, except for belting Sammy in the jaw, he was a perfect gentleman."

"Did he ever mention his background or where he works?"

"I think he was a waiter at Gaido's, so we had that in common." She shrugged. "Now he said he's looking for new opportunities."

New opportunities? Sounded like a gangster-in-training to me.

Changing the subject, I asked, "When do you start at the Hollywood Dinner Club?"

"This weekend!" She practically bounced on the bed. "Big Sam wants me to meet the staff first, so I begin training this week."

"That's swell! Bet you're excited." I knew Amanda was destined for bigger and better places than Star Diner, but worried about the mobsters and sugar daddies she'd fall for at the Hollywood.

"Can't wait to get all gussied up and wear nice clothes for a change, not this greasy spoon uniform that smells like smoky fags and burgers." She clasped her hands, her fingernails shining with fresh polish. "You never know who could show up—maybe a film producer or a movie star?"

"Fitting that the film crowd would flock to the *Hollywood.*"

"Hope so." She looked at me coyly. "Do you suppose your big brother could give me a ride to work on my first day? I hate to get all dolled up just to get windblown on the trolley."

"Why not ask him yourself?" I smiled. "I'm sure he'd be thrilled." Thrilled he could keep an eye on her, as long as he didn't beat up her admirers every night.

Golliwogg greeted me the next day at the *Gazette*, and I rewarded her with scraps of ham from Eva's dinner. At my desk, I tried to drum up the nerve to call Charles Howard for an "interview," but then I chickened out.

First, I decided to do a little digging and find out more about the ghost bride's fiancé and his upcoming nuptials. According to Lily, the engagement announcement appeared two months earlier, and I had no trouble locating it in the *Gazette*. At that time, I had no idea about the sordid story behind their happy news.

The photo depicted a handsome fair-haired couple who beamed at the camera in their Sunday best, her hand on his chest, displaying a big sparkling diamond ring. Side by side, Charles Howard looked much older than his fresh-faced fiancée with his sun-weathered skin, but in reality he was only about ten years older, a common age difference. They'd set the date for mid-June and I wondered if they also planned to get married at the Hotel Galvez?

His bride-to-be, Diana Thomas, worked as an elementary school teacher and appeared to be as sweet and innocent as Marilyn Foster. I felt nothing but sympathy for this pretty young gal, originally from Fort Worth, Texas.

Did Diana have any idea that Charles had been engaged once before and his bride had died a mysterious death? What if he was indeed a killer—would she be his next victim? Was she suspicious of his sideline business at all or just in the dark? Even if Charles turned out to be an honest and honorable husband, would she always feel like second best?

I hoped Mrs. Harper would agree to a short society piece on the couple, complete with photos, though they didn't exactly fit the high-brow mold. How could I get him alone to talk about his former fiancée? Tell the truth, I'd feel guilty trying to lure the couple for an interview under false pretenses. With Lily in town, would he figure out the ruse?

Instead I pulled out my notes from the ghost bride's so-called suicide and hid in a quiet office to call the M.E. directly through the switchboard. If I went through Mrs. Page, everyone in the office would be in the know.

A curt woman demanded, "What's your name? Does he know what this is regarding? A recently deceased family member?"

Stammering, I mumbled my name, but didn't mention the *Gazette*. Finally a Mr. Winter came on the line, grumbling, "What do you want?"

"Do you remember a case involving a young bride who drowned on her wedding day in June, 1925?" I jumped in. "A cop found her dead on the beach across from the Hotel Galvez. Apparently she was devastated because her groom never showed up for the ceremony and she assumed he died at sea."

"Vaguely. Why do you ask? Are you a relative?"

Was it my imagination or did he sound defensive? "No, but I'd like to know which officer found her body."

"I'm afraid that information is confidential. I don't remember the name of every officer on the scene of every case I investigate," he groused. "I reported my findings two years ago. As I recall, it was ruled a suicide."

"Are you sure there weren't any signs of a struggle or foul play?" I persisted, irritated by his blasé tone. "I mean, why would she kill herself on her wedding day? Doesn't that seem suspicious to you?"

"Young lady, are you questioning my report? My integrity?" he huffed. "I'll have you know I have twenty years of experience with John Sealy Hospital. The Galveston County Morgue has trusted me with their cases since...."

"Not at all," I interrupted. "I just wonder if there's more to the story, some details that were overlooked."

"Why? Is there an official investigation? On what grounds? I can assure you, the young woman died by drowning. Her lungs were filled with water and she was obviously asphyxiated."

For someone who could scarcely remember the case, his memory certainly was improving.

"That doesn't mean she killed herself...Maybe she was strangled to death or someone held her head under water," I challenged him, then immediately regretted opening my mouth.

"What are you getting at, miss? Are you saying that I don't know how to do my job—that the whole police force is incompetent? Let me tell you something, young lady..."

"Thanks for your time." Panicking, I cut him off and hung up the receiver—very professional, I know. Would he try to trace the call back to the *Galveston Gazette?* I just hoped that busybody Mrs. Page hadn't eavesdropped on the line or the newshounds hadn't overheard my call.

If word got out that I was snooping around the ghost bride's suicide, what then? Would I end up like her—drowned in Galveston Bay, without even a grieving fiancé? Maybe I'd better stop investigating the ghost bride before she came back to haunt me...if her killer didn't find me first.

CHAPTER THIRTY-SEVEN

After I slunk out of the back office, I heard Mrs. Page call out my name: "Jasmine Cross! Someone is here to see you!"

Oh no—was it the cops? Was it concerning Sammy or Burton?

I peered up front, but didn't see anyone I knew, only a young boy in a news cap holding a letter. Cautiously I approached the front desk when the cute redheaded messenger thrust an embossed ivory envelope at me, with the Moodys' return address. No doubt, Lily had snagged an invite to the holiday party.

"Thanks, sport." I noticed his freckles. "Say, how old are you? Shouldn't you be in school?"

"Yes, ma'am, but I don't have time for school. I gotta help support the family. I'm eleven!" he said proudly.

Sadly, I noticed his threadbare clothes and worn mittens.

"Wait while I get my purse." I rushed to my desk, found some change and handed it to the cute urchin. Not much, I knew.

He reminded me of Finn, the newsie who sold the *Gazette* down the block. Thanks to Mr. Thomas, Finn was going to school full-time and working at the *Gazette* on weekends. Unlike the snooty Galvez valet, the boy seemed grateful for the coins.

"Gee, thanks! Now I can get some hot chocolate for lunch!"

I handed him an extra dime. "Here's enough for a sandwich. What's your name, son?"

"Baxter," he said. "Baxter Dillon."

"Nice to meet you. I'm Jazz. Hope you and your family have a merry Christmas. Come back and see me, will you?"

At my desk, I studied the formal invitation, requesting the pleasure of my company along with a guest. Saturday night, 8:00 p.m., with a small orchestra and *hors d'oeuvres*. No jazz for the Moody family. Madame Farushka's name wasn't mentioned—perhaps she'd be a surprise guest or was she too in demand? Who should I invite: Agent Burton or would my boss insist that she attend?

Nathan stopped by my desk, saluting Baxter as he left. "Who's getting married? Amanda?"

"Not yet." I smiled at his remark. "Lily came through and sent us an invite to the Moodys' party this weekend."

"Us? Count me out. Why not take your beau with you?"

"I may need photos. First I need to clear it with Mrs. Harper."

"Are you sure the Moodys will allow photos of a private party?" He looked skeptical. "I don't want to go just for jollies. I can think of better things to do this weekend, like go see Holly in Houston."

Nice he kept in touch with Miss Houston, his bathing beauty crush. "How's she doing?"

"She's OK, trying to decide what to do with her life, become an actress or go to college? She's too pretty to work a regular job."

"Too pretty to work? May be just what she needs."

"Sorry, that didn't come out quite right." Nathan leaned over my desk. "Guess where I'm headed now? Mack's shack for a snack. My treat. I figured if he's in debt to Musey, he doesn't have two nickels for fried fish and chips."

"You think he saw us last night in front of his house?"

"He didn't bring it up, but he wasn't surprised that I called."

"You haven't told him the truth about his pal Musey?" I fumed, recalling the terror of that night. "He needs to know his stooge tried to run us off the Seawall!"

"Not yet," he stalled. "I'll play it by ear, see how the conversation goes. Wish me luck."

Sad to say, Nathan needed more than luck if he expected Mack to dish the dirt. A couple of cocktails and cash might do the trick.

Mrs. Harper bustled in, her arms laden with shopping bags full of colorful wrapped packages. What a contrast to the waif delivering invitations for tips. And here I was, excited about going to a high-society holiday party at the Moody mansion.

Still, I wondered if I should show my boss the invitation or keep it to myself? I knew she'd love to attend, but she'd turn it into an assignment and make me do all the work. Quickly I stashed the envelope in my purse and slumped over my desk, watching her sit down. She waved me over, motioning to her desk.

"Jasmine, I need some help! Can you help me clear this stack?"

Groaning to myself, I picked up a tower of papers and spent the rest of the day proofing and editing and typing until I thought my head would explode. Honestly, I wanted to stick around, hoping Burton would call about Sammy, but no word so far. Since I'd skipped lunch, by five o'clock I was famished and ready for a break.

Luckily Nathan arrived a few minutes later and gave me a look as he headed to the darkroom, meaning, "We need to talk."

When he emerged, I pounced. "What happened with Mack?"

"We can't talk here. Let's take a walk around the block."

Just what I needed—some fresh air. Without asking for permission, I grabbed my coat and cloche and followed him out the door. The air was chilly and I pulled my wool coat around my neck.

"Well? Did he spill the beans?" I asked, getting worried.

Nathan seemed dazed as he walked down the sidewalk, jostling Christmas shoppers and workers rushing home. "Not exactly. He did say he owes money to the Downtown Gang but they're going to let him work it off. Face it, they have him by the short and curlies."

I had a sinking feeling. "Work it off? What does *that* mean?"

"Guess. Mack was very vague and kept trying to change the subject. He claims he's only doing small favors here and there."

"What kind of favors? Does that include visiting Madame Farushka? Passing on information or delivering packages?" I mused.

"He didn't say anything specific, but what else could he do at his age? No one would suspect an old fogey like Mack to be involved in any gang activity. We both know he's in no shape to be a hit man." Nathan looked down, visibly upset about his pal and mentor.

"Poor Mack. I'd hate to be in that position."

"I'm just worried they'll keep upping the ante. If he does one job well, they'll keep piling it on until he's totally under their control. If he refuses or fails, he's a goner."

"Yikes! Damned if you do...Did he happen to mention George Musey? Did you tell him about our run-in on the Seawall?"

"No, I think the less I say to Mack, the better, for everyone's sake." He stared at me in alarm. "Please don't say anything to your fella. If Burton finds out he's in cahoots with Musey..."

"*In cahoots?* So far we don't know if Mack has done anything wrong, yet." I considered the situation. "What if Musey wants him to plant stories or fudge facts to get the Downtown Gang off the hook? I know the police have asked us to stretch the truth or embed wrong information to fool the gangs."

"Mack draws the line at faking the news. He wouldn't jeopardize his job. I watched him over lunch. He has a good game face, but it's not *that* good."

I let out a sigh. "Mack won't last long in this business if editors find out he's falsifying news stories, especially to pay off the gangs."

Nathan stopped short, his head down, hands in his pockets.

"Exactly what I'm afraid of—that he won't last long, period."

By the time we got back to the office, the newsroom was abuzz.

"What's the ruckus?" I asked Chuck and Pete, who were grabbing their notepads and coats.

"A fishing boat crashed right into the Seawall," Chuck said.

"At least fish can swim," Nathan cracked. "Is the crew OK?"

"They must've jumped overboard 'cause there's no sign of them." Pete said. "Maybe the Coast Guard or cops will pick them up. A wet fisherman or two won't be hard to spot along the Seawall. Nathan, got your camera ready?"

He nodded. "Jazz, you up for a little fishing trip?"

"No, thanks, I've got bigger fish to fry," I cracked back.

"Suit yourself." Pete shrugged. "Just thought your Probie beau might be interested in the cargo."

"What cargo? I thought you said it was a fishing boat."

"A fishy fishing boat." Chuck smirked. "Guess what was hidden under all those boxes of smelly fish? Brand-new bottles of Canadian Club Whisky."

CHAPTER THIRTY-EIGHT

"A fishing boat full of booze?" I smiled. "Sounds promising."

"No wonder they jumped ship," Nathan said. "Bet they helped themselves to the cargo, got zozzled and crashed on the rocks."

"What else do you expect on a booze boat?" I grinned at Nathan. "Sure, I'll tag along. Let's hurry before they disappear."

If they caught the sailors, maybe they'd know Charles or how to find him? Had Burton heard the news?

"Coming, Nathan?" I held the door open as he struggled with his camera equipment, and reached for his tripod.

"How'd you guys find out about this shipwreck?" Nathan asked.

"An off-duty officer was eating at Gaido's and saw it happen. Lucky for us, he called us on the spot." Pete waved as he rushed toward his jalopy. "Hey, I'd love to chat, but we've got a story to cover. See you there."

"I hope there's a few bottles left for evidence—or to celebrate."

"Celebrate what?"

"A boat full of whiskey." Nathan winked.

A fire truck and a couple of cop cars beat us to the scene. We parked along the Seawall and peered down at the jetty: a mid-sized fishing boat leant precariously against the jagged granite rocks, its bow buried between the boulders. Luckily the boat seemed secure, positioned so we could step aboard, if we were careful.

Thankfully, Nathan held a flashlight as we gingerly made our way across the rocks down to the boat. Seemed steady enough. I was balancing on a boulder, about to step inside the cabin when a voice demanded, "Who are you and why are you here?"

A cocky young police officer on board shone a flashlight in our faces. "Be careful, miss, you could fall on the rocks."

"So could you," I retorted, squaring my shoulders. "I'm a reporter for the *Gazette*, just doing my job—or trying to."

A wave crashed against the jetty, saltwater spraying our faces, and I held onto Nathan's arm.

"Let her in, Mike." I heard a familiar voice calling out from the boulevard. "She's my contact at the *Gazette*." Burton to the rescue.

"Your contact or your squeeze?" The cop smirked.

"She's a reporter, like she said. Show her some courtesy. Are you going to move out of the way or will I have to push you overboard?"

In a flash, Burton crept down the boulders, took my hand and nudged Nathan onto the boat. "This is my department, Mike, so I'm in charge here," he told the young cop. "I heard you saw the crash. What happened?"

Mike backed away, looking sheepish. "The boat was struggling, slowing down until the motor gave out. The minute it crashed, a couple of fellas jumped off and ran down the Seawall, shaking like wet dogs."

From fear or the booze, I wondered?

"Thanks for the report, but I'll take it from here," Burton said.

"Sure you don't want me to help carry out the crates?"

"We can remove the cargo later. Wait out here and signal if you recognize the crew or anyone suspicious shows up," he told the cop.

"Say, where are Chuck and Pete?" Nathan asked.

"Those two reporters? They're searching for the fishermen, checking bars, restaurants and flophouses on the Seawall," Mike said.

The boat was too small for the four of us and the smell of dead fish so overpowering, I was tempted to follow Mike outside.

Still, after Burton's show of chivalry, I decided to hold my breath and face the fish. "You showed up just in time," I smiled at Burton with gratitude. "Thanks for coming to my rescue."

"I don't think you need to be rescued." He grinned.

"Only by you. Say, how did this rinky-dink boat make it all the way to Canada?" I asked.

"I suspect it met a Canadian bootlegger out in the ocean, far enough away to elude the Coast Guard." Burton glanced over both shoulders. "Let's do a quick search before the other cops get here."

"What are we looking for besides the liquor?"

"Evidence. Hurry, before half the force shows up, strips the ship bare—and swipes the booze."

"Good idea." We squeezed on board like Cracker Jacks in a box, with the booze as the prize. Crates of fish covered the crowded deck, probably hiding more bottles of whiskey.

"Any idea who owns the boat?" I asked.

Overhead a lantern swung wildly back and forth as waves struck the boat, and I held on for dear life.

"That's what I'm looking for, some form of ID." Burton's eyes darted around the small cabin.

Poking around the stern, quickly I rummaged through some drawers in the cabin and gasped when I pulled out the bottom one. Inside, folded neatly under a towel, was the distinctive white uniform of the KKK.

CHAPTER THIRTY-NINE

Stunned, I pulled out the robe, clean and creamy as cotton, and waved it like a white flag. "Look what I found. This bootlegger must supply the Klansmen." I eyed Burton. "Now do you believe me?"

"Quick, put it back." Burton frowned. "You don't want anyone to know you found that...outfit. Least of all a Klansmen."

"Think he's part of the KKK ring we saw?" Nathan piped up. "Who else carries around white hoods and robes for fun?"

"Makes sense. Maybe the crew meets the KKK offshore and they go directly to their storage place, like the cemetery," I added.

"Could also be bootleggers who belong to the Klan," Burton said. "Lots of hoods around town."

"I wouldn't be surprised." Nathan held up his camera. "I'll take some pics of the cargo and damaged hull and bow. You reporters are always talking about proof. If we don't catch these guys, maybe a reader can ID the boat?"

"Can you take some for me in case our shutterbug doesn't show up?" Burton said. "Might help in the police investigation if we can't locate the owner."

Nathan maneuvered around the tiny boat taking interior shots of the cabin and one of the white robes in the drawer, for my own use. Outside, the sky was turning gray, but lights from Murdoch's and the street lamps illuminated the crushed bow, some drama for our readers. Burton looked for eye-witnesses on the scene, but no one had seen the crash or crew.

A cop car parked on the Seawall, and a rotund older officer came over and saluted Agent Burton. "How can I be of service, sir?"

"Will, would you mind guarding this boat for the night?" Burton asked. "We'll cordon it off to keep thieves away. Will you be OK here by yourself?"

"I'm fine, sir. Don't worry about me."

"Be careful. If anyone recognizes this boat or knows what's on board, they may try to confiscate the cargo," Burton said. "I'll get you some back-up."

As Nathan turned to take one last photo, the burly cop blocked him and snatched at his camera. "What do you think you're doing, boy?" he demanded.

Nathan clutched his camera to his chest, and dodged the heavyset cop. "If you have a problem, take it up with Agent Burton."

Will scowled at us, then glanced at Burton, who nodded his consent. "They're with me, Will. I asked him to take photos."

Nathan shook his head and muttered, "What a palooka."

Why were cops so suspicious of the press? We only wanted to help solve crimes, just like they did.

Looking up, I noticed a few people peering at us from Murdoch's and nudged Burton. "Say, maybe they saw the crash? Why don't we ask them some questions?"

"You know it's considered a mob hang-out, don't you?"

"Yes, that's why I want to go." I grinned at his surprised expression. "I wouldn't mind eating at Gaido's. Besides, I need to talk to you..."

Nathan walked up then and Burton motioned to Gaido's. "How about a bite to eat? I'll treat since you took all those photos."

"You know me, always ready for a hot meal. Sure I won't be a fifth wheel?" Nathan's eyes shifted back and forth between us.

"Not at all," I told him. "We need to tell Burton about our wild ride on the Seawall."

"Go on ahead and I'll catch up with you two."

"What wild ride?" Burton asked as we strolled along the Seawall.

"Gotta hand it to Nathan. He saved our lives," I admitted. "Musey's stooge chased us down Beach Boulevard in his Bentley like a race car driver."

"When did this happen?" Burton looked upset. "Are you OK?"

"For now." I was about to give him a brief account when Will, the burly cop, came over and whispered something to Burton, then walked off.

A salty breeze blew my hair around and I held it away from my face. "You look swell, all wind-blown." His expression softened.

I smiled back at him. "You look pretty good yourself."

Still, I didn't want to get mushy with cops around so I changed the subject, fast. "Say, what happened after you dropped off Sammy yesterday? He never showed up at the boarding house. Guess he didn't want to be under the same roof as Sheriff Sanders."

"Can you blame him, after Sanders interrogated Sammy at the station? Walt may look like a harmless Teddy Bear, but the guy can be a bruno, a real brute."

"Sammy didn't tell me. Sanders didn't try to hurt him, did he?"

"No, but..." Burton stalled. "Walt thought Sammy withheld information about the hit on the grand jury witness, so he applied some pressure."

"Pressure?" I fumed. "Damn it, he had no right to intimidate Sammy. Doesn't he know Sammy broke free of the Downtown Gang, thanks to you?"

"That's why I intervened. Walt means well, but he's old-fashioned, very by-the-book."

I'd heard terrible tales of interrogation tactics gone wrong. "Was he rough or violent?"

"Just loud, yelling in his face, like a drill sergeant."

"Figures. Eva mentioned he fought in the Great War." I shook my head, frustrated, wondering if Eva should call off their romance.

At Murdoch's, Nathan caught up with us. "Before we go in, did Jazz tell you what happened last night?" I nodded for him to continue. "Let's just say we saw George Musey threatening someone. Next thing you know, he and his henchman followed us down the Seawall and tried to run us off the road."

So he *was* threatening Mack, a fact Nathan had left out earlier.

"Who's someone?" Burton glanced at me, concern etched on his face. "Where were you, at some gangster's speakeasy, doing *research*?"

"Let's keep it quiet for now," Nathan said. "We'll tell you later if it becomes a problem."

"Up to you. But it might be too late for your friend." Burton's eyes narrowed. "So who was Musey's pal? Anyone we know?"

"Remember the lothario who locked horns with Sammy at the Hollywood? He looked a lot like Amanda's date."

"All those hoods look the same to me." Burton shrugged. "They acted like hooligans so I had to throw them out. Know his name?"

"He goes by Marco Polo." I rolled my eyes. "A made-up moniker if I've ever heard one."

"It's not unusual in that business. These small-time hoods give themselves nicknames that are easy to remember. Makes them stand out from the crowd of thugs." Burton rubbed his chin. "I suspect Musey is grooming him to be his right-hand man."

"You mean right-arm man," Nathan cracked.

Burton's blue eyes clouded over as he held my gaze.

"Believe it or not, I still feel bad about that night. I didn't mean to blow his arm to bits...it was self-defense. Jazz, you were there. It was him or me. I was trying to knock the gun out of his hand, but he moved just when I fired."

My heart went out to him. He had a haunted look and sadly, seemed to be reliving that night.

Nathan looked uncomfortable and started walking up the stairs into Murdoch's. "I'm famished. Ready to eat, you two?"

The diners at Gaido's appeared to be their regular crowd, mostly families and couples, no gangsters or sinister wiseguys. After we ordered—the seafood platter for Nathan, salmon for me and Burton—Burton stood up and made an announcement: "Did anyone see the fishing boat crash on the Seawall this evening? It happened right outside the window."

The crowd got quiet as the diners stared at each other, eyes wide. "We believe one or two men jumped overboard," Burton explained. "They might be injured and need medical attention."

Everyone shook their heads and resumed eating, speaking in low whispers, glancing at our table as if we were the main attraction. Maybe they recognized Burton from his frequent mention and photos in the papers?

Luckily the waiter appeared swiftly with our dinners and Nathan dove in as if it were his last meal on earth. Burton grinned, saying, "Glad you're enjoying yourself."

Nathan looked up, pieces of fried cornmeal crust plastered around his mouth. "Want any? There's enough here to feed a horse."

"Or just you," I teased him, then began to worry about my own appearance. "Excuse me, fellas. Need to freshen my lipstick."

Fishing in my bag, I pulled out my vanity compact, ready for my close-up. Passing by the kitchen, I heard a commotion, loud voices, pots and pans crashing to the floor. What was going on?

I couldn't resist taking a peek inside, standing on my tiptoes to see inside the smudged window. Without warning, the door swung open and a man's hand grabbed me by the arm, dirty fingernails pressing into my flesh.

"Ouch! Let go of me!" I twisted around, trying to pry his ragged nails loose. "Stop—you're hurting me!"

I looked up to see a damp, disheveled fisherman with skin like a worn baseball mitt, a bloody slash on his forehead, wet hair and muddy boots, reeking of fish and saltwater and booze.

CHAPTER FORTY

"Tell your fella to stop lookin' for me," the sailor hissed. "Don't breathe a word about this to anyone. I was never here."

I tried to squirm free of his tight grasp. "Let go of me or I'll scream. You're scratching my arm!" I noticed a shiny reflection and realized he was holding a huge kitchen knife in his free hand.

An older bald man in an apron stepped between us and shoved the fisherman back inside.

"Leave the diners alone, Harry. Let the lady go."

"Thank you!" I yanked my arm out of his clutches and rushed into the ladies room to catch my breath, rubbing the red streaks on my skin.

Now I realized why the diners seemed so reluctant to talk. Either they were part of the cover-up or they'd been warned to keep quiet. Taking a deep breath, I smoothed out my frock and tried to regain my composure and my wits. Then I returned to the dining room, forcing myself to act calm as I sat down at the table.

Burton took one look at my face and asked, "Everything jake?"

I pulled him closer and whispered, "A fisherman is hiding in the kitchen. Be careful. He has a weapon."

"Well, so do I." In a flash, Burton removed his gun from its holster and stormed into the kitchen.

"Federal Agent James Burton. This is a raid. I have reason to believe there's a fugitive trying to sell liquor on these premises."

Nathan stopped licking his fingers, roused from his seafood bacchanalia. "The sailor's here in the kitchen?" He jumped up as if yanked by marionette strings and charged toward the kitchen. "Let me at him!"

The fisherman bolted though the dining room holding the large kitchen knife with Burton at his heels, his gun drawn. I sucked in my breath. Damn, I hoped that thing wasn't loaded. Surely he wouldn't fire in a crowd of civilians?

Nathan tried to block the fisherman but he knocked him down like a bowling pin. On instinct, I stuck out my leg and he tripped, falling face-down, the knife clattering across the wood floor.

Burton pulled out his handcuffs, planted a knee on the sailor's back, pinned his arms behind him and clicked on the steel bracelets. Nathan pressed his boot on the man's neck, in case he tried to run.

"Is that your boat on the Seawall?" Burton demanded as the fisherman struggled on the floor.

"Maybe it is and maybe it ain't."

Burton tried yanking up the big guy but he rolled back and forth, cursing under his breath in a foreign language. Polish?

"You're under arrest for evading a police officer," Burton began, then... "Oh, hell. Never mind. Nathan, help me load this suspect into my car."

I scrambled to get the kitchen knife—at least ten inches long—and held it up for Burton to see. "Need this?" I called out.

"Naw, we've got the suspect in custody."

Barely, from the looks of it.

The sailor kept struggling, trying to shake off Nathan and Burton as they dragged him to the door. Finally the burly cook came out to help and it took all three men to hoist up the feisty fisherman and push him out of the restaurant.

"Hey, my hands are kind of tied," Burton told the cook, puffing under the suspect's weight. "Can you put the meals on my bill?"

"We didn't even get to finish," I wailed, suddenly famished. "Can we wrap it up to go?"

"Will do, little lady." The cook nodded. "It's on the house, Agent Burton. Thanks for your help. He was holding us hostage in the kitchen."

Flanking the foul-mouthed and foul-smelling fisherman, Agent Burton and Nathan headed toward the cop cars lined up on the Seawall. I couldn't help but laugh when I saw Burton make a face, turning his head away from the fishy fella who still struggled and twisted in their grasp. I kept my distance, cringing each time a gust of wind blew his scent in my direction.

"What happened to your boat?" Burton demanded.

The man just shrugged. "What do you think?"

"I think you helped yourself to the cargo and wrecked the boat." Burton gave a smug smile. "Tell me. Who's your supplier? Who's your local contact?"

Suddenly mute, the fisherman stared at a tugboat churning past.

"Who else was on board?" When the man didn't reply, Burton said, "If you're cooperative, we'll make it worth your while."

"You don't want to spend a night in a Galveston jail cell," Nathan added in a menacing tone.

Burton flashed him a warning look while I suppressed a smile. Boy, was Nate playing up his role as...as what? Crime fighter? Burton's new sidekick?

Luckily Mike still stood sentry on the Seawall and Burton waved him over. "Say, pal, can you do me a favor and take in this suspect? Are you parked nearby?" Now they were pals?

Eager to please, Mike nodded, smiling until he got closer to the suspect. The he visibly reeled as Burton handed him off, and helped escort him to a squad car parked nearby.

Mike opened his car door and Burton shoved the fisherman inside, giving his head a hard push.

"One more chance. Where'd you get this bootleg? Who's your buyer?" Burton asked.

Finally the smelly fella piped up. "If I talk, what's in it for me?"

"Your life will be a whole lot easier, I assure you."

The man opened his mouth to speak, then pointed down the Seawall. "Why don't you ask him? It's his boat. He can tell you a lot more than me."

We squinted in the dark and saw two familiar faces half-carrying, half-dragging a man by the arms down the Seawall. What a shock!

Somehow Chuck and Pete managed to lasso the wayward boat captain. He appeared to be injured—or sloshed, or both—and limped along like a wounded steer, dragging his feet. Was he really hurt or faking an injury?

"Well, I'll be damned." Nathan peered down the boulevard. "Is that our newsboys?" He rushed to his car, grabbed his camera and darted toward the trio, a grin on his face. Tempted to follow his lead, I held back when I realized the boat captain was in no shape to talk to anyone. Not yet.

Burton jumped onto the granite boulders and called out to Will, still on board. "Will, I think we found our missing boat captain. Come help me bring him in. Jazz, would you mind keeping an eye on the boat?"

Would I? "Aye, aye, sir," I saluted.

With the cops gone, now I could do a more thorough search.

Burton turned to Mike before he ran down the Seawall. "Wait till we return. We still need your services."

"Yes, sir." Mike seemed reluctant as he waited by the car for the fellas and fisherman to return.

Standing on the Seawall, I watched the waves crash against the ship, seagulls dipping and landing on the deck, looking for fish. When the coast was clear, I crept along the boulders and stepped carefully back onto the boat, holding onto the sides.

"Say, what are you doing? You can't go there!" Mike yelled from the Seawall, approaching the boat.

"Says who? Why don't you mind your own beeswax? Your suspect is on the loose!" I retorted, pointing at his squad car.

With Mike's back turned, the fisherman managed to sneak out of the car and stumble down the Seawall. Mike didn't seem to know which way to turn, and began flailing his arms, calling out to Burton for help like a lost boy. I felt like I was watching the Keystone Kops in action.

Burton raced back down the Seawall in a hurry, stopping to ask, "Are you OK, Jazz? What happened?"

"Mike was paying more attention to me than his charge." Pointing down the Seawall, I said, "Hurry, they went thataway!" feeling like an extra in a Tom Mix Western.

While they were trying to locate the fishermen, I quickly perused the drawers and bins in the cabin. For what, I wasn't sure, but I did come across a few more bottles stashed away. Poking around the stern, I went below deck and peered under the cots, finding dirty boots and more bottles of booze.

Reaching underneath a cot, I felt something hard wrapped in an Indian blanket and pulled it out. Inside the blanket, I found a handsome box, decorated with ornate brass fittings and an Art Nouveau design on top, obviously a prized possession. Maybe it held personal papers, some form of ID, lists of names and numbers, something incriminating, I hoped.

Curious, I studied the handcrafted box, trying to decide what to do. Should I turn it over to Burton as evidence or put it back or open it now? Who was I kidding? Of course my nosy Nellie self won out.

Balanced on the rickety cot, I slowly opened the box, feeling like an intruder. Slowly I sifted through the contents, fingering a man's gold wedding ring and a dainty heart necklace.

A small faded photo was taped to the top: the fisherman and his fiancée posing for their engagement photo, the same one in the newspaper with a date on back: April, 1925.

CHAPTER FORTY-ONE

Honestly, I wanted to hold onto the box but it wouldn't fit in my purse and I didn't want to get Burton, or myself, in trouble. When he was in full cop mode, he played by all the rules.

Still I couldn't resist taking the gold necklace and ring for safekeeping. What if the cops found it and stole the jewelry? Carefully I wrapped them in a hanky and hid it in my purse, then covered the box with the blanket and shoved it farther back under the cot. Then I crept out onto the jetty, trying to balance on the jagged granite boulders while the wind roared and whipped.

Finally Chuck and Pete and Nathan showed up, holding the fugitive fisherman by the arms, looking triumphant.

"Guess who we found," said Chuck proudly.

"A runaway captain." Pete grinned. "Trying to escape."

"Good work, guys!" I smiled at the newsboys-turned-rookie cops. Then I stole a look at the boat captain. His face had aged, his lines were deeper, but I recognized the features of the once hopelessly-in-love sailor in the photograph, now sadder and wiser, and perhaps just plain hopeless.

"Are you Charles Howard?" I asked. "Is this your boat?"

The captain's head jerked up from his drunken stupor. "Who are you?" he slurred. "How'd you know my name?"

"I think we have a mutual friend..." I began, ready to mention Lily, but Burton appeared and gave me a stern look.

"Jasmine, wait till we get to the police station. We can interview the suspect then." We? Did that mean I was included?

Burton smiled at the newshounds still grasping the boat captain. "Thanks for your help, fellas."

Mike and Will, the older cop, followed behind, holding the first fisherman by his handcuffs.

The captain shrugged off the reporters and managed to throw a few punches at his pal before Burton pinned back his arms and handcuffed him.

"Sorry, Charlie, but you're under arrest," Burton said. "You're coming with us downtown."

The two fishermen faced off, glaring at each other like a couple of pit bulls. "Look what you've gotten us into now!" Harry snarled.

"You sonuvabitch, this is all your fault!" Charles yelled. "If you'd done your job instead of drinking our profits, we'd be in the clear."

"Oh yeah?" The fisherman charged at his captain.

"Yeah. You're the bastard who wrecked my boat."

The cops laughed while Burton fended off the fishermen. "Break it up, you two. You'll have lots of time to talk in jail."

The cops yanked on the fishermen's arms, leading them to a squad car. I saw the suspects exchange looks that I interpreted as signals. Were they keeping an oath of silence or ready to rat each other out?

"Let's put him in your car, Mike, next to his friend," Burton commanded. "They can keep each other company in jail."

"He's an ornery fella," Will said, yanking Harry, the first guy, by the collar and shoving him inside the squad car. "We need to keep a close eye on these two crooks."

"I'll say!" Mike pushed the captain into the opposite door.

"He was almost to the Galvez when we caught up with this lug. He's as mean and slippery as a rattlesnake."

"Need any help bringing them downtown?" Nathan asked. From his buoyant tone, he clearly enjoyed the danger and excitement, of being a faux cop, if only for one night.

"You've done enough. I owe you boys. Thanks, all of you." He nodded his appreciation to the newshounds, who shuffled their feet, looking pleased. "Mike and Will can take over from here."

Pete looked over at Nathan. "Hope you've gotten some good shots of this whole ruckus so we can write it up for tomorrow's paper. Are you coming?"

Damn, of course the newsboys beat me to the story. No doubt they already had time to drill the captain after his capture.

Even so, I wanted to do more in-depth digging and write a follow-up story, perhaps on the ghost bride.

"Still want me to stay on board, Burton?" Will moved closer to the stern. I nudged Burton and pointed toward the boat. Luckily he got my message.

"Why don't you follow Mike down to the station? He'll need a hand with these two Houdini's. I'll guard the boat till you get back."

Burton waved at their tail lights as they drove off, letting out a whistle. "Boy, what an adventure. Those two sots sure know how to put up a good fight, considering they're three sheets to the wind."

"You said it," Nathan agreed. "Guess lugging all those crates of fish and booze around builds muscles, not to mention thick skulls."

"Thanks for the assist, sport," Burton told Nathan.

"Anytime."

"Before you go, I want to show you some interesting things hidden away inside the boat." I motioned for Nathan to climb on board. "I think we may have caught two fish in one net."

"Let's see what you found," Burton said, curious. "Make it fast, before the cops come back."

Like a sleight-of-hand trick, I pulled out the hanky and revealed the gold ring and necklace.

Nathan's eyes opened wide. "Where'd you get the loot?"

Below deck, Burton kept mum as I retrieved the wood box under the cot and handed it to him like a Christmas gift.

"The box was hidden under here."

"You removed the jewelry from this box?" Burton blinked.

"Wouldn't you, with all these crooks around?" I tilted my head toward Murdoch's for emphasis. "Remember the séance I mentioned for the ghost bride? I wanted to interview her fiancé and find out if he knew what really happened."

"And your boss approved of all this?" Burton seemed skeptical.

"Not exactly..." I took the box and opened it, tapping the faded photo. "Recognize anyone?"

"Holy Moses!" Nathan exclaimed. "Looks like we found our KKK bootleggers and the missing fiancé all on one boat!"

CHAPTER FORTY-TWO

"Hope I get to interview the boat captain face-to-face." I smiled at Burton, trying to soften his "I'm on the job" expression.

He examined the items. "So what does this prove?"

"Proves that our fisherman fiancé is actually a bootlegger, with possible ties to the mob and the KKK. What can you charge them with?" I asked Burton.

"For starters, evading arrest and assaulting an officer, not to mention violation of the Volstead act."

"Could I possibly talk to the boat captain—in private?" I asked. "I want to find out if they're the group we saw at the cemetery the other night."

"I doubt the chief will approve." Burton frowned. "You know he doesn't want to get civilians involved in criminal cases."

"Remind him how I helped with Sammy's case the other day. That may convince him to change his mind."

"I'll see what I can do," he said. "But don't get your hopes up."

"Why not tell him we're eye-witnesses? That we saw the KKK hide the hooch at the cemetery." I had an idea. "Are you going to fingerprint the fishermen and see if they're on file? If not, you can try to match the prints with the ones on the bottle we found."

Nathan nodded. "Wouldn't that be swell if we caught these bootleggers red-handed? I think Jazz and I are getting good at this crime-fighting stuff."

Burton stifled a smile. "Don't get carried away. These fishermen may look harmless, but they're considered dangerous criminals."

"A fella who's still so in love with his dead fiancé can't be all bad," I pointed out. "He cared enough to keep her photo and his wedding ring on his boat. I wonder what he did with *her* ring?"

"Bet he's saving it for his next bride," Nathan said.

There went my romantic fantasies.

"Ready to go, Nathan?"

"Sure you don't need me anymore?" Nathan asked.

"You're going to leave me out here all by my lonesome, Jazz?" Burton looked disappointed.

"Seems you've got everything under control."

As I turned to go, I saw a squad car park on the Seawall and Will called out to Burton as he made his way to the boat.

"Boy, those sailors sure know how to fight. They were brawling the minute we put them in jail. We planned to put them in the same cell, but they'd probably kill each other by morning."

"Glad you all made it there in one piece," Burton grinned. "Let's hope they settle down or no one will get any sleep."

"I don't know how Mike managed to keep his eyes on the road." Will guffawed. "Poor kid. Now his Tin Lizzie smells like a can of sardines." They shared a laugh, while Will playfully punched Burton's arm. Nathan and I took it as an excuse to exit the boat.

"Say, I'd better head back to the paper and develop these photos. You're welcome to see them tomorrow."

"I'll be glad to stop by." Burton nodded. "See you then, Jazz."

"Sure, tomorrow." I tried to sound cheerful but honestly, I was getting annoyed with Burton, my so-called beau. When would he ever take me and my career seriously? Seems he couldn't be bothered to ask his captain for a favor, no matter how important it was to me.

With a little luck and a lot of legwork, we were on our way to solving two mysteries in one fell swoop.

"What a night." Nathan let out a happy sigh as he parked in front of the boarding house. "Say, I could get used to being a junior Prohibition agent. Let me know if Burton ever needs a partner."

I smiled in the dark. "I think you need formal training to be a Treasury agent. May be easier to be a local cop. I doubt most of these knuckleheads even have a high school diploma. They reminded me of the Keystone Kops tonight!"

"Don't underestimate these cops or the gangsters," Nathan said. "I'd say both groups equally get away with murder, often literally."

The next morning, I huddled with the newshawks as we compared notes about last night's adventure.

"You should've seen the look on the boat captain's face when he realized we were chasing him," Chuck said, snorting. "I think he sprained his ankle running away."

"I'm surprised he didn't break his neck," Pete added. "He tried to jump onto the boulders and got his leg stuck. He was a sitting duck—or should I say a lame duck?" The guys hooted over that stupid pun.

"Being a Prohibition agent isn't such a bad job. I wouldn't mind all the perks, like the free booze," Nathan cracked.

"I don't think Burton takes home any liquor after a raid as pay or a reward," I reminded him. "You know he's a straight arrow."

"Unfortunately." Nathan grinned. "Otherwise we'd be kicking up our heels on that booze boat."

I rolled my eyes while they slapped each other's backs. "Thanks for all your help, boys. I know Burton appreciates you catching the boat captain."

"No problem. Your fella ain't too bad for a Fed. If he really wants to thank us, tell him to give us a head's up before his next booze bust," Pete said.

"I can't promise anything, but I'll pass on the word," I replied. "By the way, did you have a chance to talk to the boat captain after you caught him?"

"Not really," Chuck said. "I asked who he worked for and he didn't really answer. But I heard him mumbling to his partner about Johnny Jack."

"You don't say. What else?"

"Said he'd have his hide if he ever found out. I got the distinct impression that there's no love lost between those fellas."

Interesting. Sounded like he may be a rum-runner for the Downtown Gang, pocketing a few bottles on the side. "Hey, would you mind if I read over your story before it goes to press?"

"OK, why not? Let us know if we left anything out," Pete said.

"Great, thanks." I mulled over his words, wondering what was the connection with the fishermen and Johnny Jack.

Were they bootleggers for hire or officially part of the gang—or had they gone rogue?

If only Burton had allowed me to question the captain...but why would he spill the beans to *me*?

After I returned to my desk, I couldn't concentrate, replaying the night's events over and over in my mind. Should I call Lily and tell her I'd located her sister's fiancé? Then what would I say—by the way, he was caught rum-running with a boatload of booze and got arrested? Too bad I didn't have a chance to "interview" him before they stuck him in jail.

I riffled through the papers on my desk, wondering if I should work on my seer story or wait until after the Moody party. Would the Moodys mind if we invaded their private world of wealth and privilege and parties with a society story complete with pictures—or did I need their permission in advance?

Tell the truth, I couldn't do much of anything while worrying about Sammy and Burton and wondering what would happen to the fishermen in jail. Then I heard Mrs. Page yell across the room: "Jasmine! Your agent beau is on the phone for you!"

Predictably, I heard smooching noises across the newsroom and headed to the back office to take the call.

"How are you?" I asked Burton. "Did you have to stay on the boat all night or did you get any sleep?"

"Will and I took turns keeping watch. We didn't want any gangsters showing up and trying to confiscate the goods."

"So did you finally clear the boat?"

"Yes, we got a crew there early this morning and picked up everything." He paused. "Well, almost everything."

"Where's the wooden box?"

"Don't worry, it's safe." He cleared his throat. "Say, I've got someone here who's all sobered up now and ready to talk."

"Who—the boat captain?" My heart leapt in appreciation and all was forgiven. "Chief Jones said it was OK?"

"Lucky for us, he's out this afternoon." I could imagine Burton smiling on his end.

"What about the other sailor who tried to get away?"

"Harry? He's still sleeping it off. I found out that he's just hired help, not a real partner. We'll get to him later."

"Has Charles told you anything yet?"

"Not yet. You're the journalist. I'd rather you do the honors."

CHAPTER FORTY-THREE

"Really?" I was excited. "Can I interview the boat captain now?" Like Sammy, Agent Burton rarely let me into his world, saying it was too risky. No doubt he thought I couldn't handle the inherent danger and wanted to protect me—or did he want me to mind my own business?

"The sooner, the better."

Before she could interfere, I told Mrs. Harper I had an emergency and nabbed Nathan leaving the dark room.

In the car, he asked, "Where's the fire?"

"Burton is giving us a chance to talk to the boat captain before Chief Jones returns. I'm hoping he'll answer a few questions about his ghost bride—and the KKK bootleggers. You can back me up."

Nathan raced to the station as fast as his Tin Lizzie could go, and I jotted down a few bumpy notes along the way.

Burton met us at the door and took me down the hall to the back room where I'd spoken up for Sammy.

"Glad you two made it here so fast. Under different circumstances, I might've given you a speeding ticket." He grinned.

The captain looked as weather-beaten as his wrecked boat, his face as worn and bloated as an old stuffed suitcase.

Obviously he hadn't slept well, and still had on his disheveled clothes from the previous night. Unfortunately he needed a shower and a shave, plus a clean change of clothes. Despite the fishy odor, I was determined to try to get some answers.

Nathan and I got settled, facing Charles and Burton across the long oak table. Burton took the lead, asking, "What happened last night? Sampled too much of that rotgut and hit the rocks?"

Charles just shrugged and looked away.

"Where'd you get the liquor? Who's your source?"

Charles cracked his knuckles.

"If you refuse to talk, I'll have no other option but to lock you up until you do. Sorry, Charlie, but you leave me no choice."

"What choice do I have? Seems I'm screwed either way."

"The way I see it, if you cooperate, we may be able to work out a deal with the police chief."

"What do you want to know?"

"Who's your contact? Who are your suppliers? Can you provide a list of customers?" Burton leaned over the table, glaring at Charles.

The captain stroked his chin. "Let me think it over."

"Sure, you'll have plenty of time to think in jail." Burton let out a sigh. "Shame since I hoped we could cut you a deal. You help us, we help you."

"What kind of deal?"

"Depends on your cooperation. Tell me, are you mixed up with the local gangs or do you mainly operate a booze boat for hire?"

"Whoever pays me the most," Charles said, avoiding his gaze.

"Who pays best, which gang or group? Tell me their names."

"If I do, they'll kill me." Charles made a slicing motion across his neck.

"Are you a member of the KKK?"

"Hell, no! I don't believe in killing people based on their God-given skin color. People can't choose if they're black or white."

I thought of all the Negroes who helped stock my dad's store and lent a hand over the years. He considered them friends and trusted employees, not third-class riffraff. Despite Charles' belligerent tone, I began to like this fella.

Burton didn't buy it. "So why do you have a KKK uniform hidden on your boat? Does the Klan deal in hooch?"

"What? You cops searched my boat?"

"What did you expect?" Burton stood up, impatient. "Who wears the outfit if it's not yours?"

Charles shrugged. "Belongs to a pal of mine. I keep it around for emergencies. No one messes with you in those robes."

"I'll bet." Burton frowned. "Well, be glad we confiscated the loot before some rival gang found it and burned the boat."

"So what? Useless piece of firewood. Can I have a fag now?"

Burton raised his brows. "We have evidence that the KKK is involved in bootlegging. Are you involved or are you their supplier?"

Charles' face registered surprise. "What evidence?"

In a way, I wanted to reveal that we'd actually witnessed the Klansmen in the act, but knew it would be like putting a noose around our necks.

"Let's just say we know where the bottles are buried." Burton looked smug.

"Where?" Charles smirked.

"Why don't you ask your Klan buddies?"

"Can you butt me now?" Charles asked. "I need a smoke."

"You'd do a lot better if you worked with us."

"Why should I? What do I get out of the deal?" Charles leaned back, crossed his arms, and plunked his heavy boots on the desk. "I'd rather take my chances and stay here in jail. Safer that way."

"If your partner in crime, Harry, cooperates, he may get off with a rap on the knuckles."

"Go ahead, drill him," Charles challenged. "He's a Reuben, straight off the farm."

"This is a waste of time." Burton gave me a nudge, then paced the room. "I'm not getting anywhere. He's all yours."

Charles perked up. "You don't say. And who are you, toots?"

"Your friend." I smiled, taking the cue.

Burton gave me sly wink and moved to the back of the room, behind Charles' chair.

"What about this lollygagger?" He shaded his eyes at Nathan, who scurried over to join Burton.

"Don't mind me." Nathan held up his hands. "I'm part of the wallpaper."

"We're here to help you, I promise." I reached across the table to shake his hand. "I'm Jasmine Cross."

"Nice to meet you," he said, wary.

"Say, aren't you the same Charles Howard who's engaged to a teacher named Diana Thomas? She's very attractive."

He sat up straight. "How do you know about Diana?"

"I work for the *Gazette*. I saw your photo in the paper."

"What do you know? A lady crime reporter. Well, I ain't talking to any newspaper hack, even if she's a pretty dame."

Honestly, I was flattered, except for the hack part.

"Actually, I'm a society reporter. This isn't for the paper."

"Says you. How can I trust you?"

"We have a mutual friend, Lily Leavenworth. You can ask her about me."

His face twisted, a mixture of shock and suspicion. "H-h-how do you know Lily?"

I figured telling the truth might encourage him to do likewise. "She called the paper and wanted us to do a story."

"What kind of story?"

"A story about her late sister, Marilyn Foster. Is it true you two were engaged, but you shipwrecked your boat, and never made it to your wedding?"

Charles stared at me and blinked. "That was a long time ago. I'm engaged to Diana now."

I pulled his faded photo and postcard from my purse. "Will this help jog your memory?"

The blood drained from his face. "Such a beauty. God rest her soul. Why are you bringing this up now?"

"Lily wanted us to investigate her sister's death. She read about your engagement and wanted to get in touch with you, but couldn't reach you."

Charles hung his head in grief. "I want to forget the past. Marilyn's gone and I can't bring her back."

"You can help us prove she was murdered. Lily thinks the M.E fudged his findings," I pressed. "She doesn't believe Marilyn drowned herself. As Lily explained, they come from a religious family and her sister had no reason to take her own life."

"Why are you telling me all this? Why are you dredging up this mess from the past?" Seeing his heartbroken reaction, my instincts told me there was no possibility that this fella killed Marilyn.

"Lily wants justice for Marilyn. She want you to help her find the real killer. She thinks that's why her spirit roams the Hotel Galvez, searching for the truth, so she can rest in peace. Did you know they call her the ghost bride?"

Charles began to sweat. "Those are just rumors."

"I've heard ghosts will roam the earth if they have unfinished business," I added. "Such a tragic story."

Silent, he crossed his heart and pulled out a long chain with a stunning diamond and ruby platinum ring—the bee's knees!—from beneath his T-shirt, hidden under his raincoat. Then he bowed his head, hands clasped together, as if in prayer. Was this an act or was he truly reliving his grief?

"It's all my fault. She was a beautiful, sweet angel," he muttered, fingering the ring. "She didn't deserve to die that way. Lily is right. They murdered her in that goddamn ocean."

CHAPTER FORTY-FOUR

So he knew. "They? Who's they?" I tried to meet Charles' eyes. "Why do you think she was murdered?"

I exchanged looks with the fellas and scooted my chair closer to the table. When he didn't reply, I took note of the stunning ring on his chain: vibrant rubies around a marquis diamond, set in platinum. Boy, that sparkler must have set Charles back a grand or two.

"How pretty!" I exclaimed. "Is that Marilyn's ring?"

Silently he nodded. "I always wear it close to my heart." He eyed me, sounding defensive. "I bet you're wondering what a nice young lady like Marilyn ever saw in me. Diana too, for that matter. I wasn't always a fish monger, you know. I was enrolled at Texas A&M College studying to be a mechanical engineer when my pop had an accident at the boot factory. Damn near tore his right hand off. How could he work after that?" He blinked, his eyes misting.

"All he wanted was a better life for us, a good education, to have a chance to do the things he couldn't So I had to drop out my sophomore year and support the family...It was my duty."

"I'm sorry," I nodded in sympathy. "You did the right thing. My father died when I was in college, too."

"Did you ever finish?" he asked quietly.

"Not yet. I'm trying to save enough to pay for tuition at the University of Texas."

"So you understand." We had a moment of solidarity, his eyes bright before they went dull again.

Nathan added, "Tough luck, sport."

Impatient, Burton motioned for us to continue.

"Why do you think Marilyn was murdered? Any ideas?"

"She saw something she wasn't supposed to."

"Like what?"

"A booze drop, what else?" Charles' face turned to stone. "Boats often stopped near Murdoch's or the Hotel Galvez to deliver cases of liquor. She probably got a good look at the bootlegger and his crew before the sun set."

Finally, a motive for murder. I'd had the same thought so he'd confirmed my suspicion. But I wanted to test him, find out what he knew. "You're sure she didn't drown?"

"I know my Marilyn. She wouldn't take her life. She told me she'd wait for me forever. My gal believed in happy endings."

When he spoke, his expression softened, his whole demeanor changed, like he was lit from within. What a horrific ending to a sweet love story. My heart seized and I stole a look at Burton, wondering if he'd noticed.

"Do you have any evidence? Are there any eye-witnesses?"

"No one will admit what they saw. I just got a hunch."

Charles shifted in his chair, acting uncomfortable. "The way the fellas acted around me, guilty, like they were keeping a secret. They'd say they were sorry but wouldn't look me in the eye. At first, I was in shock, confused, you know? I didn't get it. I didn't want to believe she was gone. But the bosses brought it up all the time to keep me in line, the bastards."

"Keep you in line?"

"Yeah, to shut me up so I'd stop asking questions about Marilyn. The goons made these threats, warning me to back off."

Burton jerked to attention and leaned over the desk. "Who? Who threatened you?"

Charles ignored him, as if he hadn't heard. "They'd even threaten my pals, my crew. If anyone complained, they'd say things like, 'Look what happened to Marilyn.' You know, clear warnings."

"Did you tell anyone your suspicions? Or talk to the coroner?"

"I tried to ask the M.E.: Didn't you check her neck for bruises? Did you check her lungs? But I got back too late. I swear, they forced her head into the ocean until she was drinking saltwater!"

He leapt up, straining against his handcuffs, his eyes like wildfire. Burton tried to contain him, but Charles pushed him away.

Startled, I said, "I believe you," to pacify him. "All Lily wants is justice for her sister so she can rest in peace."

"What can I do? They've already killed my Marilyn and if I open my trap, I'll be next."

"Anything you can recall will be helpful," I prodded. "You don't want to stay locked up and miss your wedding, do you?"

A siren sounded outside, and we heard tires crunch on the gravel lot. "Wait. I think Chief Jones just arrived. He always likes to make an entrance." Burton winked at me behind Charles' back. I wondered if he made that up to spook the suspect.

"Let me tell you, he won't be as lenient or generous as I am. Sure you don't want a deal?"

"If I talk, I don't want to see the inside of a jail cell, got it? If word gets out I'm a squealer, then I'm a goner."

"We can offer you protection."

"Yeah, right. You don't know who you're dealing with." Charles started fidgeting, eyes darting around the room.

"Can you ID the KKK bootleggers or not?"

"Hell, no. I can't see their faces under those hoods."

Burton heaved a sigh. "You expect me to believe you? You'll have to do better if you want to skip jail time. Who's your contact?"

He shrugged. "Some white guy."

"OK, smart ass, here's my deal. You take me to your next meeting and you're out on bail."

"Are you loony? It ain't a party." Charles squirmed in his seat.

"Hear me out. I've got a couple of conditions." Burton was solemn. "First, I'll need to borrow that...uh..*outfit* we took off your boat. And the booze stays here till we deliver the crates. Under cover, of course."

"Then you'll let me go?"

"After you post bail."

I frowned at Burton, wondering how he'd talk Chief Jones into releasing Charles since they'd confiscated his booze boat.

"Hey, I'm broke till I get squared away." Charles mulled it over, biting his chapped lips. "OK, Fed, you're in luck. I'm gonna meet the guys tonight."

Burton perked up. "Tonight? Short notice, but I can manage."

"Not so fast. I've got my own condition." Charles paused. "Make that two conditions."

"What's that?"

"You'd better keep your trap shut or you'll blow our cover. If you arrest us, put the cuffs on me, too. Or the guys will get wise."

"Not a word. Swear you'll hold up your end?"

"Hey, Fed, my life is in your hands. If word gets out we made a deal, they'll string me up in the trees."

"You tell me where and when to bring the booze." Skeptical, Burton eyed Charles.

"That's between us." He glanced at us sideways. "I don't need an audience. Give me your word before I change my mind."

"You expect me to let you go, just like that?"

"That's up to you, Fed." Charles said. "It works two ways."

"First we need to make the arrangements." Burton motioned toward the door. "Nathan, Jazz, time to go."

As we walked down the hallway, Burton squeezed my hand. "Nice job reeling in a big fish, Jazz," he said, smiling at his own pun. "Hope I don't regret this. I'm taking a big risk, but Charlie's no use to us in jail."

"True," I agreed. "One of these Klansmen may know who killed the grand jury witness. Two birds, one stone."

"Make that two bottles of booze, one lush," Nathan added. "Or two drunks, one bottle of booze?"

"Hurry, let's get out of here before Chief Jones sees you." Burton ushered us out of the station, hands on our backs, shielding us from view.

As we left, I saw the chief in his office, staring at a stack of papers. So Burton was telling the truth. The second sailor, Harry, seemed to be sleeping it off in a cell. Now that Jones was back, the rowdy cops were on their best behavior.

Outside, Burton said, "Thanks for your help. That interview turned out better than expected. Frankly, I'm surprised he agreed to the deal."

"Not every day you get invited to a bootleg delivery run by the Klan." I smiled up at Burton. "Glad we could help out."

"I only hope nothing goes wrong and he gets away. We'll have men on guard, hidden in the area, just in case."

"Good idea. Let me know what you find out about the meet."

"Sorry, doll. I'm grateful you got Charles to spill the beans, but from now on it's our case. We can't risk getting civilians involved."

"Don't forget," I pointed out, "Nathan and I brought this KKK case to your attention in the first place."

"Yes, but you two need to stay away. Let me and my department handle these Klansmen. For all we know, they work for Johnny Jack and he ordered them to kill the grand jury witness."

"As I recall, you don't have a department," I told Burton. "We're just trying to help."

"Help, how? By getting killed? Blowing our cover?" He wagged a finger at me. "Jazz, this isn't some joke or a crazy assignment. These Klansmen are killers. They've got to take off their hoods at some point so I can ID them."

"Yes, sir!" Deflated, I gave a mock-salute. I didn't want Burton, or anyone for that matter, giving me orders. "Thanks for the chance to interview the captain. Good luck." Irritated, I turned on my heel.

Burton's face fell. "Jazz, I didn't mean to sound so..."

I whirled around like a mad dervish. "Bossy? Rude? I don't want you barking orders at me, not now, not ever. I'm not your servant or your slave." With that, I stomped out to the car, while Nathan trailed meekly behind. Poor guy, having to see us spat.

Burton grabbed my arm. "Jazz, listen. You know how important this is to my career. If I can prove the KKK is bootlegging hooch, we can arrest them for violating the 18th Amendment."

"Great. We can help you catch them in the act."

His expression softened. "Like I said, it's too dangerous for civilians. Don't you get it? I don't want anything to happen to you. Or Nathan."

"Sure, I get it, loud and clear," I huffed. "Your career is more important than mine."

Still fuming, I got into Nathan's car and slammed the door, shaking poor Lizzie. "Who cares what he says? The only reason he even *has* a case is because of us. We're the ones who saw the KKK storing liquor at the cemetery."

"Sorry to say, Jazz, but he's right. What in hell can we do?"

"You've got a gun, don't you? Burton will need back-up."

"Are you kidding? He'll need more than two nosy newshounds to help if he's surrounded by the KKK. They'll get a good laugh before they kill us."

"But Burton is risking his life! He needs us more than ever."

"Stop and think—we're no match for bloodthirsty, out of control Klansmen. If they catch us spying on them, no telling what they'll do to us."

"Come on, Nathan. All I want to do is watch, from a safe distance. I don't expect us to rush in like Douglas Fairbanks and save the day."

"Right, like we did at the docks." He scowled. "We almost got burnt alive in that damn warehouse."

"You're the one who ran into the flames," I said, feeling guilty since I'd actually started the warehouse fire to escape Black Jack's goons. "Fine, I understand if you're afraid. I'll go by myself."

"Who, me? I'm not afraid." He snapped his suspenders. "Honest Injun, I'd love to catch the KKK in action. I'd get some great shots for the paper."

"No cameras! They'd hang you for sure."

"Don't worry, I'll keep my distance. But even if I wanted to go, we don't know where they're meeting or when."

I began to feel hopeful. "So you're interested?"

"Guess I could ask Chuck or Pete if they've heard anything," Nathan said. "They *did* help round up the runaway captain."

"No, this is our story!" I insisted. "If you tell them what we're up to, they'll take over the whole thing and probably get us killed in the process."

"You got that right."

"Why not drive by the cemetery tonight and see if they turn up? Go on a stakeout, like we did on the docks."

He had a gleam in his eyes. "Same cemetery, same time?"

"Sure." I returned his smile. "I admit, this could be another wild goose chase. But bring your gun, just in case."

CHAPTER FORTY-FIVE

That evening, Nathan picked me up around eight o'clock and we acted like it was all newspaper business as usual in front of my aunt Eva and Sheriff Sanders. Since he got into town, she didn't have much time to pay attention to my antics. Did he know about the KKK booze drop tonight?

As we were leaving, Sanders sauntered up, drawling, "I heard you were at the Seawall after that booze boat crashed. Did you see anything unusual?"

I froze, wondering if he heard about my interview with Charles. "Only two bruised and beaten sailors running for their lives. Why, what's new?"

"Thought maybe your beau had some information that might help this investigation." He worked his jaw. "Strange the suspect was released so early into Burton's custody. Weren't you there today?"

Did he know about the meet tonight? I tried to look blank. "Yes, he wanted me to identify the suspects, make sure they were the same sailors we saw. I found a fisherman hiding at Gaido's and alerted Burton."

"Jasmine, you didn't tell me anything about this!" Eva scolded. "Did that bully try to hurt you?"

"I didn't want to upset you." I glared at Sanders for blabbing. "Don't worry, Burton arrested the fishermen and took them down to the police station."

"Thank goodness," she sighed. "Well, you two stay out of trouble. Nathan, maybe you can talk some sense into her."

"I doubt that, ma'am, but I'll try my best."

"I'd better be on my way, honey pie." Sanders followed us out the door and gave Eva a quick peck. "See you tomorrow?"

I had to admit, it was disconcerting to see my aunt light up like a Christmas tree. Naturally, I was happy for her, but I kept Burton's warning in mind. No one needed a drill sergeant for a beau.

Luckily, Nathan found a quiet place to park, away from the street lamps, yet facing the Broadway cemetery. "I'll wait half an hour tops, then if no one shows up, we'll blow, OK?"

"Hope they didn't find a new location. Can you keep a lookout while I change my clothes? A boarder left these behind."

"My duds aren't fancy enough for you?"

Despite the December chill, the night was so humid and sticky that I practically had to peel off my clothes. Twisting and turning in the cramped car, I elbowed Nathan in the face a few times.

"Ouch, watch out!" he yelped. "Say, how are you going to explain that top and trousers to your aunt and the sheriff? He already seems suspicious."

"I'll say. Burton doesn't confide in me at all. He likes to keep his work private. I wonder what he told Jones when he took the booze and KKK uniform? Maybe he never turned them over to the cops."

"He only wants to protect you. He's not trying to be a louse."

"Oh yeah? He doesn't trust me."

Nathan snorted. "Can you blame him? Here we are, sitting outside a cemetery, hoping to catch him at a booze drop with a bunch of KKK bootleggers."

"Well, when you put it like that..."

Suddenly he turned around. "I think we've got company."

"Where?" I saw a flash of headlights turn around and park close to the guard shack. Peering out, I saw a flashy hayburner, the kind of wheels gangsters like to show off along with their glamorous gun molls. "Hope we can see their faces. Surely they don't drive around in those ghost costumes."

We watched in silence as more cars drove up and parked on a side street. A few fellas in street clothes filed out, carrying plain white sacks. What was inside—KKK robes or cash or weapons or all of the above? Whatever was going on, this sure looked like a good place and time for crime.

From our vantage point, I watched out for Burton's Roadster—or did he switch cars? I hoped he'd gotten one of his few trusted cop buddies to help, if only to drive and act as back-up. The thought comforted me, though I was still angry at him. He needed to take me—and my career—seriously.

"I can't see much from this distance. Can we get closer?" I let out a sigh. "I'd feel better if I knew Burton was here."

"Me, too," Nathan admitted.

"I wonder if Captain Jones caught wind of this meet and cancelled the deal with Charles," I worried. "If Burton shows, he'll be outnumbered, unless he brings help."

A Cadillac raced down Broadway and I crouched down in my seat, hiding from the bright headlights. But as the car got closer to the cemetery, the driver dimmed the lights, then flashed them three times at the entrance. Clearly a signal—but what, and to whom? Who was in the Cadillac—the leader, a Klansman or a mobster?

Frozen, we watched for a few minutes, but nothing happened.

"What are they doing?" I wondered.

"Who knows? Let's wait and see." The minutes ticked by.

"We're not getting anywhere just sitting here," I complained.

"I'll say. My legs are cramping. Ready to make a move?"

I was getting cold feet. "Where's Burton? What if the gang caught him?"

"Only one way to find out."

Slowly we got out of the car, quietly shut the doors and crouched down as we made our way toward the mausoleum with the angel. No chants or loud noises. Heads down, we hid behind a shroud of bushes surrounding a tall headstone and saw a small group of fellas in the familiar white robes, murmuring in low voices.

We exchanged wary glances, relieved we'd found the right spot, but afraid of what the Klansmen had planned. Had Charles tipped them off? A thought hit me—was Burton walking into a trap?

I assumed Charles had been kept under watch until the meet could be finalized. Honestly, I hoped tonight would only involve an exchange of money and booze—please, no violence or dead bodies.

My heart began a slow thud as Nathan and I watched in silence, waiting for their standard ritual, a secret handshake or chant or whatever the hell those Klansmen did in their robes.

They shuffled their feet, speaking so low we couldn't hear actual words. What did these thugs accomplish at their meetings anyway: brag about their kills, compare war stories, show off their prison tattoos, insult other members or plan their next attack?

To me, this band of boozers seemed off somehow—disjointed, disorganized. The Klansmen acted nervous, twitchy, clumps talking amongst themselves. I remember seeing photos of the KKK forming a circle, burning white crosses, terrorizing neighborhoods and churches full of Negroes before they set them afire.

Apparently this secret group of men didn't play by the regular rules. Were they rebels and rogues, robbing Peter to pay themselves?

A slight figure in civilian clothes approached the group, hesitant, as the hooded figures circled him. Charles? Angry voices, slowly getting louder as they closed in. No doubt it had to be the boat captain, who arrived empty-handed, probably as Burton instructed.

"So where is he, huh?" a Klansman with a deep voice demanded. "You said he'd be here by now."

"Don't worry. He knows the way." We recognized Charles' shaky voice, unlike the bold and brazen fella we'd met earlier today.

"What happened to our hooch?" A man demanded.

"You know I lost it when I wrecked my boat," Charles lied. "Crates of top-notch liquor, buried in the ocean. All gone to waste."

"Why couldn't you save the booze, you palooka?"

"The boat was filling up with water so fast, I had to throw it overboard," Charles fibbed. "If we stopped to save the booze, we coulda drowned."

"So who's this new crook?" the man asked. "How d'ya know his stuff's any good?"

"He's on the level," Charles snarled. "I take all the risks, so don't give me none of your lip."

Oh no—was he trying to pass off Agent Burton as the new bootlegger in town?

CHAPTER FORTY-SIX

The night was pitch-dark, a silver half-moon highlighting the Klansmen's flowing white robes, like a mirage of black and white.

What was taking Burton so long? He was punctual to a fault, so did something go wrong?

Then I heard a motor and saw a delivery van park near the guard shack. All heads turned as doors slammed, twigs snapped and two hooded figures emerged from the darkness. One tall, one medium height. Nathan and I were riveted to the cloaked men striding up to the KKK gang. No hesitation, no fear.

"Did you start without us?" I heard a familiar voice.

Maybe I was mistaken, but the short fella sounded exactly like Sheriff Sanders. I hoped the tall man was Burton. As long as he kept his Yankee mouth shut, they might actually pull off this caper.

I nudged Nathan. "Is that...?"

"Sure sounds like Sanders. Makes sense to bring him along."

"He put on a good act, pretending not to know about the meet. Burton needs all the help he can get."

I strained to listen to the ghostly group. The lawmen seemed to be outnumbered—unless more cops were hiding under those robes? Not the best odds, but I knew the men had faced bigger challenges.

"Sorry to keep you waiting, fellas. Let's take a head count first. Who's who?"

"And who are you, wiseguy?"

Sanders stammered, "The fellas call me Bear Claws 'cause I like to get my paws on the honey pot." Bear Claws and honey, like Winnie the Pooh? The men snickered, and I wondered how he came up with that corny line on the spot.

"How about you, boys? What are your names? Tell me who ordered how many cases."

Seems Sanders was trying to trick the spooks into revealing their identities—did they use code words or nicknames?

"That's not how it works," one man growled. "You can't barge in here and give us orders." Guess they weren't falling for his ruse.

"Back off, Butch," Charles told him. "Give the guy a chance."

"That's right, son," Sanders said. "Just trying to do my job. So how does it work?" Too bad Charles hadn't given the cops any pointers. If Sanders wasn't careful, he'd single-handedly blow their cover. I assumed Burton stood by his side, silent, perhaps trying to identify the Klansmen's voices, waiting to make a move. Who knew exactly who was who under those hoods?

Butch marched over to Burton. "Whatcha doing here, boy?"

"He's my assistant." Sanders cut him off. "Pay him no mind. His English ain't so hot, but he's here to help load the crates."

If that wasn't Agent Burton, who was it?

Sanders' act of submission seemed to appease the wiseguy. "Give me my usual. Ten cases of whiskey."

"Sorry, boys, no Canadian whiskey tonight," Sanders said, to cries of disappointment.

Butch told Charles, "Oh, yeah. You had to go and wreck your boat and bring in this no-name hood to fill in."

"Forget it, then. What are we here for anyway?"

"Hold your horses." Sanders held up his hands. "Got something even better. A fresh load of rum straight from Cuba."

Cuban rum? That sounded familiar.

"Oh yeah?" Butch poked Sanders in the chest. "This better not be like the bathtub booze going around town last summer. Let me take a swig, make sure you're not selling me crap moonshine."

We waited to see how Sanders and Burton would react—not that we could actually see them. How in hell were they going to handle this—actually let them sample the rum? Burton retreated to the van while Sanders kept up a steady stream of sales talk.

"This rum will grow hair on your chest and keep your customers coming back for more!" he exclaimed. Boy, if Sanders ever wanted to retire, he could easily find work as a carnival barker.

Burton returned with an open crate and Sanders handed each Klansman a bottle of rum, passing around a bottle opener. Looked like they'd thought of everything.

I'm sure it pained the cops to actually turn over the rum to these hoods—whoever they were. Maybe they were trying to gain their trust, slowly infiltrate the group from the inside out.

So far the strategy seemed to be working. Soon the Klansmen were joking and laughing, getting plastered, open to dealing with the new bootleggers. If they only knew.

"OK, boys, let's get down to numbers. Who wants how many crates?" With Charles' help, Sanders made the rounds with a pad and pencil, taking orders, I assumed.

Sanders and Burton retreated to the van, while Charles whispered a few words to the gang before he followed. Were the Klansmen getting suspicious? Was Charles ratting out the cops, warning the gang—or trying to reassure them?

Thank goodness Burton had an experienced partner like Sanders along, instead of a dirty cop. Was that part of their plan: to hand over the full crates of rum now and try to ambush the men later?

Sanders and Burton returned with a wheelbarrow haphazardly stacked with crates of liquor. I couldn't believe my eyes. What was going on? Were the lawmen actually going through with this charade?

The duo began to distribute the liquor while the Klansmen fished in their pockets for cash. What struck me was each man seemed to have a different method of payment, confirming my suspicion that they weren't one cohesive group or gang at all. Seemed to me each operated independently, not as part of the KKK. Who in the world were these guys?

I noticed most men paid with bills, while a couple had silver dollars. One man handed over a sheet of paper that I assumed was a marker with a written IOU. I watched a Klansman pull out a small pale cloth bag and dump the glittering contents in Sanders' hands. Jewelry, watches, chains, coins? Shuddering, I nudged Nathan—was he one of the grave robbers?

Charles and the lawmen took turns carrying crates from the van with the wheelbarrow, making sure someone was keeping an eye on the gang. After each got his share, the men tried to carry the crates, but they weren't prepared for the heavy load. Only one wheelbarrow to split among eight men?

"I'll be back for the rest," said Butch, picking up a crate. "Watch my load, will you, boys?"

Suddenly tires screeched on Broadway and gunshots rang out overhead in the dark. Panicked, Nathan and I looked up to see a Cadillac—the same one as earlier?—race down the street and make a U-turn. Nathan and I instinctively flattened on the ground, crawling behind a large tombstone. Breathing hard, I looked around to see what had happened to Agent Burton—was he OK?

The Klansmen ducked for cover, hiding behind a mausoleum as the cops removed their guns from under the robes. Did Charles and the gang notice or did they pack their own pistols?

The Cadillac barreled down Broadway again, and this time I saw a flashing gleam of metal. I couldn't help it: I screamed just as a Tommy gun slid out and took aim, firing at the Klansmen.

CHAPTER FORTY-SEVEN

"Watch out!" Charles yelled. A second round of gunfire erupted, and the Klansmen scattered in all directions, like a frightened pack of coyotes. Shaking, I covered my mouth to silence my screams. No need—the shots were deafening.

The scene was utter chaos. Some men dropped the booze, while a few clutched the crates to their chests, hobbling away from the Cadillac. Everything seemed to move in slow motion as the Klansmen disappeared in the darkness. Was it a rival gang, the KKK or bad cops? Who had tipped them off?

A tall hooded man ran toward the Cadillac, his gun drawn. James? I followed him a few yards with Nathan in tow as he ran along Broadway and jumped into his Roadster. The Victorian street lamps helped light the way.

My heart leapt when he yanked off his hood and I realized that it *was* Burton. I watched while he gunned his engine and followed the Cadillac down Broadway until the red tail lights disappeared. Thank goodness Burton was there, protecting us, keeping us safe.

When all was still, I noticed only a few men were left, guarding their crates, dazed, checking to make sure they weren't hit. So far the Klansmen didn't seem to realize that Sanders and Burton were actually undercover cops. All they cared about was grabbing their share of rum.

Butch, the so-called leader, charged at Charles, grabbing his collar. "You bastard, you set us up!"

"Hell, how was I to know someone would take potshots at us? Maybe you're the asshole who nearly got us all killed!" Charles yelled out before he ran off into the night.

"Should we follow him?" I asked Nathan.

"Not our problem." Nathan shook his head.

Two men darted out of the bushes, holding guns, racing to catch the bootleggers. Squinting to see by the dim moonlight, I recognized the cops from the boat crash, Mike and Will. I assumed they stopped to talk to Sanders, but how could I tell in the dark?

"Damn, wish I had my camera on me. What a scene."

Heading back to our hiding place, I gasped when we saw a Klansman staggering toward us. He stumbled in the dark a few steps, until he finally fell, clutching at his leg.

"He must be shot. Should we get help?" I asked Nathan.

"If we stop to help this fella, the men will find us here, accuse us of spying," he said. "His pals may try to retaliate."

"No one else is around. We can't stay here, hiding in the shadows." Indeed the cemetery seemed quiet now. Guess the cops were still chasing after the suspects on foot or had caught and arrested a few by now.

"If we get shot too, it's on your head. Could be a trick."

Nathan leaned over the big man, who was writhing in pain on the ground. A dark red stain seeped onto the lower half of his robes. Nathan pulled out a handgun and pointed it at the man's heart.

I inhaled sharply—I didn't realize he'd been carrying his gun.

"Who are you?" he demanded. "Show yourself, you coward."

The hooded man lay still, motionless, and refused to answer. Was he pretending or had he passed out from pain or loss of blood?

Still, Nathan couldn't hide his contempt for the Klan. "Are you so chicken shit you can't show your face?" His hands shook as he pressed the gun into the man's chest. "Take off your hood—or I'll do it for you!"

Holding his gun with his right hand, Nathan bent down and yanked off the Klansman's pointed hood with his left.

The man grunted and rubbed his eyes, trying to focus.

"Mack?!" We both gasped at once. "Is that you?"

"Are you OK?" Nathan asked. "Are you hurt?"

"Just a flesh wound, that's all." He clutched at his leg. "Believe me, I endured a lot worse during the Great War. This is nothing."

"Nothing?" I glanced at him, dubious. Mack's grimace told me otherwise. "We'd better take you to Big Red, get you checked out."

"Is that you, Jasmine? Dressed like a fella?" He tried to smile. "It's not safe here for anyone, especially you two kids. Better scram before the lawmen catch up to us. Isn't your beau here too?"

"He drove off after the shooters. Any idea who took those potshots? Were you followed here?" My money was on George Musey and Marco, his malicious henchman.

"Neither gang would cotton to more rivals," Mack muttered.

"What in hell are you doing mixed up in a KKK bootlegging ring?" Nathan snapped. "You almost got killed!"

"This isn't what it looks like." Mack reached for his leg.

"Try me. You owe us an explanation."

"I had no idea you're part of the KKK," I hissed. "Hell, you've written enough articles about their lynchings and murders." I had a few more choice words, but reined in my temper since he was hurt.

"Hey, back off. For your information, I'm working undercover," Mack said. "For an article. Swear to God. I had to infiltrate this group for my research." He grimaced. "Helps that I fit the bill. A white Southern male."

"Sure you're not working for George Musey?" Nathan asked.

"That's what *he* thinks," Mack said. "I'm humoring him till I can finish this piece."

What did that mean? Was he working for Musey or not?

"Well, you can explain on the way to Big Red," Nathan said, trying to lift the big man.

As I sagged beneath Mack's weight, I heard a deep voice bark, "What are you boys doing?" I felt the hard barrel of a rifle pressed in my back, and knew this nightmare could get even worse if they found out I was female. "What about you, fella?" The man turned his attention to Nathan. "Were you two hooligans *spying* on us?

Turning around, I realized it was Charles, relieved he'd returned, and wondered how he'd react if he knew we'd witnessed the whole scenario. Obviously he didn't recognize us in these duds, but I kept my mouth shut as I eyed his weapon. Where'd he get that rifle—from a dead cop?

"We're trying to help our pal," Nathan said, taken by surprise.

"Sure you're not trying to pickpocket an old man?"

Mack piped up. "They're my friends, Charlie. And I'm not old."

Nathan and I stifled our smiles.

"Wanna bet, *old* sport?" he said. "Where're you taking him?"

"Big Red. Can you help lift him to my car?" Nathan said.

"Sure." Charles set the trigger on safety and slung the rifle over his shoulder before bending down to get Mack. Seems he'd gained some strength after years of handling boats and crates of booze.

"Hang in there, pal." Nathan gently shook Mack's arm as they hoisted him up like a scarecrow. Mack limped along on his semi-good leg, the wounded limb dragging.

Sure, we'd had our disputes, but I pitied the old codger, who only had one good leg after the Great War. Now it seemed both legs had suffered serious injury. Still, I hoped his days as a crime reporter weren't over. I held the car door open while they dragged Mack to Nathan's ragtop, and tried to gently position him in the back.

Imagine trying to stuff a Longhorn bull into a suitcase.

Carefully they propped him up against the door, his legs spread across the back seat, a tight squeeze for the stocky fella.

"So how do you know Mack?" I asked Charles, curious.

"Mack's my poker pal. We met playing cards at the Kit Kat."

Johnny Jack's notorious nightclub and casino. I wondered what else, and who else, they might have in common.

"Wait." He peered at me closely. "Have we met before?"

"The police station, earlier today. Jasmine Cross."

"You're the dame. The gal who knows Lily." Charles frowned. "Say, I told Burton to keep this quiet."

"Sorry, lucky guess. This was our idea. Need me to come too?"

"I think we're OK," Nathan said. "You'd have a lot of explaining to do if you got caught at Big Red looking like a fella."

He was right. Surely my boss would get wind of Mack's injury and hospital stay. Guess I'd have to hitch a ride with Sheriff Sanders or his posse.

"What do you boys think you're doing?" a deep voice said.

I looked up to see my handsome Yankee beau, looking tall and muscular, thankfully wearing jeans and a cowboy hat instead of white robes and a hood.

CHAPTER FORTY-EIGHT

Relief, then guilt, surged through me: Burton caught me and Nathan spying on the Klan, after he insisted we mind our own beeswax. Yikes!

"We're trying to save Mack's life!" I explained, hoping he'd consider this a rescue mission, not my typical stakeout.

Burton snapped to attention. "Jazz, is that you? I told you two to stay away. I should've known you and Nathan would show up."

"Thank God, these kids probably saved my life," Mack cut in.

Then Burton did a double-take when he spotted Charles. "You're still here? Thought you'd run like the wind."

"Remember our deal?" Charles looked frantic. "You gotta lock me up. It's not safe out here with these animals. They blame me for the shooting *and* the booze bust!"

"Say, where's Sanders? Mike? Will?" Burton glanced around the cemetery. "What happened to the rum? I'll take a look."

"I'll go with you," I offered.

"You don't take no for an answer, do you?"

"Why should I when yes is more fun?"

"Don't let the cops see you. They may get some funny ideas about me," Burton teased, grabbing at my cap and tousling my hair.

No doubt I looked a fright—like a muddy, unkempt ragamuffin, especially without my face paint.

"So what happened? Did you catch the thugs in the Cadillac?"

"No, they got away, but I may have an idea who they were."

"Beach or Downtown Gang?"

"Jazz, you know I can't tell you anything. Not yet."

Such a straight arrow. Slowly we circled the area, but aside from a few busted wooden crates, all the booze appeared to be gone.

"Let's hope Sanders and the cops loaded the rum into the van."

"Gotta admit, I was shocked when I saw you actually distributing the bottles to the Klansmen. Whose idea was that?"

"You liked it, huh? All mine. In fact, we marked these bottles after Johnny Jack's bust a month ago." Burton looked smug. "Figured we'd put them to good use, gain the guys' trust before we nab them. After all, we can't arrest them for dealing in soda pop."

"Right. I wonder how many men got away with the rum?"

"We'll take a tally back at the station."

"Why don't I try to talk to Charles on the way?" I offered. "Besides, Nathan's car is full."

"Sure, but remember Charles is a prime suspect. I know you feel a connection with him and all, but he's still in police custody."

In case his gang was watching, Charles put up a good fight when Burton clicked on the handcuffs and shoved him into his car. I wiped off my clothes before I got into Burton's Roadster, hating to dirty his spotless interior. Luckily, he had the Army blankets spread over the front and back seats.

"Nice set of wheels for a Fed." Charles sounded impressed.

"It's my company car," Burton half-joked. "Gotta fit in with you rich guys."

"Say, who were all those fellas?" I asked Charles. "Your pals?"

Burton tilted his head, listening. I noticed he'd slowed way down, giving me plenty of time to grill Charles, who seemed flattered by my interest.

"The boys are my crew, former shipmates, back when I was rum-running for Johnny Jack," he said. "We worked so hard without a break over the years, I wanted to let them in on the haul." His speech sounded slurred, no doubt from sampling too much rum.

"You're skimming from the Downtown Gang?" I asked.

"Hell, no. I don't work for the gangs no more. This load is for me and my friends. I swear, the mobsters liked to stiff us, hold back our pay or say the load wasn't good enough or incomplete, then give us half the take they promised." His face darkened.

"Me and the boys got tired of always being bamboozled. We wanted to start our own gang, be independent."

Burton nodded at me, encouraging me to keep Charles talking.

"You could say I went into business for myself. After Marilyn died, I just couldn't put up with the bullshit anymore."

"I don't blame you." I paused, hoping to keep him on his blue streak. "So are the guys actually gangsters or Klansmen?"

"A mix of both. Some got fed up and kept the robes out of spite. Most of the guys had run-ins with the gangs or the KKK." He scowled. "Shame what those bums will do if they don't like the way some folks look or talk or act."

"I'll say." Was it possible to drop out of the Klan without retribution? Ever since Sammy left the Downtown Gang, he always had to watch his back. "What do you mean run-ins?"

"Well, don't tell anyone..." he drawled. "Take Butch, the bully. A couple of Klansmen he knew took a fancy to his sister, but when she turned them down, they raped her and left her for dead. Thank God she's OK. This group of bootleggers was all his idea."

"How sad. No wonder he's got a chip on his shoulder."

"More like a boulder." Charles leaned forward. "Let's just say this is our payback, a way of getting revenge. A frame job."

Now I understood, even sympathized. Prohibition brought together friends and enemies alike for a common goal: to exploit the public and profit from a nonsensical and impossible-to-uphold law. Bankers buddied up with bootleggers, and rum-runners risked their lives to venture onto foreign soil, all to chase the mighty dollar.

"Say, any idea who took potshots at us from the Cadillac?"

Charles shrugged. "I suspect one of Musey's flunkies was behind the drive-by. The big boys don't like it when the small fry muscles in on their racket."

Made sense. Clearly, it hadn't sunk in that he'd been arrested by a Prohibition agent and was on his way to a police station.

Since he was dishing dirt, I wondered if Charles had an inside track on Johnny Jack. "Say, did you hear about that recent gang slaying? A body was dropped off at the Broadway cemetery a few days ago, left on a grave."

"You mean the wiseguy tied to the headstone?"

CHAPTER FORTY-NINE

I'd never mentioned O'Brien was tied to anything. I exchanged knowing looks with Burton. So Charles *had* been there the night O'Brien turned up dead. What a shocker. Observer or participant?

"Do you know anything about it?" I coaxed, trying to act calm.

"Damn snitch shoulda minded his own business."

What else did he know? I had to ask: "Did you see who left the body—or who killed him?"

Charles shook his head and leaned back, clamming up the rest of the way. I wondered: did any of his gang witness the murder?

Burton gave me a grateful smile as he led Charles into the police station. I wanted to follow, but knew that wasn't proper protocol. Let Burton bask in his own glory after a semi-successful booze bust.

As I waited, I freshened up my face paint, squinting in my tiny compact mirror. I made a note to go shopping for a new tango vanity the next day—didn't I deserve a treat?

I ducked when I saw the delivery van drive up, and slid down in the seat, trying to make myself invisible. Mike got out, opened the back and proceeded to carry a crate of rum into the station. Looked like most of the load had been recovered. Was that a smart idea, flaunting the crates of booze in front of both bootleggers and cops? Then Mike reappeared with Will and unloaded the van, leaving a couple of crates behind.

Were they keeping it for themselves? And what was taking Burton so long?

Finally Burton appeared with a smile and started the car. "That was very interesting. How'd you get Charlie to spill?"

Pleased, I turned pink. "Easy. He was blotto."

"Not blotto enough. He refused to answer any more questions tonight. Crawled into a cell and fell asleep."

"No wonder. His friends accused him of betraying the gang and setting them up."

"I'll say. The fellas we arrested blamed him for everything, like he said."

"I wonder if they know who killed O'Brien?"

"The Downtown Gang may have hired them to kill O'Brien so he wouldn't testify against Johnny Jack," Burton said.

"Sounds like there's no love lost between those men." I paused. "You think Charles is telling the truth about his bootlegger buddies?"

Burton shrugged. "They appear to be a ragtag bunch of disgruntled thugs trying to form a new gang. For them, it's not only about profit or justice, it's revenge. They probably steal from the Downtown and Beach gangs so they can fund their own band of criminals. Call it a mutiny."

"What better way to fight your enemies than to beat them at their own game?"

Burton nodded. "They may try for a small slice of the pie, not enough to topple the kings but enough for them to notice."

"Those hoods sure hide a lot of secrets under their hoods. Charles has already lost the love of his life. Go easy on him. I think he's suffered enough."

"He still broke the law. But if his men cooperate, we may be able to work out a deal. They're already behind bars, so what do they have to lose?"

A white fuzzy animal started to dart across the street. I yelled out, "Stop! It's a cute opossum."

Luckily, Burton braked just in time. "Cute? To me, they look like big rats."

"They're harmless, really gentle if they're not provoked. Can't you see his big eyes and fluffy fur? He looks like a fuzzy white Mickey Mouse." I watched to make sure the frightened creature crossed the street safely.

"Maybe you should adopt one as a pet," he teased.

"I leave out scraps in the backyard," I admitted. "They're just trying to survive, like the wild animals you locked up tonight."

Burton rolled his eyes. "Say, I was surprised to see Mack there at the meet. Did he say what he was doing with this bunch of crooks?"

"We think he's somehow...involved with George Musey."

"I hear he's deep in debt to the Downtown Gang."

I let out a sigh. "OK, so what else do you know?"

"He must be acting as Musey's watchdog, keeping an eye out for rogue gangsters. Musey takes his debts seriously."

"Mack told us he was there undercover, working on an article."

"If that's true, then he may as well put a bullet in his brain. Musey doesn't like traitors or rats." Burton smiled. "Even if he's a cute opossum."

"I'm sure Mack knows the consequences. Seems he'll do anything to get his old job back, even risk his life."

"Mack's been around the block a few times."

"I'll say—including Madame Farushka's block."

"Who, that gypsy, the fortune teller dame?"

I gave him a sly smile. "Turns out they're sharing secrets."

"Interesting. What kind of secrets?"

"I think she's feeding him tips about the society set and who knows what else. He said she's privy to all sorts of information—for a price."

"I wonder how he pays her if he's broke. Tell him to be careful."

"You can't stop an old war horse like Mack," I said. "He'll do as he pleases."

Burton parked in front of the boarding house and turned off the engine. Luckily the old Victorian was dark, so that meant Aunt Eva wasn't waiting up for me. "This is your stop, missy. I've tried dissuading you from investigating these crimes, but you're determined to disobey direct orders."

"Disobey who?" I bristled, then realized he was teasing me. Again. "I can't wait around for plum assignments with all this excitement going on. I need to chase after leads myself. Isn't that the mark of a good journalist?"

"Sure. If I were in your pretty shoes, I'd do the same thing."

I lifted up the muddy men's shoes I'd borrowed. "These?"

"Very nice."

"Say, let me know what you find out later, if Charles is willing to ID any of the gangsters or ex-Klansmen."

I leaned over to kiss Burton on the cheek.

"You'll have to do better than that if you really want inside information." Then he leaned in and gave me a deep kiss that knocked my dirty socks off.

"Thanks, mister. Now you've made my head swim."

"That was the plan." Burton grinned. "This case gets more complicated and confusing. I'm afraid to say much since you journalists were there on the scene. Speaking of, let me know what Mack says if you see him."

I nodded. "Nathan and I may visit him at the hospital tomorrow. Say, don't forget, we've got the Moodys' party coming up. Madame Farushka is supposed to be there, reading palms and spouting fortunes."

"Swell," he groaned. "Sure they want a Prohibition agent there to see them swilling hooch?"

"The Moodys don't drink," I reminded him.

"Maybe not, but I'll bet their guests bring full flasks."

CHAPTER FIFTY

Carefully, I tiptoed into the boarding house and up the stairs, exhausted. I tapped on Amanda's door, hoping she was still up. Boy, did I need someone to talk to. Still I worried she might blab to the wrong customers at Star Diner—like her gangster pal Marco Polo.

"Was that James? Where'd you go tonight? Tell me!" She patted the bed by her.

"Nathan and I went on a stakeout and saw a lot more than we bargained for. Exciting night." I was dying to describe the whole frightening escapade, but bit my tongue.

"That's all?" She could tell I was holding back. "Well, don't forget I start at the Hollywood this weekend, on Saturday night! Why don't you and Burton come by and wish me luck?"

"Sure, we'll be there..." I began. "Damn, that's the same night as the Moodys' Christmas party. Maybe we can stop by afterwards?"

"Swell! I knew I could count on you."

All night, I dreamt of ghouls with white skin and haunted eyes popping up out of fresh graves, waving Tommy guns. Thank goodness more people weren't hurt—the cemetery could have become a bloodbath of bodies. Who was taking random potshots at the bootleggers—and why?

At work the next day, I felt like I was sleepwalking. I admit, it was dangerous, and even stupid, for me and Nathan to put ourselves in such a vulnerable position at the cemetery, but hadn't it paid off?

Not only did we help save Mack, I found out more about Charles and his band of half-baked thieves—and a possible lead in the O'Brien murder. Not to mention I saw my daring beau in action, even if he hadn't caught the culprits who did the drive-by shooting.

Still disoriented, I was passing the darkroom when Nathan pulled me inside. Eerie red lights and the black-and-white photos hanging from a wire reminded me of the cemetery all over again—or a tiny haunted house. Was I hallucinating?

"How's Mack? How serious was the wound?"

"Mack got lucky, very lucky. The bullet just missed his thigh bone so it's only a flesh wound, as he said, but the hole is as big as a walnut, so it took out a lot of flesh. Nothing that can't be fixed."

I felt faint, trying not to imagine his bloodied leg. "What a relief. Poor old guy doesn't need any more war wounds."

"I'll say. I wanted to check on him after surgery. Want to go?"

Surprised, I frowned. "Sure he doesn't mind an extra visitor?"

"Not at all. After he came to last night, he mentioned you. Said you had balls for showing up at the meet, like a real reporter."

"Balls? Mack actually said I had balls?" Strange, but I knew it was a compliment coming from Mack.

After we exited the darkroom, I scanned the office, glad Mrs. Harper had left early for an "appointment." She probably wanted to hit the Christmas sales at Eiband's before the tearoom opened. Less competition for hats and hosiery.

"Sounds good. Maybe we can grab a bite at Star Diner on the way back? Might be fun to see her one last time before she starts her new job at the Hollywood Dinner Club."

"Amanda?" He nodded. "She'd make a great gun moll."

In Nathan's Tin Lizzie, I tightened my wool shawl around my shoulders. The old *Gazette* building was behind the times, with a decrepit heating system always on the blink. Due to late payments, the staff suffered through several cold weeks as a result. Galveston rarely got snow, but the icy winds could be brutal. I'd had plenty of sore throats and the sniffles during the short winter.

"Say, do you really think Mack is working undercover for the *Daily News*? Or did he make that up to impress us?"

Nathan shrugged. "Probably both. If he can't pay off his gambling debt to Musey, at least he can cash in on his story. Imagine how the KKK would react if they knew a reporter infiltrated their stupid secret society."

"Sorry to tell you, but I doubt the actual KKK was involved."

"What? How do you know?"

"Well, for one thing, Charles told me they're mostly ex-Klansmen and gangsters and sailors who have a beef with the KKK and the local gangs."

"You got to interview Charles?"

"I mainly listened. He was in a talkative mood—in other words, totally smashed."

"Maybe Mack has a different take on the whole situation."

At Big Red, I felt a sense of déjà vu as we tiptoed around the hospital, its interior as pale as its patients. Heads down, we managed to sidestep the nurses and go directly to Mack's room.

This time, his craggy face lit up when we came in. "Thanks for stopping by, kids. Uncle Mack needs to be cheered up."

Uncle Mack? What kind of medicine were they giving poor old delusional Mack?

"Don't look so surprised, you two." He flashed a wide grin, a sight I'd never seen. "I've just dodged a bullet, literally. I feel like I've been given a new lease on life, a second chance."

And a whole bunch of happy pills?

"Whatever it is, the medicine seems to be working." I smiled.

"I'll say! I could take these all day long."

"Careful, Mack," Nathan admonished him. "Your bad habits got you in trouble before."

"Not to worry, old sport, young sport, whatever you want to be called. The nurses are giving me their undivided attention, making sure I take my pills on time and get three square meals a day."

Mack shifted his bulk, the springs creaking under the weight. Short and stout, he was built like a tank, fitting for an old general.

"Good to hear." Nathan lowered his voice. "Does Musey know you're laid up in the hospital?"

"Sure, but he doesn't care. You'd think he'd give me a break since my leg almost got blown to bits." Flustered, he clammed up and took a sip of water, obviously uncomfortable.

To keep him talking, I asked, "Say, how long have you known Madame Farushka? I heard she has special powers and hobnobs with Galveston's movers and shakers."

"A few months. They say she's pals with all the local bigwigs and gives them advice for the future. She told me they consult with her before they make any major business decisions or investments."

"Even the Moodys?" I was skeptical. "Say, we're going to the Moodys' annual Christmas party and she's the featured guest."

"Is it a piece for Mrs. Harper? I'm surprised the old biddy didn't invite herself to that fancy society shindig."

"Our friend Lily Leavenworth asked us to attend. You may recall seeing Lily at Madame's house that day?"

"Her name sounds familiar." He snapped his fingers. "That's right! Franny just asked me to look into the death of Lily's sister. She mentioned Charles Howard, her fiancé, the boat captain. Did you know we play poker together?"

"What else?" I was all ears.

"I found out Charles was rum-running for the Downtown Gang when his boat capsized over two years ago. Everyone assumed the sailors were dead, the cargo lost. Turns out some fishermen rescued the crew and ship, so the sailors rewarded them with all the booze."

Mack whistled. "When Johnny Jack got word they'd pawned off his precious cargo, he was livid and vowed revenge."

"Revenge? Did you tell Madame Farushka?"

Before Mack could elaborate, two nurses came in holding a lunch tray. "My favorite girls!" he said, perking up.

Clearly, the combination of pills and pretty young things had its own healing effect on a crabby curmudgeon like Mack.

After we said our goodbyes, we headed outside.

"What's gotten into Mack? I hardly recognized the old grouch."

"You know—lots of drugs." Nathan said. "Hope he takes some home. He may actually be pleasant for a change."

Surprised, I replied, "But you've always liked Mack and looked up to him, even after he was canned."

"True, but he can be a real Scrooge. I just feel for the fella, divorced, no children, only his job to keep him busy—and that went up in smoke."

"Seems he's turned over a new leaf. When he gave me a compliment, I almost fell over from shock."

"I'll bet." Nathan nodded. "Glad Mack is back on track."

CHAPTER FIFTY-ONE

After a quick lunch at Star Diner—a mini-celebration before Amanda quit her job there—we arrived at the paper before our bosses returned. When Mrs. Harper and Mr. Thomas walked in later, looking flustered and wind-blown, I wondered: What was going on with those two? The mere thought of a romantic rendezvous made my stomach queasy.

More likely, my bosses had attended a boring meeting with the mayor or city council who tried to control the paper's contents from afar—but not far enough. Through the Galveston grapevine, I'd heard constant battles erupted between our Honest Abe editor and the city officials who wanted to keep our beach town a profitable and popular tourist spot.

They'd be better off consulting with gang leaders Ollie Quinn, the Maceos and Johnny Jack, whose clubs and casinos were Galveston's main attraction and the reason for the town's prosperity.

I pretended to be working on my Madame Farushka story when Mrs. Harper stopped by my desk. "Did you have a nice time at lunch?" I asked with a straight face.

"Oh, just a dull meeting with a local politician who wants us to favor certain businesses in our coverage," she said, rolling her eyes. "Why should this bozo and his cronies get special treatment?"

"What did you tell him?"

"I informed him the ads are the only parts of the paper that are for sale," she huffed. "He had some nerve."

Good for her. Maybe there was more to Mrs. Harper than I'd thought. "By the way, are you attending the Moodys' holiday party?"

The Mrs. Harper I knew and resented returned, all aflutter about a snobby society shindig. "I hear Madame Farushka will be on hand to tell fortunes and read palms. Wonder if she'll bring her crystal ball?" I joked.

"I do hope so!" she exclaimed. "Wouldn't that be a hoot?"

Surprised, I asked, "Are you going too?"

"Yes, of course. I wouldn't miss it for the world. What a wonderful chance to see Madame in her element." She paused. "That reminds me. Are you almost finished with your story?"

"Almost," I fibbed. "I may need to ask her a few more questions about her past. Unless you want me to wait until after the party?"

"No need. Your article will only add excitement to the Moody celebration, a preview of treats to come."

"You mean like candy canes and gingerbread cookies?"

"Miss Cross, you do have a funny way of describing things," she murmured. "I suppose it's one of your endearing little quirks."

Was that a compliment or an insult?

"Thanks, I guess. I'll try to have the story to you by tonight."

"If you can turn it in today, we can make the morning edition."

"I'll try to stop by her place right away. Maybe Nathan can take more photos?"

"Good. I look forward to seeing it as soon as possible."

I added a couple of lines to my draft, then searched for Nathan. What a busy day! Personally, I enjoyed the thrill of seeking out stories, interviewing sources, pounding the pavement—not spending my days covering debutante parties and holiday galas.

Mack and Mrs. Harper had piqued my curiosity about the mysterious Madame Farushka. They spoke so highly of her, perhaps I'd underestimated her skills, her talent, her purpose.

No longer did she appear to be a spiritual charlatan, I wondered if she truly had insights and vision. Was she a fake fortune teller or a divine diviner? I hoped to find out, once and for all.

This time, Nathan seemed glad to visit Madame again. He seemed buoyed by Mack's new lease on life and curious about his relationship with the seer, as I was. I couldn't wait to ask her more questions, specifically about her "friendship" with Mack.

As we approached the foreboding mansion, with its steep front entrance, I noticed the windows seemed dark, the curtains closed.

Maybe Madame was holding a séance or reading Tarot cards? I hated to interrupt, but I did have a deadline to meet. Timidly, I tapped on the door, then knocked harder, louder. No answer.

Damn, maybe I should have called first.

"Should we come back?" I tugged on the massive front door.

To my surprise, the doorknob turned and we cautiously entered the dim hallway and gasped. The entire interior had been stripped bare: the furniture and frippery, paintings, adornments and crystal chandeliers and statues were all gone.

In shock, we tiptoed through the rooms of the massive Victorian, with its fine walnut wood paneling and massive winding staircase. I listened for movement, any type of noise or activity, but there were no signs of Madame Farushka.

"Do you think she's upstairs?" I wondered, tempted to explore, but afraid of what I'd find. Our voices and footsteps echoed in the empty rooms, reverberating against the thick walls and high ceilings.

"Let's take a look." Nathan bounded upstairs and I followed behind, curious yet cautious. I felt like a trespasser, a burglar, a voyeur all at once, but there was literally nothing to see or to steal.

My hand trembled as I climbed the staircase, transported back to an earlier era, when ladies of the manor had servants and maids and wore corsets so tight they required fainting couches. Luckily, we dames no longer had to be harnessed into such antiquated torture devices designed—no doubt by a man—for the sake of "beauty."

Uneasily, we crept through each room, surveying each angle, each corner, yet nothing remained of its previous owner. Sad to say, Madame Farushka and all of her elegant trappings seemed to have disappeared, vanished into thin air like a sorceress's trick.

Panicky, Nathan and I took one last look and rushed downstairs.

"Whatever happened to Madame Farushka?" I asked. "Did she skip town or was she kidnapped? Was this related to her break-in?"

"Who knows? What if they return? Get me outta here!"

Before we bolted outside, I saw something in the corner by the entrance and reached down to pick it up: "The Hanged Man" Tarot card. Did she know about the gang murder? I stuck it in my bag, wondering: was it an oversight or did Madame leave a clue?

CHAPTER FIFTY-TWO

"Stop the presses!" I cried out dramatically when we entered the *Gazette* office. I'd always wanted to say that, and now I finally had the chance. A few reporters craned their necks to stare, thinking I'd lost my marbles.

Mrs. Harper peered at me over her spectacles, obviously worried. "What's wrong, Jazz?"

"Madame Farushka is missing!" I exclaimed. "There's no sign of her. The Victorian mansion is empty, completely cleared out. She simply vanished."

My boss glanced at Nathan for confirmation and he nodded.

"You don't say." I could see her mental gears working, and expected my story to be killed or at least postponed in case Madame turned up eventually.

"I can put off my story until later," I offered.

To be honest, I felt relieved I didn't need to rush to finish, yet irritated I'd spent so much time on a dead-end article.

"Not at all." Clutching her spectacles, my boss leapt up and began pacing the worn wooden floor. "This changes everything. We can file the story as a missing persons report, give the readers some background and clues and a mystery to solve. With the public's help, perhaps we can fill in the pieces that will lead us to our beloved Madame Farushka."

"You mean like a treasure hunt?" Sure, I liked the colorful gypsy, but did anyone else care besides the society set who could afford her services?

Animated, Mrs. Harper whirled around and pointed her glasses at me. "How fast can you write this up? If you hurry, we can make the morning paper."

"Shouldn't we notify the police first?" I pointed out. "What if she's been kidnapped or...worse?" I couldn't bring myself to say *killed*. "I've heard these first few hours are crucial."

"You're right." She nodded. "But I don't want to alert the whole police force. You never know who may be involved in her *disappearance*." She stressed the word as if she knew more than she let on, as if the cops were somehow involved and hiding crucial information. "Jasmine, why don't you call your lovely friend and tell him the news. Ask his opinion without telling the whole police force. What can we do to help locate Madame?"

"Burton? Once I place a call with the operator, everyone will know. What do you suggest?"

Mrs. Harper gave me a stern look. "I suggest you call him under different pretenses and tell him what you witnessed in person. Surely you know how to use your feminine wiles to entice Agent Burton to do your bidding."

My feminine wiles? Entice Burton to do my bidding? What century was she living in? She seemed to be reciting a Victorian romance novel with heaving bosoms and forbidden passion. Sorry to disappoint her, but all I knew how to do was pick up the phone and place a call. I hoped a simple request might do the trick.

"Well, what are you waiting for?" Mrs. Harper prompted me.

"Tell the truth, it sounds a bit sensational to me, like a death-defying stunt. Maybe she's dodging her landlord or a client and decided to move and hawk her services elsewhere."

Mrs. Harper fixed me with her: "Who asked your lowly opinion?" glare. "Don't you admit the whole scenario seems suspicious? Why on earth would she suddenly move out of town with the Moody party coming up showcasing her talents?"

"Yes, but we don't want to jump the gun and assume it's a worst-case scenario," I stalled, worried that my "Stop the presses" act might have been much ado about nothing. "Shouldn't we get the OK from Mr. Thomas?"

"If you insist, I'll get his approval first. Meanwhile, why don't you write up the story and have it on my desk in an hour. Then you can call your beau and ask him to dinner or request a favor or whatever you *modernes* call being forward these days."

Actually, we still called it being forward. To be honest, I began to relish the idea of writing about a missing persons case, hoping to help locate her and possibly save her life. I found the one-hour deadline a challenge and raced to my typewriter. As I banged on the keys, Mrs. Harper rushed out of Mr. Thomas' office with a triumphant smile and a nod of approval.

In that moment, I realized she enjoyed the fast pace and pressure of deadlines as much as any "real" reporter. Perhaps she too had a penchant for hard-boiled stories like the newshounds, but had been relegated to being a "society editor"—just as I had to write puff pieces—because she was a woman. Boy, could I sympathize.

I forced myself to focus, trying to make my words interesting and insistent, dramatic yet factual, adding a dash of color and a clear sense of urgency. After I pounded out four pages, I placed the revised copy on her desk and she glanced over it with a smile.

"Thanks, Jasmine. I do need you to fill in a few holes before it goes to press." She marked up a few pages, waving her red pen around like a baton.

Holes? What could be bigger than the black hole into which Madame Farushka had disappeared?

At a loss, I looked over my draft, trying to fill in the blanks. Since I barely knew the woman, I was unaware of her background and couldn't begin to guess her whereabouts. Plus I didn't want to reveal any personal or private information that might put her in more danger if she had indeed been kidnapped.

Then it dawned on me: I'd ask the one person who might help solve this puzzle—my old nemesis and our new best friend—Mack.

Would Mack, of all people, be willing or able to help locate Madame Farushka? I caught up with Nathan in the break room and asked him, "Do you think Mack would know anything about Madame's whereabouts?"

He shrugged. "Hope so. But may not be anything we can print."

"Can you call him at the hospital and mention that she's missing?" I suggested. "Or is that too risky, considering she might be in danger? Think of the timing. Seems coincidental she disappeared right after Musey's flunky broke into her house."

"I think it's best if we visit Mack there and get his take."

"I'll need to push back my deadline..." What was more important: Finding Madame Farushka or rushing to meet a deadline? Did Mrs. Harper need to know about their "friendship" or whatever they called their clandestine meetings?

In any case, I had to be careful since Mack was still *persona non grata* at the *Gazette*—and in hock to the Downtown Gang.

Just then Chuck popped his head into the break room. "What's this I hear about Mack getting shot? When did that happen?"

How'd he know? "Shot? You must have misunderstood."

Chuck narrowed his eyes at me. "You sure about that? There's an easy way to find out. Pick up the phone and call Big Red." Nathan and I followed him out, exchanging worried looks behind his back.

While Chuck was on the phone, I told Mrs. Harper we had a possible source who might know more about Madame Farushka's situation. "Problem is, by the time we interview this source, I'll miss the deadline. And this person may not have any additional information so it could be a false lead."

Mrs. Harper studied her soft pink nails before replying. "Who's your source? Are they credible? Will it add to the story?"

If I told her it was Mack, she'd have a fit. "I'd rather not say since it may lead nowhere. I won't know anything until I talk to him...uh...my source."

Without warning, Chuck blurted out, "You knuckleheads are right. Mack's not at Big Red so guess it was a false alarm."

Nathan and I locked eyes. Where in hell had Mack gone? Surely it was a coincidence he and Madame were both missing—or was it?

Mrs. Harper was no fool. She noticed our confused looks as her beady eyes shifted back and forth, and realized who we meant.

"Why in God's name would Mack know anything about Madame Farushka? How in the world would he even *know* her?" She harrumphed, letting out a dignified snort. "They don't exactly travel in the same social circles."

Little did she know.

My face blazed as she glared at me as if I was a turncoat. "Jasmine, I thought you, of all people, would distance yourself from that no-good lush. Why would you even rely on him for information? He's so condescending to us women for writing human-interest stories and features that he considers mere gossip!"

Honestly, I'd felt the same way about Mack and agreed with her every word. Still, he seemed so different in the hospital, sincere, like he'd actually "seen the light" and become a changed man. Or was it all an act? Maybe my boss was right, and he was still the same cynical hack she'd denounced.

"You may be right..." I glanced at Nathan, feeling like a traitor.

"Of course I'm right!" She bellowed. "I refuse to allow Mack to hold up this story and make Madame suffer in a possibly life-threatening situation."

Apparently Mr. Thomas had been listening in, and leaned against his office door, crossing his arms. "I say if Mack has valuable information to share, who are we to deny him his chance to help?"

"But we'll miss our deadline!" Mrs. Harper sputtered.

"How about this?" Mr. Thomas continued, ignoring her rant. "Jasmine, you can turn in an abbreviated version of your original story today, without mentioning the seer is missing. That gives the cops time to search for her privately—in case she *has* been taken."

"Sounds fair." I eyed my boss. "What about Mack?"

"Why don't you interview Mack later today? He's always proven to be a valuable asset to this paper and we should give him an opportunity to contribute. Then if he has anything new to report, you can do a follow-up tomorrow." Mr. Thomas was the voice of reason as he focused on Mrs. Harper, and she had to admit, albeit reluctantly, it was the best solution.

"Thanks, Mr. Thomas. I'll get on it right away."

Relieved, I beamed at him, not only for giving me a second assignment, but for silencing Mrs. Harper as well, not an easy task. His reverent tone seemed to imply that he also wanted to give his old pal Mack a second chance.

The newsroom was so quiet, you could hear pencils drop. Then Mr. Thomas ambled back to his office and the place buzzed again with activity.

I returned to my typewriter and made a few last-minute revisions, but I was too distracted, wondering: where in hell was Mack *and* Madame Farushka?

CHAPTER FIFTY-THREE

Quickly I read over my new draft before I dropped it off on Mrs. Harper's desk. She barely looked at me, tapping her pencil on my pages as if to say, "You're in the doghouse, missy."

I guess it passed muster since she gave me the silent treatment all day, glaring at me with her evil eye. At six o'clock, Nathan came by my desk, asking, "Ready to go? I wanted to stop by Mack's room to see if he's OK."

"We'd better double-check with the hospital," I suggested.

"Good idea. I'll do that and tell you what they say."

As I gathered my coat and handbag, Mrs. Page yelled out, "Jasmine! A lady's on the phone for you!"

Madame Farushka? I rushed to an empty office to answer and heard Lily's cheerful voice. "Hello, Jasmine. Haven't heard from you in a while. Hope you're going to the Moodys' party?"

"I look forward to it..." I paused, wondering how to bring up Madame's disappearance. "Say, have you talked to Madame lately?"

"Yes, as a matter of fact, I was on my way over and wondered if you'd like to go with me. The Victorian is grand, but a bit spooky at night, don't you think? Apparently she has some new information about my sister."

My heart skipped a beat. "Really? When did she call you?"

"Yesterday, before lunch. I was busy and told her I'd see her today. Why do you ask?"

How could I tell her the truth without falling down a rabbit hole? I cupped my hand over the phone. "Nathan and I stopped by today, but she didn't answer the door." I cleared my throat. "Her house was dark and she appeared to be...gone."

"Gone? What do you mean by gone?"

"That's all I know. Promise you won't tell anyone?" I took a deep breath. "The story will be in tomorrow's paper. We hope the more people know, the better chance we have of finding her."

"You think she could be in danger?" Lily's voice caught.

"Possibly. How did she sound yesterday?"

"Fine. Nothing out of the ordinary." She let out a heavy sigh. "Thanks for letting me know. Keep me posted."

I felt sympathy and admiration for the shy, yet bold woman who stayed so loyal to her sister, even after death. How horrible it must be to suspect your sister was murdered, but not be able to prove it or even confront her killer in court.

As I gathered my papers, Nathan tapped me on the shoulder. "Want a lift? I've got some good news."

"Is Mack OK?"

He put a finger to his lips, then led me outside to his rattletrap parked down the block. "Mack is still at Big Red, thank God."

"Really? How do you know?"

"Mack called me from the hospital. His leg is better, but he may need more surgery. Between us, I think he's afraid to go home. He thinks Musey and his henchmen may be waiting for him at his place."

As we raced to Big Red, Nathan filled me in. "Mack told the staff not to give out his private information to anyone. To be safe, he gave them a phony name, like Babe Ruth or some hooey."

"Good idea. Why's Mack in trouble with Musey?"

"Let's just say he's on a short leash with a tight muzzle."

At the hospital, Nathan told the nurses we were Mack's nephew and niece, and they showed us to his new room. Without any introduction, I popped in and said, "Madame Farushka is missing!"

He sat up in bed, startled. "What do you mean, missing?"

"She's disappeared. The whole mansion has been completely cleared out. Empty. You'd never know she was ever there."

"She didn't leave a note, nothing?"

I shook my head. "Just a Tarot card. What do you know about her? What she was involved in?"

CHAPTER FIFTY-THREE

Quickly I read over my new draft before I dropped it off on Mrs. Harper's desk. She barely looked at me, tapping her pencil on my pages as if to say, "You're in the doghouse, missy."

I guess it passed muster since she gave me the silent treatment all day, glaring at me with her evil eye. At six o'clock, Nathan came by my desk, asking, "Ready to go? I wanted to stop by Mack's room to see if he's OK."

"We'd better double-check with the hospital," I suggested.

"Good idea. I'll do that and tell you what they say."

As I gathered my coat and handbag, Mrs. Page yelled out, "Jasmine! A lady's on the phone for you!"

Madame Farushka? I rushed to an empty office to answer and heard Lily's cheerful voice. "Hello, Jasmine. Haven't heard from you in a while. Hope you're going to the Moodys' party?"

"I look forward to it..." I paused, wondering how to bring up Madame's disappearance. "Say, have you talked to Madame lately?"

"Yes, as a matter of fact, I was on my way over and wondered if you'd like to go with me. The Victorian is grand, but a bit spooky at night, don't you think? Apparently she has some new information about my sister."

My heart skipped a beat. "Really? When did she call you?"

"Yesterday, before lunch. I was busy and told her I'd see her today. Why do you ask?"

How could I tell her the truth without falling down a rabbit hole? I cupped my hand over the phone. "Nathan and I stopped by today, but she didn't answer the door." I cleared my throat. "Her house was dark and she appeared to be...gone."

"Gone? What do you mean by gone?"

"That's all I know. Promise you won't tell anyone?" I took a deep breath. "The story will be in tomorrow's paper. We hope the more people know, the better chance we have of finding her."

"You think she could be in danger?" Lily's voice caught.

"Possibly. How did she sound yesterday?"

"Fine. Nothing out of the ordinary." She let out a heavy sigh. "Thanks for letting me know. Keep me posted."

I felt sympathy and admiration for the shy, yet bold woman who stayed so loyal to her sister, even after death. How horrible it must be to suspect your sister was murdered, but not be able to prove it or even confront her killer in court.

As I gathered my papers, Nathan tapped me on the shoulder. "Want a lift? I've got some good news."

"Is Mack OK?"

He put a finger to his lips, then led me outside to his rattletrap parked down the block. "Mack is still at Big Red, thank God."

"Really? How do you know?"

"Mack called me from the hospital. His leg is better, but he may need more surgery. Between us, I think he's afraid to go home. He thinks Musey and his henchmen may be waiting for him at his place."

As we raced to Big Red, Nathan filled me in. "Mack told the staff not to give out his private information to anyone. To be safe, he gave them a phony name, like Babe Ruth or some hooey."

"Good idea. Why's Mack in trouble with Musey?"

"Let's just say he's on a short leash with a tight muzzle."

At the hospital, Nathan told the nurses we were Mack's nephew and niece, and they showed us to his new room. Without any introduction, I popped in and said, "Madame Farushka is missing!"

He sat up in bed, startled. "What do you mean, missing?"

"She's disappeared. The whole mansion has been completely cleared out. Empty. You'd never know she was ever there."

"She didn't leave a note, nothing?"

I shook my head. "Just a Tarot card. What do you know about her? What she was involved in?"

Mack gulped. "I tried to warn her..."

"Warn her about what?" Nathan asked.

"She's been advising the gangs, giving them information. Both the Downtown and Beach gangs. No one was supposed to know."

"What kind of advice? She tells their fortunes?" Nathan joked.

"You slay me. I may as well fill you in since it may be too late."

"Too late?"

Mack shifted in his bed, rearranging his pillows.

"Keep this under your hats. Franny was the go-between for the gangs and bootleggers. The rum-runners told her when and where to expect their next shipments, then she'd pass on the information to the delivery men or their messengers—guys like me."

"You?" Nathan frowned. "You were the main contact?"

"Why not? Who'd suspect an old journalist of relaying messages for the Downtown Gang?"

"And it worked?" I asked, incredulous. "Did anyone find out?"

"Everything was fine until Musey got greedy. He wanted to know when the Beach Gang got their shipments so he could hijack their booze. He figured I'd sweet-talk Franny into spilling the beans, but I refused. Musey tried to strong-arm her but she wouldn't give up the goods without a fight."

"A fight, huh? I'll bet that's why the goon broke into her house, looking for information," Nathan said.

Mack nodded. "Musey's men threatened to tell Ollie Quinn and the Maceos that she was a double-crosser, selling the Downtown Gang information on the Beach Gang's booze drops."

My heart sank. "What should we do—contact the police or will that make it worse?"

"Only tell the people you trust, like your agent fella." His face fell. "God, I hope they didn't try to torture it out of her."

"Mrs. Harper wants to run a piece in the paper tomorrow, requesting the public's help in locating Madame Farushka, like a real-life mystery," I said. "Do you think that will help or hurt her case?"

Mack shook his head, looking lost. "Honestly, it could go either way. All I know is you need to act fast. She could be in real danger."

I tapped Nathan's shoulder. "Hurry, let's stop by the police station and talk to Burton. He'll know what to do."

"Good idea. Thanks, Mack." Nathan tipped his hat.

As we left, we bumped into a tall, dark fella in a lab coat who bolted down the hall past us in a big rush. What was the emergency? Where had I seen him before?

I turned around to look: Yes, he was dressed like a doctor or an orderly, but something didn't seem right. That's when I noticed he wore fancy two-tone spats, made of new gleaming leather.

"It's him!" I cried out, pointing down the hall. "Marco Polo, the Bentley driver!"

We made a beeline for Mack's room and burst in just as the gangster was pressing a bed pillow onto Mack's face, sucking the life out of our friend.

CHAPTER FIFTY-FOUR

Nathan jumped on the goon's back, grabbing him around the neck. "What in hell are you doing? Leave him alone!"

The thug cursed in Italian and shook off Nathan's arms, throwing him to the floor. As he lunged for Mack, I grabbed the empty bedpan and whacked him on the head, hard. Sure enough, it was Marco Polo, Amanda's good-for-nothing gangster.

"I'm not finished with you, old man!" He shook a fist at Mack, who coughed and gasped for breath. Then he gave Nathan a hard kick and shoved me into a metal cart before he fled out the door.

Nathan scrambled to his feet and followed the attacker, but returned moments later. "That bastard got away!"

"Don't worry, I know where to find him," Mack said.

"Are you OK?" Nathan and I flanked Mack, who gave us a weak smile and a thumb's up.

"Thanks, kids. That's the second time you've saved my life this week. If you hadn't been here, I'd be attending my own funeral."

"Why was he trying to kill you?" I asked. "Did it have to do with the meet—or Madame Farushka?"

Mack smoothed out his covers. "Probably both. Musey suspects a couple of his guys were skimming off his loads, stealing some crates of rum and keeping the stash for themselves. He wanted me to go undercover and ID the chumps."

"Rum?" Nathan and I traded looks. "Were they burying their stash in coffins, by chance?" he asked.

"How did you know?" Mack sat up, alert. "They turned out to be Charles' poker pals, a couple of guys I know and like. Odd thing about them is they always use silver dollars to bet—no funny money, they say. I wasn't about to rat them out to a killer like Musey."

After we got a nurse to tend to Mack, Nathan barged down the hall, demanding, "Who's in charge? Where's the security around here? The patients need protection!"

Nathan managed to create quite a scene, and the embarrassed staff arranged for an orderly to watch Mack's room until we returned with police protection. I hoped Burton could convince Chief Jones to assign one of his cops to guard duty for a day or two.

"This is getting to be a regular stop," Nathan said when we arrived at the police station.

Thank goodness Burton was in his office. Noting our grim expressions, he shut the door. "Not another dead body, I hope?"

"We almost had to say good-bye to Mack..." I began.

"Did they botch his leg operation?"

"Musey's goon snuck into his hospital room and tried to smother him to death!" Nathan cried out. "The same guy who tried to run us off Beach Boulevard. Luckily, we fended off the attacker."

"Jazz, you too? What did you do?"

"Hit him with a bedpan. What else?"

"A bedpan?" Burton seemed amused.

"Mack could have been killed!" Nathan piped up. "He needs some kind of police protection—now."

"I'll see if Jones agrees. If not, I'll sit there all night myself."

"We can take turns," Nathan offered. "Thanks."

"Hey, I like the old guy." Burton smiled. "He comes across like a mad bulldog, but his bark is definitely worse than his bite."

"You can say that again." Nathan nodded.

"We think this may be connected to Madame Farushka. Did you know she's missing? We went over there today and her place was totally empty. Nothing was left." Then I remembered the Tarot card still in my handbag and held it up. "This is all I found. Can it be a clue?" I showed him the image. "The Hanged Man." "How could she possibly know about the graveyard victim?"

"Seems coincidental," he said. "Did Mack provide any insights?"

"And how!" I couldn't wait to fill him in. "Believe it or not, our fortune-hunting fortune teller works on the side as a go-between for the gangs and their bootleggers. They tell her their drop-off points and she passes on the information to the gangs."

"No wonder she's so popular." His eyes lit up. "Explains a lot."

"Exactly. And guess who Mack represents? The Downtown Gang. He said Musey and Nounes are getting greedy, trying to coerce her into giving up the Beach Gang's next big booze drops. I'm afraid they've taken it too far. What good will she be to them if she's..." I could barely say the word... "dead?"

"Sounds like she's too valuable an asset," he replied. "They may be trying to scare her into submission, only take orders from them."

"Maybe she decided to pick up and move," Nathan suggested.

"Right before the Moodys' party? That's like her big introduction to Galveston society." I turned to Burton. "I know this isn't your area, but could you investigate her disappearance and keep us posted?"

"First I'll get a rookie out to protect your pal Mack. Then I'll try to track down this gypsy woman."

"Thanks, Burton." I was tempted to give him a proper kiss, but didn't want to embarrass him in public. "Say, should we mention Madame is missing in the newspaper? My boss thinks it may help locate her, but I think she wants to try to bring in more readers."

"I'd be careful," Burton said. "The gangs are trying to show who's in control. You don't want to make her a bigger target."

"True. I'll tell Mrs. Harper this isn't a game of hide-and-seek with Madame as bait. Don't forget, the Moody party is tomorrow night. We'll see if she turns up by then. Pick me up at six?"

"Swell. Does that mean I have to wear my penguin suit?"

"You make such a handsome penguin. How about you, Nate?"

"Sure, I can tag along. Guess I'll have to show up as the ugly duckling since I don't own a penguin suit," Nathan said. "By choice."

Before we left Burton's office, I looked around the station.

"By the way, what happened with Charles and his sailor friend? Were they released?"

He nodded. "They posted bail and are supposed to appear in court in a week or two. So far Charlie's been very cooperative. He's ID'd most of his pals and they don't seem to have records. These guys are as slippery as an ice rink."

Back at the *Gazette*, I didn't have the heart to break the bad news to my boss, that her beloved Madame Farushka was in cahoots with the local crime bosses.

To make her happy, I quickly wrote up a sanitized version of events and showed it to Mrs. Harper. "Thanks, Jazz, this is all very nice, but what about the mystery? The missing persons angle and the appeal to the public for help?"

"After consulting with Agent Burton, I thought it might put Madame Farushka in greater danger. So I merely implied she was moving her business instead of admitting that she's actually missing."

Yes, I was playing it safe, but I didn't want to harm or endanger the seer for the sake of selling more papers.

"That was Agent Burton's conclusion? Smart thinking." My boss nodded as she skimmed my article. "We certainly wouldn't want anything to happen to our dear Madame Farushka. Let's pray she can untangle herself in time for the Moodys' party tomorrow night."

What? Did Mrs. Harper know more than she pretended?

Madame Farushka needed more than our prayers if she was entangled with Johnny Jack and the Downtown Gang.

CHAPTER FIFTY-FIVE

Agent Burton was true to his word and spent the afternoon and early evening guarding Mack's hospital room. Nathan relieved him around eight o'clock, followed by a rookie cop at midnight. Mack appeared to be safe, at least for one more night.

On Saturday, my article appeared without much fanfare since, in all honesty, I'd turned it into the flattering puffy profile I normally abhorred—all to save Madame Farushka's neck. I made no mention of her disappearance or empty mansion, but simply stated she was relocating to a new address.

Despite my coveted invitation to the Moodys' party, I was half-dreading the festivities, afraid to face the chamber music. How could we make merry believing Madame Farushka had been kidnapped or tortured by gangsters—and very possibly killed? I felt guilty and ashamed and nauseous, knowing we'd done too little, and now it was too late to save her.

Burton picked me up at six, looking dashing in a bow tie and tails, the epitome of the suave, sophisticated New Yorker. In keeping with the holiday theme, I wore a silky maroon gown cut on the bias with a huge bow on one hip and a semi-low-cut back, a bit risqué for the Moody crowd but still subdued. My new Mandalian mesh bag sparkled as bright as our Christmas decorations.

For the finishing touch, I wore my latest splurge—an elegant cocoon coat, a patterned gold velvet gem finished with long silky tassels. I bought the coat at a small boutique off Tremont street, where talented Asian seamstresses recreated the latest Paris fashions at a fraction of the cost. Leave it to my aunt Eva to stumble on such a treasure trove while shopping at the corner meat market.

"You look like the tiger's stripes!" Burton whistled.

"Well, sir, you look like the leopard's spots."

Burton even brought me a Christmas corsage with deep maroon roses he carefully attached to my cocoon coat. Eva's eyes watered when she saw us. "What an attractive couple you make. I hope Nathan can take photos of you at the party." Not a bad idea. Honestly, I didn't want to leave her alone, but she assured me she had plans to dine out with Sheriff Sanders at Gaido's.

Towering over Broadway, the imposing Moody Mansion appeared like a red-brick fairy tale castle, known for its Romanesque structure, arched windows and witches hat roofs. Broadway was so busy, we had to park a few blocks away, but I enjoyed the cool night air. Gallant as usual, Burton took my arm as we entered the four-story home, admiring its tasteful décor.

We wandered through the magnificent building, nodding to guests, noting the gleaming banisters and mahogany staircase adorned with garlands of evergreens and holly berries. Frosted wall sconces illuminated the colorful stained glass window in an alcove above the stairway. A twenty-foot tall Christmas tree filled the parlor, dressed with simple glistening red glass balls.

The thirty-one-room mansion contained a ballroom, but guests congregated in the living room and parlor. A long lace-covered dining table held an array of cold meats and a tempting display of pastries and cakes.

My stomach was in knots as I searched for Madame Farushka— sadly she was absent. I spied my boss in a hallway, making nice with the head of the Ladies' Library Association. To my surprise, Mr. Thomas, the editor-in-chief, stood at her elbow. Mrs. Harper actually looked pretty, with her hair in an upswept 'do and dusty rose frock that flattered her pale pink complexion.

"Would you get a load of those two?" I nudged Burton.

"Are they on an actual *date*—or is this an official outing?"

"Who knows? May be more pleasure than business."

A trio of musicians played classical music along with Christmas carols and a few folks gathered to sing along, reminding me of an old-fashioned scene straight out of Dickens.

Tuxedoed butlers holding trays of canapés and sweets threaded their way through the dignified crowd—not a gangster in sight. Obviously the Moodys preferred to keep their business and private lives separate.

Burton and I made the rounds, enjoying glasses of eggnog and spiced apple cider, even wassail, a new drink for me. Nathan looked spiffy in a tweed jacket and slacks, discreetly taking photos from an alcove with a good view of the living room. Burton excused himself to talk to Chief Jones while I filled two plates of finger sandwiches and snacks for Nathan, as a reward.

"Thanks, I was starving." He grabbed the plates and grinned.

"Seen anything interesting? Any sign of Madame Farushka?"

"Not yet." He shook his head. "Nothing salacious. Maybe we can stir things up? Dance the tango?"

"I wish, but our bosses are here. Together."

"I noticed. No hanky-panky so far."

"Good to hear." Glancing around the lively room, I finally spotted Lily Leavenworth in a corner, decorating a round table with a crystal ball and Tarot cards. Poor Lily. Did she insist on going through with this charade, pretending Madame Farushka was OK? Was the colorful table a tribute to her?

"Lily, so good to see you." I squeezed her arm. "I'm so sorry about Madame Farushka. Have you heard anything?"

"She's fine." Lily looked startled. "Everything is fine."

"What do you mean?" I stared at her in shock. "Her mansion is completely empty, like she's vanished."

"Jasmine, I'm so sorry to mislead you, but I had to find out what you and the reporters knew, if anything." She blushed. "You see, we had to keep everything hush-hush for Madame Farushka's safety."

"She's OK? Why didn't you tell me? I was worried sick!"

"I'm so sorry for the ruse but it was necessary." Lily had the decency to sound apologetic. "Luckily she got a tip from a friend— Max, I think his name is?—that she was in danger."

"You mean Mack Brown, the reporter?"

So Mack was in on the whole charade...

"I think that's his name. She's gaga over the fella, especially since he helped saved her life. I wish Mack could have joined us tonight. Then I called in a favor from Charles..."

"Charles? Marilyn's fiancé?"

She nodded. "He and his friends spent a whole day moving her belongings into a storage facility. Just in time, luckily."

"She got away? Is she safe now?"

"Yes, thank God. Franny has been staying with me at the Hotel Galvez for the past two days."

Dumbfounded, I wanted to ask her so many questions, but suddenly the music stopped and, as if on cue, Colonel Moody took center stage and held out his hand. "We're pleased to present our featured guest, the incomparable Madame Farushka."

Incomparable indeed—and devious to boot.

All heads turned to gape at the divine diviner commanding the stage. Like the diva that she was, Madame Farushka descended the grand winding staircase dressed to the nines in her flamboyant fortune teller's finery, complete with brilliant scarves, gold bangles and a smug Cheshire-cat smile.

CHAPTER FIFTY-SIX

Madame Farushka *was* alive! I felt like clapping while the mysterious Madame made her entrance, slowly descending the stairs like the silent film star, Lillian Gish. The stodgy guests became animated as they flocked to have their Tarot cards and palms read by the fortunate fortune teller.

The line was so long that I was afraid I'd never get a chance to speak to her, to ask about her ordeal and her plans for the future. Sitting nearby, Lily assisted the seer, organizing the cards, making sure the line kept moving.

Even Mrs. Harper seemed excited as we exchanged smiles across the room. Elated, I rushed over to Nathan. "Can you believe Madame is here? I almost had a heart attack when I saw her float down the stairs, acting like nothing was wrong."

I caught Burton's eye and he came over to my side. "What's going on? From what you described, I honestly thought the woman was a goner."

Hoping no one overheard us, we found a private corner to talk. "I hated to think the worst, but all signs pointed to..."

Burton nodded. "I even asked around the station, but the cops claimed they hadn't heard of her."

"How strange. So what did you and Chief Jones gab about?"

"Shop talk. Wheeling and dealing." He flashed a cryptic smile.

At last I could relax, and we mingled among the guests, trying to make small talk. Burton eyed the bountiful spread. "Don't mind me."

With relish, he piled on his plate and fed me bites of crackers and cookies which I tried not to spill on my favorite new outfit.

While he nibbled, I finally found a break in Madame Farushka's line. Beaming, I reached out to hug her, feeling like I was greeting an old friend. "How are you? I'm so happy to see you! Did you know we went by your house and it was totally empty?"

"I'm so sorry to worry you, but Lily and I thought it was safest under the circumstances." She patted my hands, as if comforting a frightened child.

"I was so upset, you can imagine what we thought." I sighed. "All I could find was this Tarot card." I pulled out the "The Hanged Man" Tarot card from my cocoon coat. "What does it mean?"

"How observant you are." She lowered her voice. "I believe you saw a similar image—at the cemetery, am I right?"

"How did you know?" I froze.

"My crystal ball gives me glimpses into the past *and* future. The vision of the hanged man appeared after the séance."

"I have no idea what it means, so I took it literally."

She nodded. "The man was rightfully punished for his sins."

Did she mean Mick O'Brien?

"Do you know who did it?" I had to ask, but she only shrugged. "So what's next for you? How will you...get away?"

"I'm going to visit friends out of state." She winked at Lily. "Please tell Mack I'll be in touch when I'm settled."

"Mack will be disappointed. Will you really have to relocate?"

"I have no choice. Galveston is wonderful but I'm afraid my affairs have gotten out of control." She took my hand. "Thank you for the lovely article."

"My pleasure." I paused. "While I'm here, would you mind telling my fortune...again?"

"Of course. How about a Tarot card reading this time, Jasmine?"

She shuffled the cards and with a magician's flair, pulled one off the deck: "The World."

"Aha! I predict new beginnings for your future, a chance to see the world, explore new opportunities."

Entranced, I studied the card, wanting to keep it in my purse, then stood up to leave. "Wish it would come true." I shook her hand, sad to see her go. "Thanks for the good news. I wish you all the best, wherever you end up."

"Same to you, Jasmine. May you always enjoy good fortune."

A pushy dowager hovered over the table and Lily tried to distract her, but she plopped down in my seat. "I believe I was next?"

Lily tapped Madame's elbow. "There's time for only one more reading. Then we really must leave."

I took Lily aside while the seer read the woman's palm. "You're leaving for the hotel?"

"I'm heading back to Minnesota on the train. Tonight."

"Tonight? So soon?"

"We think it's safest that way. Franny will accompany me on the train. I invited her to be my houseguest for a while. We're all packed up and leaving directly for the station after the party."

"Sounds like a great idea," I said, glad I'd introduced the two women who appeared to be fast friends. "I wish you all the best."

"By the way, I saw your article in the paper. Such a nice homage. Franny was delighted."

Burton pulled me into the parlor, draping his arm over my shoulder. "I saw you talking to Madame Farushka...did she explain what happened?"

"I think she's in safe hands. Seems she's not only outsmarted the gangs, she found a way to get out from under their control for now."

"Good for her." Burton smiled.

"The best part is she gave me a wonderful fortune. I got "The World" Tarot card. My luck is about to change."

"I'll give you the world," Burton said, only half-joking.

"Thank you." I smiled at him. "Say, before we leave, let's take a few photos with Nathan. Then I need to check in with my bosses."

Nathan was happy to oblige, making funny faces as we posed with Lily and Madame Farushka, then Mrs. Harper and Mr. Thomas. Finally he snapped a few photos of us alone together in front of the Christmas tree.

Burton and I shook hands with the Moodys as we were leaving, thanking them for the lovely party. "Will we be featured in your newspaper?" Mrs. Moody asked shyly.

"Only if you want to be," I replied, knowing the Moodys had considerable clout.

"Oh my, yes!" she exclaimed. "How exciting!"

After we said our goodbyes, I suggested to Burton: "Say, why don't we stop by the Hollywood Dinner Club before we head home? Tonight is Amanda's first day on the job and I promised we'd wish her well."

"Sounds fun." He squeezed my waist. "Can't wait to show you off to the high living high-rollers. These goody-two-shoes teetotalers are cramping my style."

"And how!" Making our exit, we stepped outside when a four-door Ford pulled up. A handsome blond gent in a nice suit got out and stood on the curb.

I clasped Burton's hand and whispered, "Wait—is that Charles Howard? What in the world is he doing here?"

Charles seemed as shocked to see us. I had to bite my tongue to keep from blurting out my first thoughts: What in hell?

Heaven forbid the church-going, law-abiding Moodys allowed rumrunners or hoods into their private abode. He looked so dapper, I almost didn't recognize him—what a transformation from the sloshed boat captain to this proper gent in a snazzy suit and tie.

"Hello, Charles. Fancy seeing you here." Agent Burton shook his hand as if greeting jailbirds at the Moody Mansion was *de rigueur*. "Excuse me while I pick up the car. See you later, Charlie."

I pasted on a sunny smile, saying, "Good to see you, Charles. Are you here for the party?"

"Hell, no. These top-hat parties aren't for me." He grinned. "I'm taking Lily and Franny to the train station tonight. I'm riding with them to Houston to make sure they arrive...safely. But I'll be back tomorrow."

"How nice." I smiled, glad Lily and Charles had made up. "I was so happy to see Madame Farushka here tonight. We heard she got out just in time, thanks to you."

"When Lily called, I was happy to help. See, Franny is an old friend from the past...you know, when I was tight with Johnny Jack."

I nodded in understanding. So Charles had *also* passed on information to the fortune teller. "When is your court hearing?"

"They decided to drop the charges."

"What?" I was floored. "But they caught you with a boatload of booze. Remember, I was there."

He shrugged. "I cut a deal with the D.A. and the Feds."

"The Feds? What kind of deal?"

He shuffled his feet, looking up and down Broadway as cars roared past. "This is all supposed to be under wraps. Hell, your fella will probably spill the beans anyway."

"What? Agent Burton knows?"

"I think he came up with the plan. Promise not to tell a soul? I'm scheduled to testify at Johnny Jack's grand jury hearing next week. Let's just say Ollie Quinn sweetened the pot."

"You don't say." That meant Sammy was off the hook! I knew Charles was a bootlegger and a criminal, but I had a soft spot for the romantic sailor who'd lost his beautiful bride-to-be. Torn, I warned, "Are you sure? You know what happened to the last snitch."

He looked grim. "He got what he deserved."

From his bitter tone, I sensed the men had a history.

"What do you mean?" When he didn't reply, I asked, "Why did he turn up at the Hollywood Dinner Club later?"

"That wasn't my doing. Some guys lost big at poker there and decided to get payback. They wanted to start a gang war and take the heat off of us."

Was he telling the truth? I gave him the once-over. That's when I noticed his tie, eerily similar to the one I saw on the dead man—the hanged man.

"Nice tie," I said cautiously. "Where'd you get it?"

"From an old pal. I wear it like a badge of honor," he boasted.

Was that a confession? We locked eyes and that's when he realized that I knew.

I stared at him, trying to comprehend. "Were you trying to protect Johnny Jack? Who hired you? George Musey?"

"Hell no, it was all my idea. I wanted that bastard to know how Marilyn felt when he choked the life out of her in the ocean."

CHAPTER FIFTY-SEVEN

Stunned, I was speechless. Guess I should have felt frightened, threatened or upset. But I felt nothing but sympathy for Charles, this heartbroken man who'd done the wrong things for the right reasons.

"Why'd you wait so long?"

"My friends on the boat saw him choke her, hold her head under water. But he disappeared afterwards without a trace. I tried to hunt down that devil, but he was on the run. So I waited here two years for that killer to return, to confess."

"Did he know you were looking for him?"

"I'd bet on it. When I heard Ollie Quinn brought him back in town to testify, I made my move. I confronted him, made him admit he killed Marilyn, while I choked that murdering bastard to death."

Charles paced the pavement. "He had no right to take her life. Word is, she witnessed Mick at a booze drop on our wedding day, but I doubt she even knew what she'd seen. She was an innocent, so sweet, my angel. That day, she was waiting for me on the beach, praying I was safe, that I'd come back to her. If I hadn't left, she'd still be alive." He hung his head, ashamed.

"I'm so sorry. She didn't deserve to die that way."

His eyes widened in alarm. "What are you going to do? Tell the Fed, talk to the cops? I had to kill him. Even the Bible preaches: "an eye for an eye.""

"You've already been punished." I handed him the Tarot card: "The Hanged Man." "I'm not the judge or jury or witness. It's between you and your maker."

What else could I do, but let him go? Was turning him in now really the best option?

"Does Lily know?" I asked softly.

"I had to tell her the truth. She believes justice was done."

"What about your upcoming wedding?" I asked, curious.

Charles shrugged. "I don't think it's fair to marry Diana when I'm still in love with Marilyn. If all goes well, after the hearing, I may be leaving Galveston permanently."

Lily appeared with a slight woman grappling with trunks and a train case, hobbling under the weight. I didn't know she traveled with a companion— was it her housekeeper or one of the Moodys' maids?

"Let me help you." Charles rushed over and lifted the cases, loading the baggage into his trunk.

"Where's Madame Farushka?" I asked, puzzled. "I thought she was traveling with you?"

"Jasmine, meet Franny Bellows." The petite woman held out her hand with a sly smile. "Also known as Madame Farushka."

I blinked, studying her delicate features. Without her thick face paint, fake eyelashes and elaborate costumes, Madame Farushka had been transformed into a modest and—to be quite frank—rather Plain Jane.

"Lovely to meet you, Franny. My best wishes to all of you."

Lily seemed amused by my stunned reaction. "Thanks again for your help, Jasmine," Lily said. "I've already said my goodbyes to Marilyn. Now she can finally rest in peace."

Charles nodded at me with gratitude as he helped the women into his Ford. I waved at them until the red tail lights disappeared into the inky night.

As they drove off, Burton pulled up to the curb.

"Did you talk to Charles? What did I miss?"

"A whole boatload of surprises," I added, wondering if Burton planned to tell me about the plea deal. "Do you know they dropped the charges?"

"He told you that? The terms of our agreement are supposed to be kept quiet."

"So you knew all about it—that *Charles* agreed to be the key witness in Johnny Jack's grand jury hearing?"

"Guess who came up with the idea? I had you and Sammy in mind when I suggested it to the D.A. Sort of an early Christmas gift."

"Thanks, James. I can't wait to tell Sammy the good news!"

"Jazz, this is supposed to be hush-hush. That's the point of a grand jury hearing. No one else knows but a handful of people."

"Please, I need to tell Sammy that he's off the hook."

"OK, we can both tell him, together." He smiled. "You must have bewitched Charles into giving up the goods. Maybe you remind him of his lost bride?"

In due time, I knew I'd have to tell Burton about Charles' crime of passion—for what else was it?—but I wanted to give him a good head start. After his testimony, no doubt Johnny Jack would hunt Charles down and try to exact revenge. Hadn't he suffered enough?

Spotlights illuminated the Hollywood Dinner Club, highlighting the elegant nightspot and casino as if it were the Taj Mahal. As we drove up, I noticed a lot of activity, cars coming and going. A few goons had their feet planted on the running boards of their Cadillacs and Bentleys. A couple of squad cars parked at odd angles by the entrance, the cops positioned behind their doors.

"What's going on?" I asked Burton, alarmed. "A turf war?"

"Looks like a stand-off." He sucked in his breath. "We heard rumblings of an attempted take-over of a Beach Gang speakeasy. Naturally they want to take down their flagship club, the Hollywood. Seems Johnny Jack and his gang made good on their threat."

I scanned the parking lot, busy for nine o'clock. A row of hoods stood by their showboat cars, aiming at the Hollywood's entrance. Frantic, I clutched Burton's arm. "Sammy and Amanda are inside."

"I think Sammy is the intended target. Hate to admit, this may all be a ploy to scare Sammy, to keep him from testifying."

I flared up. "Why didn't you tell me so I could've warned them in advance?"

"These were rumors, private police business I can't discuss with the public." The public? Now I knew how Amanda felt.

"If the Downtown Gang didn't strike tonight, then another time." He pulled his gun out of its holster. "I'm going in."

"James, be careful!" I reached for him but he'd exited the car and crouched down, making his way over to a squad car.

Trembling, I watched the scene unfold like a cops-and-robbers drama, but in real life, real time. Guards stood at the door, pointing rifles at the parking lot, daring their rivals to take a shot.

Suddenly the double-doors burst open and a thug backed out, holding a gun with one hand, his arm wrapped around a female hostage in a long gown. How had he managed to sneak into the club without being observed? Surely he had help from the inside. If word spread that the Maceos couldn't protect their own patrons, business would die off and the infamous club would be shuttered.

The hostage struggled against her attacker, but he kept his arm pressed against her throat in a chokehold.

"Let her go!" Sammy pushed through the doors, holding up his arms in surrender. "Don't shoot!" Luckily Big Sam and Rose Maceo followed behind, both clutching guns aimed at the gangster.

Caught off guard, the goon turned sideways and I caught a glimpse of their faces: Marco Polo and his hostage, Amanda.

Oh no, not Amanda! My head spun as I watched the rival gangs face off—all this for nothing? The Downtown Gang had no idea that Charles planned to testify instead of Sammy. Damn it, why couldn't I have warned him in time? What could I do?

Then it hit me. Acting on impulse, I moved behind the wheel of the Roadster, the engine still running, slammed the car into gear and floored the gas pedal, aiming for the Hollywood's grand entrance.

CHAPTER FIFTY-EIGHT

Gangsters and cops alike scattered in different directions. Luckily, I barely grazed Marco, braking just in time. The mobster dropped Amanda on the front steps, and pointed the gun at me. Burton tackled him from behind, yelling, "Don't shoot!" A loud boom erupted as a shot went off. My heart seized—was James OK?

I stuck my head out to make sure James wasn't hurt, relieved to see him pinning Marco down, holding a gun to the goon's neck. Sammy stood over Marco, one slick black shoe on his back, the conquerors claiming victory.

"Get in!" I yelled to Amanda, who scrambled into the Roadster.

"I hope they blow his damn head off!" she cried, breathing hard.

Dazed, we ducked as shots flew across the parking lot.

Rose Maceo stormed onto the veranda now holding a Tommy gun, shouting, "Get off our property!"—shooting out a few tires as the hoods ran for cover.

The gangsters and a handful of cops sprayed bullets while the others dashed away. I swear, a bullet whizzed by my left ear so loud it sounded like an airplane.

"Cuff him, Leo," Burton commanded an older officer. The cops sprang into action, handcuffing Marco and a few hoods, leading them to the squad cars nearby. The rest of Johnny Jack's gang jumped into their Cadillacs and Roadsters and raced off into the night.

Like sheep, the frightened guests poured out onto the front steps, hiding their faces, hurrying to their fancy cars. Apologetic, Sam Maceo followed his patrons to the parking lot, where I overheard him inviting them to enjoy cocktails on the house.

"Are you OK? What happened?" I asked Amanda.

"It was all my fault." She blinked back tears. "Marco said he wanted to apologize and I let him inside the club. Sammy saw him trying to get fresh and that's when Marco grabbed me and yanked me out the door. I feel so stupid!"

"You didn't know this would happen," I consoled her.

"Thanks for rescuing me. You and Sammy saved my life."

After the cops took Marco and his gangster pals away in handcuffs, Burton flung open the car door. "Jazz, where in hell did you learn to drive like that?"

I flashed a coy smile. "My father taught me a few tricks."

Thank goodness my dad gave me driving lessons when I was twelve. Sure came in handy tonight.

When the commotion died down, Burton and I sat with Sammy at a private table in back, a bottle of Champagne cooling in an ice bucket, courtesy of Sam Maceo.

"Boy, was that a surprise," Big Sam laughed. "I looked up and saw this fancy Ford coming at us like a runaway train. Thank God you stopped in time."

"I didn't mean to scare you." I blushed. "Was anyone hurt?"

"A couple of my men got flesh wounds, nothing serious. Some of Johnny Jack's guys got hit, but I think they're OK."

"Hope so." I cringed. "Next time I'll aim for Johnny Jack."

"Without your quick thinking, things could have been a lot worse." Sam patted my back. "Thanks for saving the day, all of you."

After he left, Burton grinned at me. "Attagirl, Jazz. You sure have moxie. I had no idea you could drive a car."

"You never asked me." I beamed with pride. "Sorry I used your car as a weapon, but you told me to stay put. I couldn't just sit there twiddling my thumbs while my pals were in trouble."

"Glad you didn't wreck my Roadster, or you'd be in jail next to Marco Polo," Burton teased.

"This is the thanks I get?" I pretended to act miffed.

Then I noticed Sammy's hangdog expression. "Say, we've got something to share that'll cheer you up."

"I could use some good news for a change," he sulked. "Because of me, the Hollywood could have been history."

"You're not to blame," I insisted. "You did your best."

Sammy glanced over at Amanda, who seemed to be in deep discussion with the Maceos. Was she going to quit her job after only one night—or were they convincing her to stay?

"Oh yeah? If I hadn't lost my temper over that dizzy dame, that goon might never have shown up here again," he scowled. "He knows Amanda is my Achilles' heel."

"I think this news will make up for tonight," Burton said. "Fact is, we have a new key witness who's agreed to testify during Johnny Jack's hearing."

"Oh yeah? You're not pulling a fast one, just to cheer me up?"

"Approved and confirmed by the D.A. and Chief Jones," Burton nodded. "But keep this quiet or we may have to relive this nightmare again."

"Well, I'll be damned." A bright smile flashed across Sammy's handsome features. "I swear, I thought my life was over."

Driving to the boarding house, James and I compared notes about the evening. "Talk about a night to remember! So many surprises, good and bad."

"I'll say. When I saw you gunning my car, aiming for the front door, I thought you'd gone bonkers. Little did I know this was all part of your plan."

"Thank God I didn't kill Marco, though I was tempted. I may be rusty, but your car hits on all sixes."

"Remind me never to get on your bad side," he teased. "I almost hate to call it a night."

"Why don't you come in for a while and relax?"

At the boarding house, I noticed all the lights were on, and Eva seemed to have company. Aunt Eva was usually in bed by ten o'clock so I knew this was a special occasion—or an emergency.

Rushing up the walkway with Burton, I opened the door and stared in shock: My mother stood there after all this time, looking chic in a smart wool suit and coat, as if she'd never left. After my father died, she was so heartbroken, she'd flown to Europe and stayed for months with relatives.

"Mother!" I rushed to hug her. "What are you doing here?" My mother rarely made impromptu trips from Europe. "You were in Rome last I heard."

"That's right," she beamed at me. "I came to visit my favorite daughter and sister for the holidays. I wanted it to be a surprise."

A private joke since I was her only child.

"You surprised me all right. I'm so glad to see you!"

Eva smiled coyly. "I tried to keep it a secret."

"You knew all along?" I pretended to scold her. Then I turned to James, who stood by me holding his hat, politely waiting his turn. "Mother, I'd like you to meet Agent James Burton." I stopped short of saying my beau or fiancé since we hadn't made it official.

My mother warmly clasped James' hand. "So glad to meet you at last. I've heard a lot about you, in Jazz's letters."

"You have?" James seemed pleased. "Good things, I hope."

"Of course," I reassured him. "How long can you stay?"

"That depends on you." She brightened. "I wanted to ask if you'd like to travel to Europe with me after the holidays. Honestly, it's getting a little lonely for me over there. I know you'd love visiting the famous European capitals. We'll call it our own private Grand Tour, like the Victorians used to do."

"Would I? I'd love to!" I hugged her tight, realizing how much I'd missed her. "Isn't it...expensive?"

"We have relatives all over the world who'd be happy to put us up for as long as we'd like."

"How nice. I can't wait!" I let out a happy sigh. "Madame Farushka's prediction came true, after all."

"What about your job?" Burton spoke up, looking pensive.

Was he disappointed I'd agreed to leave Galveston so readily?

"I can give them advance notice or take a leave of absence." Honestly, I wasn't ready to express or explore my feelings. Not now, not yet. Still, Burton knew how much I wanted to travel, to see the world—even become a foreign correspondent, like Nellie Bly or Hemingway. Meanwhile, I'd try to convince my editors to publish a piece on the murdered ghost bride or the faux-KKK cemetery bootleggers—or both—perhaps as my swan song?

"Wonderful. We can start making plans after Christmas."

"Great! We have so much to catch up on," I told my mother.

"I'll be here, waiting for you," Burton said, downcast.

"I hope so." I smiled, taking his hand. "Maybe you can join us in London or Paris? I hear Paris is so romantic in the springtime."

1920s JAZZ AGE SLANG

All wet - Wrong, incorrect ("You're all wet!" "That's nuts!")

And how! - I strongly agree!

Applesauce! – Nonsense, Horsefeathers (e.g. "That's ridiculous!")

Attaboy! - Well done! Bravo! Also: Attagirl!

Baby grand - A heavily-built, muscular man

Balled up - Confused, Unsure

Baloney - Nonsense, Hogwash, Bullshit

Bathtub Booze - Home-brewed liquor, Hooch (often in tubs)

Bearcat - A hot-blooded or fiery girl

"Beat it!" - Scram, Get lost

Bee's Knees - An extraordinary person, thing or idea

Berries - Attractive or pleasing; Swell ("It's the berries!")

Big Cheese - Big shot, an important or influential person

Blotto - Very drunk, smashed

Blow - (a) A wild, crazy party (b) To leave

Bluenose - A prim, puritanical person; a prude, a killjoy

Bohunk - A racist name for Eastern Europeans, a dumb guy

Bootleg - Illegal liquor, Hooch, Booze

Breezer (1925) - A convertible car

Bruno - Tough guy, Enforcer

Bug-eyed Betty - An unattractive girl or student

Bum's rush - Ejection by force from an establishment

Bump Off - To murder, to kill

"Butt me" - Give me a cigarette ("I need a smoke.")

Cake-eater - A lady's man, a gigolo; an effeminate male

Carry a Torch - To have a crush on someone

Cat's Meow/Whiskers - Splendid, Stylish, Swell

Cat's Pajamas - Terrific, Wonderful, Great

Clams - Money, Dollars, Bucks

Coffin varnish - Bootleg liquor, Hooch (often poisonous)

Copacetic - Excellent, all in order

Crush - An infatuation, attraction

Dame/Doll - A female, woman, girl

Dolled up - Dressed up in "glad rags"

Don't know from nothing - Don't have any information

Don't take any wooden nickels - Don't do anything stupid

Dough - Money, Cash

Drugstore Cowboy - A guy who picks up girls in public places

Dry up - Shut up; Get lost
Ducky - Fine, very good (Also: Peachy)
Dumb Dora - An idiot, a dumbbell; a stupid female
Egg - Nice person (Good egg); One who likes the big life
Fall Guy - Victim of a frame
Fella - Fellow, man, guy (very common in the 1920s)
Fire extinguisher - A chaperone, a fifth wheel
Flat Tire - A dull, boring date (Also: Pill, Pickle, Oilcan)
Frame - To give false evidence, to set up someone
Gams - A woman's legs
Gate-Crasher - A party crasher, an uninvited guest
Giggle Water - Liquor, Hooch, Booze, Alcohol
Gin Joint/Gin Mill - A bar, a speakeasy
Glad rags - "Going out on the town" clothes, Fancy dress attire
Go chase yourself - "Get lost, beat it, scram"
Hard-Boiled - A tough, strong guy (e.g. "He sure is hard-boiled!")
Hayburner - (a) A big gas-guzzling car (b) A losing racehorse
Heebie-jeebies (1926) - The shakes, the jitters, (from a hit song)
High-hat - Snobby, snooty
Holding the bag - To be cheated or blamed for something; framed
Hooch - Bootleg liquor, illegal alcohol
Hood - Hoodlum, Gangster, Thug
Hooey - Bullshit, Nonsense, Baloney (1925 to 1930)
Hoofer - Dancer, Chorus girl
Hotsy-Totsy - Attractive, Pleasing
Jack - Cash, Money
Jake - Great, Fine, OK (i.e. "Everything's jake.")
Jeepers creepers – Exclamation of surprise ("Jesus Christ!")
Joe Brooks - A well-groomed man, natty dresser, student
Juice Joint - A speakeasy, bar
Keen - Attractive or appealing
Killjoy - Dud, a dull, boring person, a party pooper, a spoilsport
Lollygagger - (a) A flirtatious male (b) A lazy or idle person
Lounge Lizard - A gigolo; a flirtatious, sexually-active male
Mick - A derogatory term for an Irishman
Milquetoast (1924) - A very timid person; a hen-pecked male
     (from the comic book character Casper Milquetoast)
Mrs. Grundy - A prude or killjoy; a prim, prissy (older) woman
Moll - (Gun Moll) A gangster's girlfriend
Neck - Make-out, kiss with passion

"Oh yeah?" - Expression of doubt ("Is that so?")

On a toot – On a drinking binge, Bar-hopping

On the lam - Fleeing from police

On the level - Legitimate, Honest

On the trolley – In the know, Savvy ("You're on the trolley!")

On the up and up - Trustworthy, Honest

Ossified – Drunk, Plastered

Palooka - A derogatory term for a low-class or dumb person
   (Re: Comic strip character Joe Palooka, a poor immigrant)

Piker - (a) Cheapskate (b) Coward

Pitch a little woo - To flirt, try to charm and attract the opposite sex

Rag-a-muffin - An unkempt, dirty and disheveled person/child

Razz - To tease, to insult or make fun of

Rhatz! - "Too bad!" or "Darn it!"

Ritzy - Elegant, High-class, "Putting on the Ritz" (Re: Ritz Hotel)

Rotgut - Cheap hooch, inferior alcohol, poisonous bootleg liquor

Rummy - A drunken bum, an intoxicated man, a wino

Sap - A fool, an idiot; very common term in the 1920s

"Says you!" - A reaction of disbelief or doubt (also "Hogwash!")

Screaming meemies - The shakes, the jitters, to be afraid

Screwy - Crazy, Nuts ("You're screwy!")

Sheba - An attractive and sexy woman; girlfriend
   (popularized by the film "Queen of Sheba")

Sheik - A handsome man with sex appeal
   (from Rudolph Valentino's film "The Sheik")

Scram – "Get out," "Beat it," to leave immediately

Speakeasy - An illicit bar selling bootleg liquor

Spiffy - An elegant appearance, well-dressed, fine

Stuck On - Having a crush on, attracted to

Sugar Daddy - A rich, older gentleman (usually married)

Swanky - Elegant, Ritzy

Swell - Wonderful, Great, Fine, A-OK

Take for a Ride - To try to kill someone (bump them off)

Torpedo - A hired gun, a hit man

Upchuck - To vomit, especially after drinking too much

Wet Blanket - A dud, a dull date or person, a party pooper

Whoopee - (Make whoopee) To have fun/a good time, to party

"You don't say!" – i.e. "Is that so?" "Oh, really? I didn't know"

"You slay me!" - "You're hilarious!" or "That's funny!"

Zozzled - Drunk, intoxicated, (Also: Plastered, Smashed)

BIOGRAPHY

Ellen Mansoor Collier is a Houston-based freelance writer whose articles and essays have been published in several national magazines including: FAMILY CIRCLE, MODERN BRIDE, FIRST, GLAMOUR, BIOGRAPHY, COSMOPOLITAN, COUNTRY ACCENTS, PLAYGIRL, etc. Several of her short stories have appeared in WOMAN'S WORLD. A flapper at heart, she's the owner of MODERNEMILLIE on etsy, specializing in Deco to retro vintage items.

Formerly she's worked as a magazine editor/writer, a substitute teacher and in advertising/marketing and public relations. A graduate of the University of Texas at Austin, she earned a degree in Magazine Journalism. She served on UTmost, the campus magazine, and acted as President of Women in Communications (W.I.C.I.) her senior year. During college, she worked as a reporter/intern for a Houston community newspaper and once as a cocktail waitress, a short-lived experience.

Her Jazz Age series includes: FLAPPERS, FLASKS AND FOUL PLAY (2012). BATHING BEAUTIES, BOOZE AND BULLETS (2013) GOLD DIGGERS, GAMBLERS AND GUNS (2014), VAMPS, VILLAINS AND VAUDEVILLE (2015) and DECO DAMES, DEMON RUM AND DEATH (2018).

"When you grow up in Houston, Galveston becomes like a second home. After visiting Al Capone's haunts in Chicago, I heard wild stories about Galveston's rival gangs, bootleggers and turf wars during the 1920s and beyond. My Jazz Age series attempts to capture an ambitious, adventurous flapper's life during Prohibition."

DEDICATION

I dedicate DECO DAMES to my late mother, May Mansoor Munn, whose mother (Ellen Audi Mansur) was a feisty, fashionable flapper much like Jazz. Mom inspired me to finish this novel, always encouraging me to "work on the fifth chapter." Despite her struggles with Parkinson's disease, she never lost her faith or love of writing, and her enthusiasm motivated me to continue the series.

My brother Jeff J. Mansoor contributed his artistic skills to most of my covers. My late father, Isa Mansoor, who loved Galveston, lives on in my novels, larger than life.

I couldn't have completed five novels without the help of Gary, my amazing husband, who has been there since day one and read virtually every chapter of my novels—often while I was still writing.

ACKNOWLEDGEMENTS

I'm especially grateful to Karen Muller for meticulously editing the latest draft of the manuscript, catching errors and discrepancies that I'd missed. Thanks to journalist/attorney Noreen Marcus, who read and edited DECO DAMES from the start, and also helped with legal information and jargon.

I'm indebted to the late *Texas Monthly* contributor Gary Cartwright, author of *Galveston: A History of the Island*, whose painstaking research made Galveston's past come alive.

Many thanks to all of my friends and family for your support and encouragement! Last but not least, I greatly appreciate the positive reviews from new and loyal readers.

As for the artwork, I designed the covers using vintage photos and images. The original artists and photographers are unknown.

www.ingramcontent.com/pod-product-compliance
Lightning Source LLC
Chambersburg PA
CBHW021008120726
47905CB00009B/2911